Summer SECRETS

ALSO BY JILL SANDERS

The Wildflowers Series

Summer Nights
Summer Heat

The Pride Series

Finding Pride
Discovering Pride
Returning Pride
Lasting Pride
Serving Pride
Red Hot Christmas
My Sweet Valentine
Return to Me
Rescue Me
A Pride Christmas

The Secret Series

Secret Seduction
Secret Pleasure
Secret Guardian
Secret Passions
Secret Identity
Secret Sauce

The West Series

Loving Lauren
Taming Alex
Holding Haley
Missy's Moment
Breaking Travis
Roping Ryan
Wild Bride
Corey's Catch
Tessa's Turn

Haven, Montana Series

Closer to You
Never Let Go
Holding On

The Grayton Series

Last Resort
Someday Beach
Rip Current
In Too Deep
Swept Away
High Tide
Sunset Dreams

Lucky Series

Unlucky in Love
Sweet Resolve
Best of Luck
A Little Luck

Silver Cove Series

Silver Lining
French Kiss
Happy Accident
Hidden Charm
A Silver Cove Christmas

Entangled Series: Paranormal Romance

The Awakening
The Beckoning
The Ascension

Pride, Oregon Series

A Dash of Love
My Kind of Love
Season of Love
Tis the Season
Dare to Love
Where I Belong

Stand-Alone Novel

Twisted Rock

JILL
SANDERS

Published by Montlake, Seattle
www.apub.com

Amazon, the Amazon logo, and Montlake are trademarks of Amazon.com, Inc., or its affiliates.

ISBN-13: 9781542007764
ISBN-10: 1542007763

Cover design by Vivian Monir

Cover photography by Wander Aguiar Photography

Printed in the United States of America

Summer
SECRETS

PROLOGUE

Hannah was running late to her first yoga class of the morning at River Camp—the adult camp she and her best friends owned and ran. Meeting Elle Saunders, Zoey and Scarlett Rowlett, and Aubrey Smith at the tender age of eleven here on these very campgrounds had been the single most important event in Hannah's life to date. Starting the camp back up again ten years later was their way of bringing the spirit of friendship to new groups of people.

As she ran down the wet pathway, she hurried toward the gym and cursed her new cell phone and its stupid alarm feature. She smacked right into a solid body as she came around a corner. Caught off guard, she fell backward, letting out a high-pitched screech, a sound she'd never made before in her life. She tried to catch herself before she landed on her butt in the mud. Her mother would have been mortified by her actions. After all, a Rodgers didn't screech, or even run, for that matter. They certainly didn't bump into people.

Just as she imagined herself landing in a mud puddle, strong arms closed around her and lifted her to safety.

She had closed her eyes in anticipation of landing in the water and having it splash all over her, but now she looked into a pair of dark-brown eyes. Eyes that were laughing at her instead of glaring at her for bumping into him.

"Sorry," she started to say, but then she realized it was Owen Rhodes holding her. Zoey had hired him and his two younger brothers a few weeks back, before she and her friends had reopened their childhood summer camp to be for adults instead. The three men were tall, dark, and handsome as sin and, lately, seemed to be up to no good. At least according to Zoey.

"Are you okay?" he asked instead of letting her go immediately.

"Yes." She straightened herself and pulled away from his light hold. "I'm sorry," she said again and then noticed the instant smile he gave her.

"You said that already," he joked.

"Right." She took a deep breath and glanced down at her phone when it chimed. "Thank you for your assistance." She started to move past him but stopped when he chuckled. Glancing back over at him, she frowned. She didn't think she'd said anything funny, but he was looking at her as if she'd just made a joke. "What?" She turned fully toward him. He shook his head, still chuckling. "What's so funny?" she prodded, her nerves running high all of a sudden.

He might be one of the sexiest men she'd ever run into, but she'd never had anyone laugh at her before.

He motioned around them to the dirt pathways surrounded by the greenness and beauty of the Florida Panhandle. "You run this outdoorsy place, yet you talk like you're in the White House."

Her eyes narrowed even more. "You're an employee." She tilted her head, wondering how he expected her to talk.

He looked at her. "Am I?" With the heat of his gaze, she realized just how close he was to her still.

"Well, since I own this camp . . ." She waited, but instead of backing off, he continued to smile at her.

"Part of it," he corrected her. "With four of your best friends."

"Still," she said, moving closer until they were almost nose to nose, "if you don't like the way I talk—"

"I never said that," he interrupted her. "I happen to like a formal tone laced with a sexy southern drawl." His eyes moved to her lips, and she sucked in her breath as she wondered for a moment what she would do if he bent down and kissed her right there on the pathway.

Swallowing, she took a step back. "Zoey thinks you and your brothers are lying," she blurted out.

His dark eyebrows shot up in question. Something flickered behind his eyes, but before she could determine what the emotion was, it was gone.

"About what?" he asked easily.

Hannah crossed her arms over her chest and shrugged. "Things, everything, something . . ." she said, thinking of how her friend had tried to explain that she just didn't trust the sexy men. She couldn't give any real reasons, other than that one of them, Dylan, got on her nerves. But Elle and Hannah believed it was because their friend was hot for the guy. Still, the jury was out on the entire situation.

But after seeing the look that had passed over Owen's face, she was beginning to have her own doubts about why the three brothers had applied for jobs.

"What do you think about all this?" he asked, again moving a little closer to her.

Just then her phone chimed again. "I think"—she glanced down at it and groaned—"I'm late for my class," she said, starting to walk backward down the pathway again.

"Let me know when you make a decision about me," he called after her.

The fact that he had made it all about her feelings toward him and not about his brothers played over in her mind as she taught the first of her many yoga classes for her guests.

What was it about Owen that had her acting like a teenager? She'd run into his brothers several times and hadn't reacted the way she had around him. It just had to be the strong sexual pull she felt toward him.

Whatever it was, she had a new business to get off the ground. If River Camp didn't become successful for her and her friends, she'd have to crawl back to her parents for help. And that was something she swore she'd never do again.

Being raised with money hadn't been her parents' biggest downfall—they had married for status and wealth, which had somehow caused the pair to end up worse. It was as if joining forces had entitled them to different rules than all the other parents. They had used those rules to govern her as if she were one of their possessions instead of a living being with her own dreams and rights.

Over the next few months, she started to grow closer to Owen. Closer than she had with anyone else before. She found herself dropping her carefully placed guard around the man and even openly flirted with him around others—something she had no experience in at all. She was sure she ended up looking like a complete dork in the process.

When she and her friends found out that the brothers had lied to them about their last name and that the Costas were only at the camp to look for their father and missing family money, she'd still found it hard to turn him away. Even when he'd made a point of not apologizing for his actions.

He promised her that he had his reasons for lying.

"We didn't know who we could trust," he told her one evening when she caught up to him after dinner. "You have to understand: all we knew was that he'd scheduled a meeting with Elle and then disappeared with close to a million dollars." He tried to pull her close, but she jerked away.

"Why didn't you tell me this earlier? Why did we have to find out from Ryan?" she spat. Her anger had been so great she'd mentally compared him to her parents at that point.

"I should have told you that first moment when I kissed you under the stars." His voice changed, growing deeper and more sincere. Just hearing the emotions in his tone almost undid her. His eyes locked with hers. "I had no right to kiss you then."

This time when he moved closer, she let him wrap his arms around her.

"You didn't," she agreed, causing him to smile.

"Spitfire," he said softly. "We didn't know who we could trust."

"Do you know now?" she asked under her breath.

"Yes. I'll never lie to you again," he said, and for some strange reason she believed him.

But then a few days later, the subject of intimacy came up, and things got . . . weird. They were in one of the cabins. He'd been called out to help Aiden Stark, the camp's head maintenance guy and chief architect for the new cabins, and she'd followed him out there, knowing that Aiden had been called to another job. She wanted—no, needed— some time alone with him.

He kissed her, and it felt so right that she blurted out that she was happy she'd waited so long. Which caused him to instantly freeze.

"You . . ." He sat up from the bed, where he'd laid her gently down moments before. "You're a virgin?" He looked so shocked that she laughed nervously.

"Yes." She tried to pull him back down to her, but he jerked away like she'd slapped him. The look on his face hurt far more than any words could have.

"I . . ." He glanced around. "Have to go." He bolted from the cabin so fast that she was left lying there, her breasts exposed to the cool night air.

A few days after that and after his father had contacted Elle but before she could sort out her new feelings completely, she learned that he'd packed up and left the camp and her. Without a word, without saying goodbye. Making her realize that she'd been a complete fool. She swore then and there to never fall for a man like Owen Costa ever again.

CHAPTER ONE

Several months later . . .

The binder Hannah clutched contained all the legal documents she would need for her meeting with the team of lawyers who were going to hopefully save her and her best friends from ruin. She stood in the late-September heat just outside the massive glass building, feeling the sweat soak into the folder from her palms.

Letting her anger drive her forward into the building, she held her head up high as she stepped into the air-conditioned lobby. Just the knowledge that their new business could be taken down by an ex-employee hell bent on destroying them practically propelled her up the elevators.

She wasn't anxious about meeting the lawyers to discuss the legal battles. River Camp had every right to fire Ryan Kinsley. After all, the woman had almost killed one of her best friends. Still, a wrongful-termination suit combined with a sexual harassment claim could mark the camp forever.

Instead, her nerves were due to the slight possibility that she would run into Owen Costa again. His family owned the building she was standing in, and it was his team of lawyers she and her friends had hired to fight against the crazed woman.

Owen had strolled out of her life as quickly as he'd walked into it. And without so much as a glance back. Which pissed her off even more.

Her anger had paved the way for her friends to talk her into becoming the camp's main liaison with the team of lawyers.

After all, she was good at negotiations. It was one of the reasons her father had allowed her to work at one of his businesses shortly after school. That and so she would be under his control once more.

But since Elle had persuaded her and her other friends to put everything they had into reopening her grandfather's old summer camp, her family problems had disappeared into the background. For the most part.

Now, as she stood outside the lawyers' offices, she was thankful Elle had suggested opening River Camp again. The business had saved her from her parents' overbearing attention.

In the weeks leading up to her departure from New York, her parents had tried to set her up with five different men. All easily double her age and either very close friends with her father or clients of his. She expected this was another attempt to control her. To keep the family money in the tight circles they wanted or to even expand it further by marrying her off to more wealth.

She preferred to choose her own man. Just not Owen Costa.

After stepping into the office, she glanced up and held in a gasp when she noticed the man she'd been dreaming of for the past few months standing just inside the office doors. It wasn't as if they had been officially dating back when he'd been at the camp. They hadn't even really been an item, in her friends' eyes. It was just that . . . she'd hoped, and that hope had caused her heart to break a little when he'd vanished.

He was facing away from her, so she took a moment to reappreciate his beauty.

During his time at the camp, he'd only worn shorts and camp T-shirts, along with flip-flops or hiking boots. Now, the perfectly tailored suit and the dress shoes on his feet should have looked foreign on him, but they didn't. Instead, he looked like he was born to wear the outfit.

Her eyes moved to his butt in the dark suit pants, and she felt herself heating even more than when she'd seen him in nothing but swim shorts. He'd been a golden-skinned god by the pool, basking in the sunlight; now, in a suit, he was something more. He was powerful.

His longer jet-black hair had always been windblown or tucked under a baseball cap. Currently it was slicked back, away from his face.

She swallowed and cleared her throat, and the two men he was talking with turned toward her, but only Owen trapped her with a look as he turned.

With his hair slicked back, his dark eyes looked even more dangerous than when they had heated upon seeing her for the first time. He still had a light stubble on his face, however, which contrasted with how he was dressed.

"Here she is now," Owen said, as if he'd just seen her an hour earlier instead of almost a full month before. The deep richness of his voice caused her insides to vibrate as she remembered all the fantasies she'd had of the man over the past few months.

Swallowing again, she raised her chin and shifted the binder in her hands so she could shake his hand. But instead, she lost control of the folder, and it slipped from her hands, sending all her organized paperwork sailing in every direction.

Bending in her pencil skirt, she started gathering the papers up, only to have Owen kneel beside her to help. Their knees brushed, and she held in another gasp as his heat transferred to her almost instantly.

"Dylan mentioned the meeting to me," he murmured as he helped pick up the papers.

Even though the interior of the building was a chilly seventy degrees, she could feel herself start to sweat the closer his body shifted to hers.

"I've got this," she said, avoiding his eyes. She tried to focus on putting everything back in its place, but her mind kept playing over the first time she'd run into Owen at the camp.

"Here." He handed her the last paper and then held out his hand to help her stand. Keeping a tight grip on the folder with everything tucked back inside it, she stood and glanced over his shoulder at the other two men. She'd somewhat expected to see them laughing at her; instead, they both stood watching her and waiting.

"Hannah Rodgers, this is Chris Schumer and his son-in-law, Jonas Cobbs."

Shifting the folder once more, this time getting one hand under the open end, she shook their hands in turn. "Nice to meet you," she said, feeling her face heat at her own embarrassment.

"We have the conference room all ready." Chris motioned behind them. The lawyer was a fit and young-looking man in his early sixties who appeared to be in far better shape than his son-in-law.

She followed the two men into the conference room and was slightly surprised when Owen followed her inside and sat directly beside her. She raised her eyebrows at him in question.

"I have a little at stake in this mess. After all, it was my brother she tried to shoot," he said softly. "Besides, I was there when Elle fired Ryan. Remember? One of the Costas needs to be here."

She took a deep breath. "Fine." She opened her folder and tried to make sure everything was in order again. For the most part, she had everything she needed on her phone as well, including notes, but she'd made copies of all of Ryan's employee records for the lawyers, including several complaints about her while she'd worked at the camp.

For the next hour and a half, she tried to ignore Owen's presence next to her. It seemed like he would be occupying the same role she was in the case. He sat back, silent for most of the meeting, as the lawyers explained that it would most likely be a cut-and-dried case since everything appeared to be in order. But there was still a hint of doubt in Chris Schumer's voice that sent her nerves spiking again near the end of the meeting.

"We'll get working on the next steps and let you know as soon as we hear back from Ms. Kinsley's lawyers."

Hannah thought of Elle's ex-fiancé, Jeff Springs. The man had called Elle to say he was representing Ryan in the case. She and her friends wanted to hog-tie the man and leave him on the side of a dirt road somewhere, but Elle had talked them out of their daydreaming, wine-induced schemes.

"I'll walk you out." Owen stood up and waited for her to gather the new paperwork the lawyers had given her. After putting everything back into the folder, she tucked it under her arm and stood.

"That won't be . . ." she started to say, but the look in Owen's eyes told her that it hadn't been a request.

"Thank you." She turned to the other two men.

"We'll be in touch," Jonas Cobbs said before they disappeared down a long hallway.

"How have you been?" Owen asked as they walked toward the elevators.

She jerked her head toward him. It was the first personal thing he'd said to her since she'd arrived.

All the anger of how he'd left her—and left the camp—surfaced again as the worry of the legal battle faded into the background.

She wanted to yell at him, to zap him with a quick retort, but instead, she answered with a short "Fine."

His eyes ran over her face as he hit the button for the elevator. "How are things at River Camp?"

"Fine," she answered again and crossed her arms, holding the folder tight over her chest like a shield over her heart.

11

She watched his eyes narrow slightly as the two stepped into the elevator.

She was so preoccupied with tracking his emotions that when they started moving upward instead of heading down to the lobby, it took her a moment to realize what was happening.

"Why are we going up?" she asked.

"Because," he said, "my office is upstairs, and I think we need to have a talk."

This time it was her eyes that narrowed. "I have nothing to say to you." She moved to punch the button for the lobby, but he stopped her by putting a hand gently over her arm.

"Hannah—"

She turned to him, waiting, expecting more, but instead, he just said her name one more time.

"What?" She shook her head. "What do you want?" she asked, hating that she could hear her own hurt in her tone.

Instead of answering, he moved closer, tucking her into the corner of the elevator and backing her up until her shoulders hit the mirrored walls. Then his lips were covering hers as his hands gripped her hips and pulled her body up tight against his.

Yet by the time the elevator doors had slid open, he'd moved back across the small space as if nothing had happened.

She had to blink a few times and breathe slowly until her heart settled back in her chest. How could the man irritate her and turn her on so much at the same time?

"This way," Owen said calmly, motioning to the right. A large reception area met the elevators as they opened, and as they walked by, a thin woman stood up and handed Owen a few notes.

"Your calls," she said to him as she eyed Hannah.

"Thank you, Nora. I'll be in a meeting for the next hour. Hold my calls."

"Yes, sir." The woman sat back down and turned back to her work.

She followed Owen down a hallway until they reached the corner office. The view of the gulf and its crystal-clear teal waters captured her attention, driving away thoughts of anything else.

It still got to her, the beauty of the area. From up here, twenty floors above the water, she could see sharks swimming in the deeper, darker waters while tourists and beachgoers played, happily unaware, in the clearer, shallower surf.

Hearing the office door shut behind her, she turned and looked at Owen. She'd never believed she could have easily fallen for a man like him before. After all, he was everything her parents had wanted for her in a husband: wealthy. Extremely so.

"So," she said, deciding to stand her ground. The kiss in the elevator hadn't been their first, but she was still finding it hard to recover from.

"So," he said, slowly moving toward her. She wished the room were larger than it was, since she felt like she was being stalked by a carnivore, ready to jump and gobble her up. She needed to take control of the situation. After all, he was the one in the wrong.

"You left," she accused him. Her words stopped him midstride.

"I did." He nodded. "You know why."

"Because your father called?" She set the folder down on a massive glass desk that sat in front of the wall of windows. When he nodded again, she cocked her head to the side. "No excuses? No explanations beyond that?"

"You know why I had to leave." As if realizing for the first time that he was about to reach out and touch her again, he turned away and looked out the window. "You know why this could never work. You knew it then."

Since he was no longer facing her, she allowed her shoulders to slump. If she'd just kept her mouth shut, maybe he would have stayed. Maybe things would have been different between them.

"Because you're stubborn?" she suggested. She moved to pick up her folder again, but he easily blocked her.

"No, because you're . . . you," he muttered as he tucked his hands into his pants pockets. "Damn it, I thought . . ." His hands emerged and ran through his hair, messing up the perfectly gelled style. "I thought you'd understand."

"Oh," she drew out, so as to make her point clear. "I understood."

"Hannah." He started to move closer, but just then his office door swung open.

"Hey, Owen, I need your signature . . ." The rest of the man's words trailed off as he spotted her from across the room. "Hannah?"

Pure shock forced a gasp from her throat at seeing the man who had broken her in so many ways walk into Owen's office as if he owned the place.

"Joel?" She hadn't thought of the man in years. Hadn't thought that there had been a hint of familiarity in Owen's appearance, but now, looking between the two, it was obvious that they were related.

Owen took her arm when she swayed as memories flooded her mind.

"You two know each other?" Owen asked, and somehow just hearing his voice helped settle her a little until she could regain her control.

"Yes," she said, again holding the folder against her chest. "We used to date." She jerked her arm out of Owen's hand and started walking toward the door, avoiding Joel's eyes as she went.

"Hannah," Joel started, but at a look that told him to shove off, he closed his mouth, glanced back at Owen, and let her pass.

She made it all the way to the elevators before the shakes started. After punching the button for the lobby, she braced for Owen to follow her. When he didn't and she stepped into the elevator alone, she relaxed as the doors shut her inside. Resting her head back against the glass, she held in the tears for all that had come before—the two men were like night and day, personality-wise. She would have never pegged them as related until she'd seen them together. They had the same dark hair and eyes. She'd been so young back when she'd been with Joel, so naive. What had happened between her and Owen must have been a step back—maybe she hadn't really grown at all, once again falling for the wrong man.

As she drove back to the camp, she took the half-hour-long trip to settle her nerves and focus on what was important: River Camp.

When she parked in her normal spot, two of her co-owners and best friends, Zoey and Elle, were waiting for her.

"So?" they both said at the same time.

"How did it go?" Elle asked.

"It went," she said. "They think we have a good chance of fighting her civil case. We have all the documentation, not to mention the complaints from the other employees." She pulled out the folder and handed it to Elle. "So, from here on—"

"Not with this." Her friend pushed the papers back at her. "With Owen."

"Oh." She sighed. "That went too." She rubbed her forehead.

"What was that?" Elle asked, sounding a little bewildered.

"Complicated!" Hannah said, leaning against her car and glancing around. It had been almost six months since they had reopened River Camp as an upscale escape for wealthy snowbirds. It was a little shocking at first, seeing how much trouble the older couples and singles could get into. She knew there were such things as swingers and wild sex parties, but she'd never imagined they would have to play host to any of that.

After the first group of guests had come and gone, they quickly revamped the camp rules and regulations. Damages were now calculated and included in guest deposits, and they'd posted many signs about nudity in public and pool areas. Designated smoking areas had been put in place, and all cabins were now smoke- and drug-free zones. She knew these steps couldn't stop all the parties, but at least they discouraged most of the wilder ones.

"That look," Elle answered finally. "I've never seen it on you before." She moved closer to her and took her shoulders.

Elle had been her best friend since she'd met her that first summer at River Camp, when Hannah had been a little girl so unhappy about her life that she'd been thinking of hurting herself. Her parents had expected perfection from her from the start. When other kids had been allowed to wear shorts and get scraped knees, Hannah had been required to remain demure and clean.

Seeing worry in her friend's eyes now had her taking a few cleansing breaths. "I'm fine," she said after a moment.

"You're not. I have a few errands to run, but then I'm going to bring up a bottle of wine, and we're going to talk. All of us." Elle threw an arm around her shoulder. "We're sisters, and we're here for you, like you've been here for all of us."

"Right," Zoey said as she walked over and added another arm to the hug. "You look shaken. It's obvious."

She relaxed into her friends' arms. "I could use some wine."

Elle giggled. "Okay, give me an hour. Go change into something more comfortable, and we'll be up soon."

"Thanks," she said, handing the folder to Elle.

"I'll put this in your office," Elle promised her. "Take a bath and relax."

She did what her friends suggested and headed up to the apartment she'd shared with Scarlett and Aubrey ever since Zoey had moved into one of the new cabins with Owen's brother Dylan and Elle had moved up to her tree house with Owen's other brother, Liam. The apartment felt lonely with the population reduced to her, Scarlett, and Aubrey. Almost two years ago, she'd had her very own apartment in New York City. She'd been working at a high-paying job at one of her father's investment firms and had, so she thought, been on her way up the ladder on her own. Then she took a business trip to Europe, and everything changed when her father sprang it on her that he expected her to make a move she wasn't prepared to in life. Being forced to merge with one of her father's business partners in her personal life was crossing the line, in her book.

Her father informed her that he was moving her to a different position, one with less freedom and directly under one of the many prospective husbands her parents were forcing on her.

She was thankful she received Elle's call the day she got back into town. Even though Elle conveyed the bad news of her grandfather Joe's death, Hannah needed to see her friends.

She expected the trip to Florida to be a fresh breath that would allow her time to recover and decide the next steps in her life. What she hadn't bargained for was that it would end up being the chance of a lifetime. The possibility for her to escape her parents' clutches once and for all.

After filling the bathtub and dropping one of Scarlett's homemade bath bombs into the warm water, she peeled off her heels, skirt, and blouse and sank below the pink-and-purple-colored fragrant water.

She didn't even tie her long hair up like she normally did when taking a bath but just let it float in the water around her face. Every time she closed her eyes and tried to relax, she thought about wanting to kiss Owen again. Memories of how she'd pretty much attacked him that last time surfaced, and she tried to avoid them even more by sinking deeper into the water.

She attempted to get the feeling of Owen kissing her from her memories by focusing on something else, but her mind kept flashing back to the first time they'd kissed.

It had been a little over a week after she'd bumped into him that first time. She'd been walking back to her apartment after dinner. Her long summer dress allowed the evening air to cool her off, and she decided to make her way around the grounds and enjoy the night.

She walked past the pool house and spotted a dark figure leaning against the wall, watching her. At first, she was prepared to approach whoever it was to shoo them out of the darkness, but then she realized he wasn't watching her. Quietly approaching, she followed his glance and noticed the deer in the clearing.

"She's giving birth," he said. "It looks like she's having a difficult time with it."

She moved closer to him and tilted her head to watch the doe. Sure enough, the small deer was making grunting noises in between heavy pants. Its large belly moved occasionally with the effort.

They watched in silence as the frogs croaked in the darkness and bugs buzzed around them. When the fawn finally arrived, Hannah let out a sigh of relief as the mother leaned in and started licking it clean.

"Amazing," she whispered. She touched his arm. "Look—it's standing already." The small fawn was trying to get up on wobbly legs.

"He," he corrected her as he tilted his head for a better look.

They watched in amazement when, after only five more minutes, both mother and fawn wandered off into the brush. She hadn't realized she'd kept her hand on his arm until he turned his head and glanced down at it.

Dropping her hand, she moved to take a step back, but he stopped her by cupping her face and quickly kissing her.

"I've wanted to do that since I got here," he whispered, then turned and disappeared into the darkness. She was so shocked by the kiss that she didn't move to stop him from leaving. Nor had she responded the way she'd wanted.

It wasn't as if she hadn't been kissed before. One moment he was leaning against the wall, and the next she was in his arms, as if he'd been planning it the entire time. No man she'd ever kissed had been that smooth before.

Feeling heated all over again, she had slowly made her way back to her apartment that evening and dreamed of Owen, much like she was doing now.

"Did you drown in there?" Zoey's voice came from just outside the bathroom door.

Chuckling, she sat up and called out, "No, but I was thinking of spending the rest of the night in here." *By myself,* she thought to say, right as the bathroom door opened and her friends spilled in. Sliding back down into the bubbles, she groaned.

"What?" Elle said, handing her a glass of wine. Elle's blonde hair lay over her shoulders in two long braids, reminding Hannah of the first summer she'd met her. "We've all seen you naked."

"You've seen all of us naked," Scarlett teased, sitting on the countertop and tucking her long legs into the sweatshirt she'd pulled over her shorts. Hannah noticed that Scarlett's brown hair was showing highlights of blonde streaked through it from all the time she spent outside in the sun.

"We know all the secrets," Aubrey said between sips of wine. It kind of frustrated Hannah slightly that of all of them, Aubrey currently didn't have a hair out of place on her head. She was wearing black yoga pants and a trendy top and looked better than any of them. She even still had earrings and makeup on. Which had Hannah thinking about how big of a mess she probably looked.

"Spill! We're all dying to hear what happened," Zoey added as she sat on the edge of the tub.

Hannah tucked her legs up and rested her elbows on her knees while she sipped the wine. "Well, the lawyers—"

"Nope," Elle broke in. "We don't care about the lawsuit."

"We *do* care about the lawsuit," Zoey corrected her with a mild glare at Elle. "We have to, but we're up to date on that and want to hear what went down with you and Owen first."

She thought about lying to her friends. Telling them that she hadn't seen Owen. After all, she wouldn't have thought twice about lying to her parents, but these were her best friends, her sisters. They had set one rule that first summer after finding each other: no lies.

Just knowing the secret she had kept from them all these years ate at her insides.

CHAPTER TWO

Why had he kissed her? Hell, for that matter, why had Owen gone down to the lawyers' floor in the first place? When he'd found out Hannah was going to be in his building, he'd lost the last strings of his control. He'd sat through the meeting knowing he had a million other items he should be doing but was focused solely on Hannah and being close to her again.

Wasn't it bad enough that he had to run his father's business because the man had disappeared months ago? Not to mention the mysterious notes he'd been receiving since returning to the office. At first, he thought that they were just messages left around the office by an employee. He tossed a few messages before actually reading them, but after receiving the last note, addressed to him directly, he realized what they were. Threats. To him and his family if they didn't step down and let the board take over the business.

Did that have something to do with his father's disappearance?

Because it had been over six months since he'd seen or spoken to his father, he was beginning to wonder if there was something more behind this disappearance compared to all the others in the past.

"Is there anything else?" he asked Joel, who had been brought on by Owen's father shortly after Owen had graduated from school. His dad had done one of his disappearing trips and then returned with this man. Instantly, everyone in the company believed Joel was Leo Costa's long-lost love child. The man certainly looked like he could be Owen's older brother, even if he didn't quite fit in with the brothers, personality-wise.

Since his father had brought Joel into the business, the man had moved up the ladder and now acted as a personal assistant to his father, which meant that he was now working directly under Owen himself.

It was strange, all this time, how Owen and his brothers just blindly accepted Joel into the family and the business without any real discussion—modeling their acceptance of him on their father's own. Yet there had always been something unspoken between Joel and Owen, as if Joel was in competition with him, especially when his father was around. Now, seeing the way the man's eyes had lit up when he'd seen Hannah, Owen felt it even more. An uneasy feeling settled over him, and he vowed to get to the bottom of what had gone on between Joel and Hannah.

"There were a few calls this morning." Owen motioned to the notes Nora had handed him earlier.

"Right." Joel glanced down at them. "I'll get on these." After a pause, he added, "Have you heard from your father?"

Owen had heard the question more than a dozen times a day from Joel since Owen had returned from the camp and taken over the company, per the board's request. "Not today." He sighed. "But I've been told he's in the state now." He'd spoken to his brothers, Dylan and Liam, yesterday evening. Liam had heard it from Elle, whom he was now officially dating.

It seemed as if their father was Elle's godfather, and she was his only confidante in his current scheme. Ever since Owen's youngest brother, Liam, had graduated high school, their father had been taking wild vacations. Leaving at the drop of a hat and disappearing for days at a time. Only to turn up on the beach in Mexico somewhere with a woman half his age. He'd fallen for a couple of ladies who had tried to persuade him to invest in their businesses or just straight up give them money.

It was as if their father was going through a midlife crisis. Maybe he was. When did a man's midlife crisis really begin? Forties? Fifties?

At one point his dad had confessed to losing the only woman he'd ever loved when their mother, Grace, had died. Owen had been four and thus had only vague memories of the soft-spoken woman. Still, their father had been there for them for the most part. As much as any single father who ran a multimillion-dollar business could be, he supposed.

But in the past few years, his father had never done anything *this* crazy—taking off without a word, emptying his bank accounts, and leaving the board of directors concerned enough that they held a meeting to determine if Leo was capable of running the business anymore.

Which was why Owen was now sitting as chairman of the board, thanks to a special vote last week. He'd dropped everything at the camp and returned to work, occupying his father's office instead of his own cubicle alongside Joel's.

"Well, that is something," Joel said, straightening the signed paperwork. "How did the meeting go downstairs?"

Owen's eyebrows shot up. He hadn't told anyone where he was going. Even Nora, his father's secretary for as long as Owen could remember, hadn't known.

"I was on the second floor delivering some paperwork to accounting when I saw you walk into the meeting room with the lawyers and Hannah. How do you two know each other, anyway?"

Owen remembered Hannah's words from earlier: *"We used to date."*

"A project we were looking into." He tried to be vague. "When did you two know each other?"

"High school," Joel answered easily.

"In Georgia?" he asked, curious now. He knew a lot about Hannah. After all, the brothers had researched the camp and its owners—Elle Saunders, Hannah Rodgers, Aubrey Smith, and Zoey and Scarlett Rowlett—after finding out that their father had had a meeting with Elle the day he'd gone missing. The brothers had taken jobs at the summer-camp-turned-snowbird-retreat before its reopening.

At first, they believed their father had invested the missing money into the camp and that Elle Saunders or one of the other ladies was their father's newest project. But when it became clear that the camp's successful finances were due to the five friends' hard work, the brothers continued to try to discern the camp's connection to their father.

It took a few months and a lot of snooping around to finally learn that only Elle Saunders was connected. She was their father's goddaughter, thanks to an old friendship between the two sets of parents.

Owen was shocked to know that his father had chosen to call Elle and fill her in briefly on what was going on rather than his own sons. Just knowing that his dad didn't trust him to run his business or help him out stung. After all, he'd been preparing Owen all his life for the day he would take over Paradise Investments.

"No, upstate New York." Joel looked at him like he was crazy.

"But Hannah's family is from Georgia," he said, remembering that sweet accent of hers.

"Right, but she was shipped off to school each year and only spent the summers at home." Joel shrugged.

"How long did you two date?" He was trying to act casual while getting as much information about Hannah as he could.

"Just a few months." Joel looked out the window behind him. "It was one of those high school romances," he added. "Then I graduated and came here and lost track of her and everyone else I knew." He shrugged as if it hadn't meant much, which had Owen relaxing. He hated to think that Joel still had a thing for Hannah, or worse, that Hannah still had a thing for Joel.

He hadn't known he had lived in New York. Actually, he didn't know much of anything about Joel—they remained mere coworkers. Over the past ten years, however, Joel had earned his own trust even with the unspoken rivalry between them. It wasn't as if they were in direct competition at the office; after all, his father hadn't owned up to being Joel's father yet. Still, the silence between them said enough. Now, however, knowing that Joel and Hannah had been an item had something beginning to build deep in his mind.

"Thanks," he said, watching him walk out of the room as the office phone rang.

Over the course of the next few days, Owen tried to get Hannah out of his mind. But every time he had a moment alone, she popped into his thoughts.

He replayed their first kiss—how quick it was and how much he wanted, more than anything, to make it last. But he'd been torn, still believing that she might know something about his father. It wasn't until after he'd confirmed that she didn't know anything that he realized he'd started having feelings for her. Three months was the longest he'd had a relationship since Kimber. With her, he'd allowed himself to ignore the warning bells. He'd been hurt beyond belief; it seemed like years before he had recovered from the betrayal of her infidelity. Even then, he vowed to never open himself up like that again to anyone.

After that, he'd stopped dating to focus on taking over for his father. Which appeared to have paid off, since the board was no longer looking to squeeze his family out, so long as Owen was stable.

He stayed in contact with his brothers and, even though he knew it was futile, continued to call his father's cell number daily. Most of the time it rang without voice mail picking up, which meant that his father had shut off his voice mail, or it was full.

The Friday after Hannah's meeting, he found the next note. This one had been stapled to his office door. Yanking it down, he glanced around the empty office. Nora wasn't even there yet. She normally got into the office around eight, and as he glanced down at his watch, he knew it would be almost thirty minutes before he'd see anyone else in the building.

After unlocking his office, he stepped inside and ripped the envelope open.

Step down or be put down.

Short and sweet, he thought as he tucked the note, along with its brothers, in the top desk drawer.

Whoever was trying to scare him didn't know him very well. His cell phone started to ring as he was sitting behind the desk, and he pulled it from his jacket pocket.

"This is Owen," he answered after seeing an unregistered number flash on his screen.

"Son?" His father's voice straightened his back.

"Dad?" He blinked a few times. "Dad?"

"I heard you took over at the office?" his father asked. The connection was terrible, and Owen thought it sounded as if he was at the airport.

"Yeah, the board . . ." He shook his head, not wanting to tell his father that the board didn't trust him anymore. "Yes," he said. "Where are you?"

"I'm in the state," he said. "Actually, I'm coming back home. I . . . can't leave you boys so exposed. I'd hoped to figure out—"

The phone started cutting out.

"Dad?" he said, standing up, as if it would help. "Dad?"

"I'm here," he said finally. "It may take me a while, but I'll be back."

"Soon?" He frowned. "I thought you said you were coming home?"

"I have to figure out—"

Again the phone chose that moment to cut out. When it went completely dead, Owen stared down at his cell and cursed.

What did his dad have to figure out? He glanced down at the drawer with the notes and pulled it open. Had his father received threats like these? Would Nora or Joel know about them?

He sat back down and dove into the calls he needed to make, then finished his normal daily work. Just after lunch, he decided to do a little research into what his father had been up to prior to his disappearance.

He hadn't meant to work past dark, but the next time he looked out the windows, the sun had already sunk below the dark waters of the gulf. He had another board meeting in the morning to discuss how things were going. He was dreading it. So, shutting everything down, he locked up and made his way down to the parking garage. His apartment was only a few blocks away, and most days he walked, but today, he'd wanted to be there for Hannah's meeting. After stepping out of the elevators, he glanced around and realized his car was one of the only employees' cars left.

"Burning the midnight oil?" a deep voice said from behind him. He jerked around and saw Joel light a cigarette as he stood against the wall.

"I could say the same about you," he joked as the man fell into step with him.

"I'm used to it." Joel shrugged. A move Owen had seen his father do more times than he could count.

"Yeah, looks like it's becoming a habit for me as well." Owen sighed. "How about grabbing drinks?" He thought of the little steak place a few doors down. He'd missed dinner and could feel his stomach growl.

"I could go for a drink." Joel motioned to his car. "I'll follow you."

Owen nodded and got into his own car. Instantly, he realized he'd sat on a piece of paper and pulled it out from behind him. Looking down at it, he tensed.

"Shit," he said out loud, scanning over the note. The threats were subtle enough, but he knew they were there.

This is your last chance to step down. Before you're removed permanently.

"Something wrong?" Joel had been walking toward his car, but he stopped when he heard Owen.

"No." He tossed the threatening note aside and started up his car. "It's nothing."

While he drove the block and a half to the steak house, he thought about turning the notes in to the police. After all, if something did happen to him, someone ought to know about it.

Deciding to make a call tomorrow to an old high school friend who was on the local police force, he pushed the notes to the back of his mind.

He'd enjoyed drinks and dinner with Joel a few times in the past. After all, Owen and his brothers wanted to show the guy they understood his situation. It wasn't as if any of them could do anything to change or force their father to fess up. God knows Owen had tried in the past to get his dad to come clean. Owen thought Joel was nice enough, if a little too eager to please his father. Still, he couldn't blame him. The unspoken competitiveness between Owen and Joel was much stronger than that between any of his brothers. Sometimes it was exhausting, but he had learned over the past year to set things aside.

As he spent the next hour with Joel, he made a point to ask more questions than he had in the past. He knew that Joel had been adopted when he was only six weeks old. The Copelands—Carl and Rhonda— had been a young couple back then. Owen had done some googling after Joel and Hannah had left his office. He had done an initial search on Joel when he'd first shown up, but after his father had found him looking into Joel's past, he had told Owen and his brothers to stop looking.

This time, he easily found some old photos of the socially elite family when they had brought Joel home. The family had moved closer to an upstate New York residence when Joel was five. But shortly after Joel's tenth birthday, his adoptive father, Carl, perished under mysterious circumstances. Less than a year after that, the family was rocked with a bunch of scandals when Carl was discovered to have been embezzling from the family business. His mother had to move in with her parents.

Still, after all the research he'd done on Joel, he knew the best way to find out more was to ask him himself.

They talked briefly about his past struggles with his own family and how, even now, he hardly ever talked to his adoptive mother.

"Rhonda kind of dropped me the moment I came to Florida with Leo," Joel said, finishing off his second beer.

Owen noted that Joel called his mother by her first name. He'd been adopted when he was six weeks old, and as far as he knew, Rhonda had been the only mother figure in Joel's life. Did that mean that Joel had never been close to the woman who had raised him?

The table had been cleared already of their empty plates, and Owen was seriously eyeing the dessert menu. He knew the chocolate lava cake was especially good at this place.

"How did Dad find you, anyway?" he asked for the first time.

"I'm not too sure of that myself." Joel shrugged. "I thought it was through the adoption agency, but I found out later that it wasn't."

"We all know . . ." He took a deep breath. "I mean, we suspect."

"Yeah," Joel broke in, "I don't think it really matters. I mean, I have parents. As flawed as they are and were, they still raised me."

"Right." Owen relaxed a little. "I mean, Dad has never said . . ."

"Right," Joel echoed. "Nor would he. At least I don't think he would own up to it. I know that Rhonda didn't know Leo before he showed up on my doorstep."

It was awkward. Talking to his half brother about why his father couldn't just step up and be a man. Here it was, twenty-six years later, and he couldn't just come forward.

"You know, Dad has never had an issue talking or opening up about things in his past before."

Joel surprised him by bursting out laughing. "He once told me a story about accidentally dropping you in a lake."

Owen was a little stunned. "He told you that story?"

"Yeah." Joel chuckled.

"It wasn't just a lake—it was an alligator-infested swamp." He chuckled himself as he remembered. "And he was the one who said it was safe to go out on the paddleboard together. I couldn't swim in anything for the rest of the summer for fear of being attacked by alligators. Even swimming pools," he added with a smile.

"Still," Joel said with a sigh, "it would have been nice. Having brothers like you three."

Owen wondered for a moment where Joel would have fit into their lives. He himself wouldn't have been the oldest, which meant he wouldn't have been trained and prepared to take over the family business. How would that have affected his life? He would have had more time to goof off, like his brothers had during school. Even now, he could be back at River Camp with Hannah, free from any obligations. Is that what he wanted?

"You've got us now," Owen said, lifting his beer so Joel could join him in a toast. "Anything you need."

"Right," Joel said again with a smile. "Thanks."

CHAPTER THREE

Hannah was just standing up from her desk to take an afternoon walk around the grounds when her phone rang. Her mother's phone number flashing on the screen had her sitting back down.

"Hi, Mom," she answered, knowing that the conversation would be a long one.

"Your father and I were just talking . . ." Her mother always jumped right into the conversation. After all, who had time for the customary greetings? "About the holidays . . ."

She tried to think of how to let her parents down easily. Even though the holiday season was months away, she knew the camp lacked the time and employees to fill in the gaps during that time. Especially since both Zoey and Elle would be taking time off to spend with Dylan and Liam. They had talked about going somewhere cold for a ski trip together. She tried not to be jealous of them or the fact that they had found the perfect guys. The fact that they were both Costa men played an even bigger part in her jealousy.

It was as if her friends' lives had fallen into place after opening River Camp back up. Sure, there had been the whole ordeal of the guys lying to them about their last name and why they had really come to the camp, but once all the secrets were out in the open, things seemed to be fixed and forgotten.

The same sort of thing she hoped could happen between her and Owen. But she'd confided one of her deepest secrets to him, and instantly, he'd pulled away. It wasn't as if being a virgin was all that shocking anymore. There were loads of people her age who chose careers over romance.

Weren't there?

Still, the moment when things had gotten so hot and heavy and she'd mentioned that she wanted him to be her first, he'd run for the hills. Well, Destin at least. Of course, the timing of his father calling Elle had coincided with the disastrous evening. Still, he'd left her heart-broken and angry. Much like Joel had done. Of course, with that case, things had been different.

Joel had been . . . well, pushy and demanding. Even though they had dated for only a few weeks, she'd been infatuated with him for almost a full year before he'd finally given her his attention.

Then, shortly before his graduation, he asked her to a dance. She was nothing more than a freshman, but being asked to a dance with an upperclassman was like a badge of honor.

That first date, he played the perfect gentlemen. Of course, it helped that her parents had insisted, since she was just shy of her sixteenth birthday, that they double-date with her friend Clara and her boyfriend, Tom. They had gone out on only two more official dates—one with Clara and Tom and a third to a movie with just the two of them.

When he drove her home after, they ended up at the vacant lot near her house instead. He embraced her, and at first, she only thought of how romantic it all was. But then he started pulling on her clothes, and she panicked. She pushed him away with a chuckle, hoping that he would get the hint. But when he kept reaching for her and tugging up her dress, she shoved him. When his fingers found their way under her silk panties and pushed inside her, she cried out, punched him in the jaw, and ran home as fast as she could.

The next day he called and apologized. But the damage was done. She told him that she didn't want to see him again. He tried to explain how some of the guys had given him a few beers before the movie, at which point she yelled at him for driving in the first place. In the end, less than three days later, graduation took place, and he moved away.

At first, no one knew where he'd gone, but she realized she no longer cared after she'd started dating Rob and found out what a man with patience could be like.

Still, seeing Joel next to Owen had been a shock. It was obvious just looking at them that they were related. She didn't know how, but she would bet that they were closer than just cousins.

She made a mental note to ask Zoey about Joel's relationship with the Costa brothers when she had a moment alone. But with Owen gone and the camp not having enough money to fill his position yet, she was running around like a chicken with its head cut off; actually, all the Wildflowers—what Elle, Zoey, Scarlett, Aubrey, and Hannah had called themselves that first summer they met—were as well. Especially since she was trying to fight the battle of Ryan Kinsley in her head.

The woman had it out for the camp and the friends. Hannah had a stack of homework to get together before the next meeting with the lawyers, which included getting more firsthand accounts of how Ryan had acted with other employees. She wanted to know everything the woman had done since stepping foot on the campgrounds. Of course, they were all doing their part to help out with this, but Hannah just had a way of getting to the bottom of things better than the others.

Each morning she woke before sunrise and rushed to either the yoga or water-aerobics classes she taught. Then, after a quick shower and change, along with a sit-down breakfast meeting with the other Wildflowers, she disappeared into her small office to coordinate all the upcoming events. She loved this part of her job. Planning fancy dinner themes, parties, and rainy-day events was her very own addiction.

She lived for it. She loved arranging every small detail, working hard to achieve it all, and then sitting back and watching people enjoy her creations. It was what she had been born to do.

Here at the camp, she could let her imagination go wild. Especially since it appeared that the snowbirds really enjoyed the wilder side of things. Sure, she wasn't going to go planning an orgy, like the first group of campers had at the pool right after their grand opening. But she could plan sexy parties beforehand, and, with the new rules in place, know that whatever happened after would take place in the privacy of someone's cabin and no longer out in the open.

Elle had been right. Once they started stocking condoms in the small lobby store, they had a whole new revenue stream to enjoy.

Scarlett and Zoey's mother, Kimberly, even suggested bringing in a third-party vendor to sell exotic toys and clothing in the little shop area. This was something Hannah had no idea how to plan but was willing to try setting up. So she spent most of her afternoon calling vendors and looking for someone to come take a look at the space.

For now, at least the little store was stocked with the basics, as well as some classy summer items from a local beach shop. She'd even bought herself a soft white pool cover-up from the store.

She had plans for adding wine and a beer cooler as well, since a lot of the guests had put in requests. But getting a permit to sell liquor by the bottle was proving more difficult than getting their license to sell glasses of alcohol in their dining hall.

"You're not listening to me." Her mother's voice broke into her thoughts.

"Sorry, Mom." She rubbed her forehead. "I just have too much on my plate here. I don't think I can . . ."

"Don't tell me you're not coming home. After all I've set up? Honestly, this little hobby of yours is going too far. You have obligations here with your family."

That statement caused Hannah's eyebrows to shoot up. "I do?"

"Yes, your father and I were just talking about Michael Ness. You remember the Ness family . . ." A statement rather than a question. "Anyway, their oldest, Michael, will be in town for the holidays, and we've arranged everything."

"What have you arranged?" she asked, knowing she'd dread the answer.

"Well, the entire time he and his family are out, we'll be entertaining them," she answered, as if she'd gone over this while Hannah hadn't been listening.

"Mom, I won't be able to make it out there. You'll just have to entertain the Ness family without me." She rubbed her forehead again as her mother started her rebuttal. Trying to convince her to change her mind. She really wished for a dip in the pool and maybe one of Britt's frozen drinks. Britt had been another great hire she'd overseen. The woman knew how to make some of the best frozen pool drinks around. She glanced at her watch and held in a groan when she realized she still had to get ready for a dinner party after she got off the phone.

She broke into her mother's complaints and stood up. "Mom, I really have to go. Can we talk about this later?"

"I'll plan on you being here. Since I'm one hundred percent sure you're going to change your mind. After all, you and Michael used to have some chemistry." Her mother sounded excited. "Just wait: he's even more handsome than he was in school."

Hannah rolled her eyes. *Handsome and conceited,* she thought.

"I've got to go," she said before hanging up. There, she'd done it. Even if it hadn't registered fully in her mother's mind, she'd communicated that she wasn't going to be home for the holidays. So when she didn't show up, they wouldn't be shocked.

After stepping out of her office, she almost ran into Damion, who maintained the pools and all the marine vessels and hosted nightly sunset boat tours for the guests. *Talk about handsome.* The younger man apologized and rushed past her.

"Is everything okay?" she asked as she followed him into the medical clinic.

"Yeah," he tossed over his shoulder. "Just have to get this stitched up." He showed her his left hand, wrapped in a white towel.

"What happened?" Keeping Dr. Lea Val on staff had proven to be one of their best moves yet. The woman was so busy sometimes that they had to use the adjoining room as a waiting room. Not that there were tons of people getting injured—just the opposite. But the older the clientele, the more aches and pains the doctor had to deal with.

"Caught it on the rigging. I've got about half an hour before I have to take a group out."

"Do you need any help?" she asked as Dr. Val took Damion's hand in hers and started checking it out. Hannah hissed and glanced away at the amount of blood that oozed from the cut.

"No, Zoey and Dylan were going to help out tonight. Thanks," he said.

"Hannah." Dr. Val's voice broke through the fog that had started messing with her mind. "Get out of here before you end up on the floor."

She didn't hesitate. As she stepped out the back entrance of the building, she closed her eyes and took several deep breaths to clear the haze that had taken over upon her seeing the blood. She'd never been able to stomach it. Even when she'd scraped her knee as a child, she'd passed out.

"What happened?" A deep voice broke into the fog. Strong hands took her shoulders and held her firm.

She must be dreaming. Owen was no longer at the camp. But when her eyes slid open, there he was, looking down at her—his dark eyes full of concern.

"Blood," she said. Her voice sounded far away, and she was still having tunnel vision.

She felt his fingers flinch on her skin. "Whose? Yours?" He examined her, his hands running up and down her arms, looking for any wounds.

"No, Damion. He . . . cut his hand." She shook her head. "I'm okay." She took a couple more deep breaths. "I just don't do well . . . around blood. What are you doing here?"

"I had a board meeting this morning and needed to talk to my brothers. I thought I'd stop in and . . . maybe we could talk about . . . the other day." She knew he was a short drive away, but she hadn't been prepared for his visit.

Then, feeling fully in control of herself again, she stepped out of his hold. "There's nothing really to talk about." She started toward her apartment so she could change for the dinner party.

"Yes, there is." He fell in step with her.

She glanced at him and stopped under a large oak tree. Even though the sun was already setting, the late-summer heat had elicited a light sheen of sweat, and she'd only been outside for about ten minutes. Wishing more than ever for a cool dip in the pool and a frozen drink, she placed her hands on her hips.

"No, I think you said everything you needed to when you left." She started to turn away, but he stopped her by placing a hand on her arm.

At least he wasn't wearing a suit here. She imagined he'd been in one for the board meeting earlier that day. Now, however, he was wearing a pair of khaki shorts and a brown V-neck T-shirt with a pair of dark sunglasses hanging from the V.

He looked like a model straight off the summer catwalk. His dark hair was longer than his brothers' hair, long enough that there was a slight curl to it. It was then that she realized that his sexy brown eyes had been roaming over her as well.

She wore one of the camp's T-shirts with her tan shorts. Nothing fancy—nothing he hadn't seen her in a million times before—but still, he was looking at her like she was wearing silk and lace.

"What?" She glanced down at his hand on her arm. "Did I miss something?"

"Yes," he said softly. "We do need to talk. If you have time?"

She huffed, mainly for show, since she didn't want him to think that he could arrive and demand her time whenever he wanted.

Glancing at her watch, she calculated that after a quick shower and change, she'd still have time to make it to the dining hall ten minutes early.

"Ten minutes," she said, and she moved over to sit on one of the many new benches his brother Liam had built and installed along the walking paths.

Owen sat next to her and, for a moment, stayed silent. "I should have talked to you before I left."

After another moment of silence, she made a move to get up. Was that all he was going to say to her about breaking her heart? Hurting her the way he had? She had felt totally humiliated and rejected when he left, and this was his explanation or attempt at an apology? "Okay, so?"

"No." He stopped her again. "It's just . . . I've never . . ." He shook his head and then ran his hands through his hair, messing up the curls even more. "You put some pretty heavy things on the table."

"Okay," she said a little slower. "Imagine how I feel." She waited, and when he turned to her, she could see something deeper behind his eyes.

"I have—the gift you were willing to give me . . . I wasn't worthy of."

"What makes you say that?" she asked. "It was mine to give. If I deemed you worthy, then you should have—"

"What?" he interrupted her. "*Allowed* you to give me your virginity?"

She quickly glanced around to make sure they were alone on the pathway. "Yes," she hissed. "Why not?"

"Because, something like that means more than just a quick . . ." He shook his head.

"Fuck?" she suggested. "Who says it had to?"

"You did." He stood up suddenly and started pacing in front of her. "Otherwise you would have . . . gotten rid of it years ago."

She laughed, and he stopped pacing. "What if I just hadn't found someone I wanted to be with?"

He tilted his head and looked at her as if she'd just grown a second head. "Really? I heard all about that mechanic you were dating from Zoey."

She winced. "Okay, hindsight, I was thankful Rob and I never . . . he cheated on me," she blurted out.

"Can you blame the guy? Without any . . ." He motioned toward her. "A guy can only wait so long."

She leaned back in the bench. "Really?" She crossed her arms over her chest and looked at him. "What about you?"

"I'm one of those guys." He shrugged. At least he was being honest.

"So, you wouldn't date a woman more than two months without needing . . . more?"

"Two months?" He frowned. "Is that how long you and what's his name went out?"

She smiled. "Yes."

"Stupid man." He shook his head and sat back down next to her. "No, two months is nothing. Hell, *we've* known each other longer."

"Right." Her smile grew as she felt her heart warm again; even though the pain was still there, she could feel that he was trying, and that was everything to her at the moment. "Which is why I was hoping to take our relationship to the next level."

She watched his Adam's apple move up and down as he swallowed. "Right." He sighed. "And I messed that up."

"Yes, you did." She stood up. "But there's nothing in the rule book that says we can't go back to being friends." He stood up as well.

"Right." His voice told her that he wasn't convinced.

"I mean, you're in Destin now, and I'm here." She motioned around her.

"We're only fifteen minutes apart. Twenty during rush hour."

"But forty during tourist times," she corrected him. That timing had messed up more than a few guest entertainers at the camp dinners.

"Right." He smiled.

"So, how about sticking around and helping out during the dinner rush? You know, for old times' sake?"

She watched his shoulders loosen. "I'd like that."

CHAPTER FOUR

Owen stood in the main dining hall at River Camp and watched the guests shuffle in. He'd borrowed a camp T-shirt from his brother's room and could instantly tell that he was seriously underdressed for the night. Most guests wore long ball gowns or suits and ties. He knew from his time working at the camp that they usually had themed dinner nights, and they'd been part of the planning when he'd been there.

But it wasn't like he had other options.

Helping out Brent, the head waiter, once again was a joy, however, as was catching up with a few of the other guys on the team. Actually, the more he thought about it, the more he realized that he enjoyed working at River Camp more than he did at his own family's business. It wasn't as if the people who worked at Paradise Investments were terrible; it was just the fact that the job here was more to his liking and a whole lot more fun.

He really had enjoyed helping out with the events and playing waiter in the evenings. He and his brothers had had real jobs throughout their lives, of course. That was one thing their father had insisted on from the moment they'd hit sixteen. Owen's first job had been mowing yards in their neighborhood. He'd dragged both Dylan and Liam around to help him out when they could. He paid them a percentage of his income, but then his brothers grew a little wiser and found out that if they set up their own jobs, they could keep all the money. When they started charging less than he was, he moved on to a real job, busing tables at a local diner. He loved to flirt with all the high school girls who came in and quickly moved up to being a waiter within a few months. He was making so much money that summer that he ended up buying his own car. Which of course once again got the attention of his brothers.

Then, the summer before he graduated, his father asked him to intern at the office. He wanted to say no, but he knew he owed a lot of what they had to his old man. Besides, it fell to him as the oldest to follow in their father's footsteps.

He found out a few things that summer. One, he hated wearing a suit, and two, he was very good at what he did for Paradise Investments. Sure, that first year his father just had him running errands, but between high school and college, his dad moved him up to a desk job in marketing. He enjoyed that job even more.

By the time he had his associate's degree in hand, he was reporting directly to his father. Joel had been brought on by then and had filled Owen's old position as his father's gofer. Which had stirred different emotions in him—not necessarily jealousy, but worry of a sort. Worry that someone was trying to move in on his position in life and on his family. Especially after rumors of Joel's connection to the family started going around. The man was either hot or cold. Sometimes he was friendly, like a brother, while other times he acted like nothing more than an employee eager to serve and stay in line. It had taken him a long time to see past the act.

Even now, he didn't believe he knew the man who could secretly be his brother.

The family business was the first place Dylan and Liam chose not to follow him. By that point, his brothers were off doing their own things, following their own paths, which made Owen even more obligated to help their father out. After all, his dad had been hinting that one day he'd take over the family business.

"You're back?" Dean Wallis, another waiter, stopped beside him. The man looked like a James Dean wannabe, and Owen wondered if Dean was even his real name. His dark hair was slicked back, and the black suit and tie he was wearing blended him into the crowd more than Owen was at the moment. The man's good looks got him enough attention from the female guests that Owen knew for a fact he'd entertained more than just the single ladies on several occasions.

"No, just for the night," he answered.

"Oh?" Dean's dark eyebrows rose; then he shot a glance toward the door.

Owen's eyes followed his, and he had to swallow as Hannah strolled into the room. Her long royal-blue dress made his mouth water. Seeing those sexy long legs of hers through the long slit in the soft material had him wishing he could pull her into a closet somewhere and . . . he shook his head.

"She's been moping around this place for days." Dean nudged his shoulder. "Until tonight." He winked at him and then strolled away to another guest.

He watched Hannah survey the room, and when her eyes landed on him, a genuine smile flashed on her face, making her more beautiful than he could remember her looking before.

He would have approached her if he could have gotten his body to move at all, but just watching her glide across the dining room toward him froze his body and mind.

"Evening," she said as she stopped next to him.

"Hi." He cleared his throat. "You look amazing." Her smile flashed.

"Thank you. You look"—she glanced down at him with a giggle—"ready to work."

He groaned. "Yeah, you could have warned me it was a fancy dinner night."

She tilted her head. "And miss seeing those legs of yours?" She wiggled her eyebrows.

"Speaking of legs . . . may I say, wow?" He crooked a brow in return.

Just then Brent walked by. "Yes, we all know Hannah looks amazing," he said with a wink, "but you have tables waiting. So stop ogling your boss and get back to work."

Hannah laughed as she turned and walked away, while he followed Brent back to the kitchen.

For the rest of the night, he caught himself scanning the crowded dining hall for Hannah. Each time, he found her talking to guests or helping out with the entertainment. Tonight a band was playing on the main stage. Guests danced on the small dance floor, and on several occasions, he even spotted Hannah dancing with a guest. Most of them were older, but still, she moved across the floor as if she'd been born to dance.

When the crowd started to thin out, he was left helping clean up. Dylan showed up halfway through the night and pitched in. It wasn't until the end of the evening that he realized they would not have made it through the evening without his help.

"Why are they so short staffed tonight?" he asked as he helped Dylan clear a table.

"Tonight?" His brother's eyebrows shot up. "Since you've left, we've all been pulling double duty."

"They haven't replaced me yet?" He frowned and put a stack of dirty dishes into the bin.

"No. They've tried, but it's hard to find good help, especially someone who'll take the low pay and work all the different jobs you did."

"Right." He thought back to all the odd jobs he'd been stuck doing. Everything from delivering food orders to cabins to making small repairs around the camp. Not to mention playing host to a bunch of fun events and keeping the guests busy and happy. He'd even taken a few couples on horseback rides around the campgrounds, filling in for their stable master, Carter, when he could. His brothers had their own jobs around the camp, and as far as he could tell, they still enjoyed working there. Dylan was head of the zip lines and other outdoor adventures, while Liam taught and worked in the wood shop most days as well as filling in when needed around the place.

"How's corporate life?" Dylan asked him as they dumped the dirty dishes in the kitchen.

He stopped and leaned on the counter. "Dad called." He had filled his brothers in on what the board had discussed earlier that morning. It hadn't been hard to convince the members who ran his family business to trust in him. A few of the members had fought against him stepping in for his father, even temporarily. Kurt Herrera and Stephen Shephard were two of the most outspoken against the move. The men had it out for him, and he had to wonder why.

"How do we know this kid"—Kurt had motioned toward Owen shortly after the meeting had been called to order—"won't take off like his father? I mean, look at him. He's barely off the tit."

This statement earned several glares from the three women and two other men in the room. But before anyone could jump in and object to the vulgar statement, Stephen added, "It seems at this point that we can't trust any of the Costas."

The entire room exploded with shouts of, "The Costas are the reason we're sitting here today. If it hadn't been for Leo Costa, there wouldn't be a Paradise Investments."

In the end, Owen had stood up and promised the group of people that he would uphold his father's integrity and forward motion, which he'd used to create the business twenty-some years earlier. Apparently, he'd been persuasive enough, because even with Kurt's and Stephen's doubting words, they had all agreed that the best thing for the business would be to have a Costa at the helm.

He hadn't had much of a chance to discuss all the requirements the board had set with his brothers, since Liam had been needed for a wood-carving class.

"He did?" Dylan looked surprised. "He hasn't called Elle again, not since the last time. At least Liam hasn't mentioned it."

"He said he'll be coming back but that he has a few things to do first." He sighed, frustrated that he couldn't just talk to his father.

"Well, that's good, then," Dylan added. "So the board is willing to keep you on even after Dad returns?"

"Yeah, that's what they decided today," he said.

"Sounds like you've earned their trust," Dylan said.

He wanted to laugh as he remembered the doubts of a few of them, but he sighed and then added, "For now." He wondered if he should tell his brother about the threatening notes he'd been receiving. The last one mentioned something about exposing him to the board as a fraud, but since that was so far fetched, he felt a little more relaxed. Still, he figured his brothers should know. "Got a moment?" he asked, nodding toward the back door. If he was going to tell him, he might as well do it in private.

"Sure." He glanced around and then waved to Brent. "We're taking a break."

Brent nodded and then rushed back out to the front dining hall.

Stepping out into the sultry night air, he was thankful he wasn't wearing a suit like Dylan was. The shorts and T-shirt allowed what little breeze there was to cool him off.

"I'd forgotten how much fun it was around here." He leaned against the railing of the back stairs.

"You could always come back," Dylan surprised him by saying.

"Sure, pull a move like Dad? I just convinced the board to trust me with the family business."

"Right." Dylan shrugged. "Just a thought. It's not like you're needed there full time."

"I've been getting threats," he blurted out.

"What?" Dylan's relaxed look turned to concern instantly. "From whom?"

"If I knew that . . ." Owen chuckled. "They're just anonymous notes."

"Right." Dylan ran his hands through his long hair. "What do they say?"

"To step down from the board."

"Or?" Dylan asked.

"Just to step down," he answered, keeping the seriousness of the threats to himself. "But the threat is obvious." He crossed his arms over his chest. "Whoever it is broke into my car the other night."

"Shit." Dylan started pacing around the landing. "You don't think that's the reason Dad left?"

"The thought had crossed my mind." After all, it had been one of the first reasons he could think of for their father's behavior.

"So, if Dad were receiving the same notes . . ." Dylan fell silent for a while. "But I just can't see Dad packing up and running because of a few threats."

"Yeah, I came to the same conclusion."

"Okay, so then . . ." Dylan started, but just then the back door opened, and Hannah stepped out.

"There you two are." She smiled at him, and instantly his conversation was forgotten. "Zoey was looking for you."

"Later," Dylan said. "We'll figure this out, together." His brother laid a hand on his shoulder before quickly disappearing.

"What was that all about?" Hannah stopped next to him. He turned and leaned against the railing, sitting on it so he could face her.

"Work." He shrugged.

"How are things going? Elle mentioned something about the board of directors putting you in charge of the business in your dad's absence."

"Yes." He reached out and touched the soft material of her dress. He'd been wanting to touch her all evening, and this was the first chance he had gotten. It was just as soft as he'd imagined it would be. Almost as soft as her skin.

"How do you feel about that?" she asked, her voice low. He could tell by the way her eyes had become unfocused that his touch had affected her just as much as it had him.

"It's what I was meant to do," he said, moving her a little closer to him. "Just like you were meant for this." He felt his heart skip a little at the thought of them living so far apart. He knew she'd mentioned starting over as just friends, but he knew as well as she did that that wasn't going to be possible. From their first kiss, they were destined to be more, and at this point, he doubted he could keep himself from feeling more about her. She was in his every waking thought, as if she'd become part of him at this point. "Hannah, tell me to go away," he murmured as his eyes moved to her lips.

"I can't." She moved closer to him, wrapping her arms around his shoulders. "Even though you left us—you left *me*—I can't tell you not to come back here. You belong here as much as you belong in a suit sitting behind a desk."

"Where do we go from here?" he asked, desperately wanting to kiss her again.

She pulled away. "I'm not sure." She shook her head and crossed her arms over her chest as if she was cold. "But I can't keep holding out for something that isn't going to be."

He could have kicked himself for saying those words to her that last night. The night she'd confided in him that she was a virgin.

"Hannah, I . . . didn't mean . . ."

Again, he was interrupted when the back door flew open, almost knocking Hannah over. He reached for her and pulled her clear of the swinging door.

"Easy," he said to Dean as he walked out.

"Sorry." Dean chuckled. "I didn't know this was the new hangout." He glanced around. "Gosh, it's still so hot. I'm going to go pull off this suit and hit the pool. Anyone want to join me?"

"No thanks," Owen mumbled. Even though a dip in the pool sounded pretty amazing at the moment.

"Your loss." Dean turned to Hannah. "You?"

"No, thanks," she said, still holding on to Owen. "Night."

"Night." Dean turned and jogged down the steps and disappeared into the darkness.

"Take a walk with me?" he asked, knowing that more employees would be coming out the back door at any moment and that their private spot was no longer going to be private.

"Sure." She followed him down the steps, and he realized instantly that her tall heels were going to be an issue on the gravel pathway.

"Why not pull those off, and we can walk in the grass?" He motioned to the small yard area near the front of the building.

She shook her head with a cringe. "I've seen a few snakes in that grass."

"Okay." He thought about it, then hoisted her up in his arms and started to carry her across the gravel.

"What are you doing?" she exclaimed as she wrapped her arms around his shoulders.

"Since you can't walk in those on the gravel, I'll carry you over to the dock area. There's cement there, and"—he shrugged—"then you can walk along the boardwalk area."

She relaxed in his arms a little. "I've never been carried before," she said, straightening her long dress over her legs. Part of it had fallen, exposing more of her leg and almost causing him to trip.

When he reached the cement pathway that surrounded the dock and boathouse, he set her back down.

"There," he said, feeling a little out of breath and disappointed at the loss of those perfect breasts of hers pressed up against his chest. "Better?"

"Yes, thank you," she answered, straightening her dress once more.

As she started walking along the path, he watched the way her hips swayed. God, he needed to stop thinking about her that way, knowing he'd broken her heart before, knowing that he didn't deserve being with her now. If she was off limits in his mind, then he should move on. Still, he just couldn't keep his eyes off her. Especially seeing the way that the moonlight was causing her skin to glow.

"So?" She turned to him so quickly he almost bumped into her. "What do you want?"

He thought about her lips, about taking her the way he'd wanted to that last night when they'd been together. It could have been so simple back then. But after touching her, after seeing the way she'd responded to him, he'd somehow known. When she'd confided in him, confirming his thoughts, he'd pulled away.

It was all too much for him to handle. He'd been fifteen when he'd first fumbled through sex with Abigail Leif, his first. Abigail had been two years older and far more experienced. Thankfully. After that, he'd enjoyed himself whenever he could, having several long-term relationships, up until Kimber had cheated on him.

"I want lots of things." He dropped his hand, remembering the hurt and betrayal of his last relationship and his current family turmoil. Turning away, he looked out over the dark waters. "But that doesn't mean I'll get them."

"Why not?" she asked, leaning on the post next to him. "If you work hard enough. I mean, look at this place. We took an old run-down summer camp for girls and turned it into something pretty amazing."

He smiled and glanced over at her. "Yes, you did. And it's a huge success."

"Not quite yet, but it will be." She shrugged.

He turned to her. "What makes you say that? Aren't you booked solid for the rest of the year?"

"Yes, but we still can't find any employees . . ." She let her sentence drop off.

"To replace me?" he asked with a smile. Her chin tipped up slightly in defiance.

"Or Ryan."

"I thought Lindsey replaced Ryan?" he asked, remembering the young blonde woman who had been hired the day after Ryan had been fired.

"She did, but she's going back to school in a week, and her hours are going to suffer. Which means"—she sighed heavily—"we need to find someone else to fill in during those times."

"The work pool isn't so great around here," he said. "My father once took almost two months to find a replacement for a secretary. Not his own—he's had Nora for as long as I can remember." He smiled as he thought about the older woman who had always been there for his father and now for him. The woman knew her job and didn't take any shit from any of the family members.

"If only the camp were closer to the city." She turned and leaned her back against the railing. "It's just so hard, being out in the country like this."

"You have housing." He motioned to the main building that housed a lot of the full-time employees on the second floor, though she shared a private apartment with Scarlett and Aubrey on the top floor. He remembered his time in the small bedroom that he had shared with his two brothers. He had tried to avoid spending as much time as he could in the small space when he'd been there.

"Yeah—glorified dorm rooms. Employees need more space when they have time off. What we really need are apartments close by." She tilted her head. "Maybe just inside Pelican Point? It's only five minutes away. Far enough away from the camp that you still get the secluded feeling we boast about. Then again," she said, her shoulders slumping, "the town isn't really big enough to support an apartment complex. We only have one gas station and a small general store."

"But isn't that a draw in and of itself?" he asked. "I mean, aren't most people looking to get out of the city? If the town starts growing . . ." He thought about it, and suddenly a plan formed in his mind. He straightened up and started pacing. "What if . . . what if someone built a small community over on the far side of Pelican Point? I'm talking about new homes, a community center, swimming pools—everything that would draw people to small-town living?"

"I don't see how that would help us out tomorrow when dinner hour comes around again and we're short staffed," she said with a skeptical glance.

"It could in the long run."

"True." She smiled. "See, you were meant to run your family's business." She walked over to him, her high heels clicking on the cement pathway. Leaning up, she placed a soft kiss on his cheek.

His hands went automatically to her bare arms to pull her closer. "Hannah, this doesn't change the fact that I still want to be with you," he said, searching her eyes. He noticed the moment she softened.

"I want you too, but . . . it seems like the timing . . ." She sighed. "With everything that's going on with your father and your work . . ."

"Screw the timing," he said with a smile. "All the greatest things in life are things worth waiting for. If we can't be together today or tomorrow . . . soon."

He heard her suck her breath in; then, as he leaned closer, she released it as his lips closed over hers.

CHAPTER FIVE

Hannah didn't understand why she was allowing her emotions to be rocked so hard by Owen. He was hot one moment and then cold as ice the next, retreating into silence and seclusion.

After that last night on the walking path by the boathouse, he'd carried her back to the front steps of the main building, left her with a quick peck on the lips, and then disappeared again for a few days. Sure, he'd texted her a few times, telling her that he'd been thinking of her, but for the most part, things had fallen back into the pattern of her being alone again.

She'd been surprised when, less than three days later, four different applications crossed her desk.

"Did you see these?" Zoey rushed into her office shortly after she received the emails.

"What?" She glanced up after reading through the last application.

"These!" She waved a stack of papers. "Applications. Real people have applied for jobs here." Her friend smiled as Elle and Aubrey walked in behind her. "And they're good ones too."

"I was just looking over them. Can they be real?" she asked. "How did they find out about us?"

"Who cares—they're hired." Elle sat on the edge of Hannah's desk. "We can't really afford all four of them . . ." Her friend frowned. "But maybe I can make things work . . ."

"What about interviewing them?" she asked.

Zoey waved the papers again. "With applications this good, who cares?"

"Need I remind you about the last employee we had to fire?" Aubrey broke in, turning to Zoey. "She turned a gun on your boyfriend."

"Fiancé," Zoey corrected with a smile.

"Right." Aubrey laughed. "Still, a gun . . ." Zoey's smile fell away.

"Right," she echoed. "Okay, interviews, then hiring."

"I'll arrange it all," Elle said, taking the stack from Zoey. "As well as working out the budget to make sure we can afford them all."

"We can't afford not to hire them all," Hannah added. "We're booked solid. Something has to give. We'll just have to find the money. Maybe pull it from somewhere else?"

Elle sighed. "I'll look."

"What about adding more items to the store? That seems to be a huge hit. How about camp T-shirts and other items like bags or cozies?" she suggested. It was an idea she'd thought of after being asked by a guest if she could buy a T-shirt like those all the employees wore.

"That's a great idea," Aubrey added. "We can even do bathrobes. I love the ones the resort in Cabo gave us when we stayed there. We could have them embroidered, along with T-shirts, maybe even with funny sayings on them like . . ." She tilted her head. "'I got into the swing of things at River Camp'?"

Everyone laughed. "What about, 'I slept around at River Camp'?" Zoey added.

"How about, 'Older and bolder at River Camp,' or 'Oldies but goldies'?" she suggested as another fit of giggles exploded in the room.

"River Camp's big tramps," Elle added with a smile.

"Getting wild in the wild," Zoey said, chuckling.

"Summer camp . . . not for kids anymore," Aubrey suggested.

"Okay," Elle said, wiping the tears of laughter from her eyes. "I'll call and set up the interviews. Aubrey, you see how much the T-shirts and other items will run us. If we can have a high markup on the items, I'd say it would be worth it. Besides, it's great marketing."

After everyone left, she wrote down a few more fun quotes as well as some more serious ideas and shot them off to the shared to-do list.

When her phone rang, she answered without even glancing at the screen.

"Hello?" Her smile evaporated as she heard her father's voice.

"Hannah, what's this your mother is saying about you not coming home for the holidays?"

Closing her eyes, she took a few deep breaths before answering.

"Yes, I've just got too much going on at work—"

"Isn't that why you went into business with your little friends? So that you could have some time off once in a while? Your family needs you. We're counting on you to help solidify this deal with the Ness family."

She knew it. There was no way her parents would have set up time with the Ness family if it hadn't had something to do with her family's investment business. After all, when she'd dated Michael, her father had been very disappointed in her choice. She'd thought it was strange that her mother had acted like they had been approving parents back then.

"Dad, I can't get away. They're counting on me. Besides, I'm seeing someone." She let the words jump out before really thinking about the consequences.

"You are?" Her father was quiet for a moment. "Do I know his family?"

"No, Dad, you don't know everyone." She rubbed her forehead. Why was it that her parents always gave her a headache?

"What's his name?" he asked.

"I'm not doing this," she said quickly. "I can't make it up there for the holidays. That's it. I have to get back to work. I'll call Mom later tonight. Bye." She hung up and slunk her head down on the desk.

There had been a time when her parents had controlled every aspect of her life. Back when they had paid for everything she had and had steered every activity. Even every boyfriend she'd had had been approved by her parents first. Of course, they'd run extensive background checks on any boy and his family. It was as if her parents hadn't wanted their only child to encounter anyone out of their tax bracket.

Everything in her life had been like that. If she wanted to take dance, they enrolled her in the best classes and vetted the teachers so that she would have only the best. At first, she'd believed that it was just parental love that had fueled them; then, after she'd found her dad berating one of her teachers about her grades not being high enough and threatening to have the woman fired, she'd realized what it actually was.

Having her eyes opened to the schemes that her parents played to get her ahead in life was almost nauseating. They didn't think twice about paying to make her bad grades go away or to remove unwanted, or poor, friends from her life.

Everyone had been affected, except the Wildflowers. The group of friends she'd met at River Camp all those years ago had gone unscathed. She didn't know if it was luck or if her parents hadn't believed they were worthy of bribing away. Either way, she was thankful her friends had stuck by her side all these years. More importantly, she was thankful they were the ones who'd allowed her to finally escape.

When her phone rang again, she smiled at seeing Owen's number pop up on the screen.

"Hi," she answered on the second ring.

"Hi." She could hear his happy tone. "Did you get the applicants?"

Her eyebrows shot up, and she frowned slightly. Her first emotion was fear that this was a step for him to control her somehow. "You . . . sent them?"

"I might have suggested to a few employees who had friends looking for your kind of work that you had openings," he said with a chuckle, causing her to relax. After all, she could tell he was just trying to help her out, and they could use all the help they could get.

"Yes, we've received four so far."

"Great." He sighed. "I hope it helps."

"It has so far. Everyone's excited about the possibility of being able to relax a little more around here."

"Good." She heard him take another breath. "Listen, I'm going to be in town tomorrow for a meeting. I was wondering if you could get the evening off? Maybe we can grab some dinner?"

"Like a date?" she asked, hope bubbling as she quickly ran through what her plans were for the evening.

"Yes, if you can get away. I thought, you know, that we should start over somewhere. You know, take it slow."

She smiled, liking that he was making a point to show her that he was interested. That he wanted more with her. "I'd like that. I'll see if I can get someone to cover for me." She thought of asking Scarlett. After all, her friend owed her one since she'd covered for her two nights ago.

"Sounds great." He must have shifted, causing the phone to be muffled for a second. "Can't wait to see you again," he said when he came back.

Just hearing the tone in his voice change had her heart skipping. He sounded sexy, as if he had been thinking about her since she'd seen him last. She'd been thinking about him, a lot.

"Me too." She smiled and sank into her chair a little more.

After hanging up with Owen, she shut down her computer and headed out to her evening hot yoga class. It wasn't one of her more popular classes, but she enjoyed it the most.

After sweating for thirty minutes, she showered off in the attached locker rooms and dressed for dinner. Tonight was a themed night, so, after putting on her swimsuit along with a grass skirt and a lei, she braided her hair down one side and bobby pinned a few flowers in her hair.

Standing back, she smiled at her reflection. Just then Andrea stepped into the locker room.

"Evening," she greeted the masseuse.

"Hi, wow, you look amazing." Andrea stopped in her tracks.

"Thanks." Andrea was about Hannah's age. Her arms bore almost full sleeves of bright tattoos. Her short-cropped blonde hair often was colored with temporary colors that matched her personality. At one point, Hannah believed Andrea had been hitting on her but chalked up the incident to Andrea's outgoing personality. But the way Andrea was looking at her now told Hannah clearly that the woman was more than interested.

Hannah had never really thought about how to discourage a woman from hitting on her before.

"Easy." Andrea smiled at her. "I don't bite. I get it. You have a thing for Owen. Too bad." She winked at her and touched her arm. "Lucky man. If you ever change your mind, though, you know where to find me." Her hand slid away from her arm, and Andrea disappeared into one of the back rooms.

As she walked into the dining hall a few minutes later, she caught another wave of flattery as Dylan shook his head at her entry.

He whistled. "If my brother could see you now, he'd never go back to Destin."

For the rest of the night, she was flooded with compliments, which she always enjoyed, and she ate up the attention. Somehow, it made dressing up even more fun. Still, the one man she had wanted to hear from had been absent, which had her wishing he was around that evening. But just knowing that she was going to see him the following night had her in a good mood. Especially after Scarlett had assured her that she could fill in for her tomorrow night.

She even thought about an outfit for the evening. This time, when the dining hall became empty, she was rushing around helping Brent and the rest of the crew clean up. The waitstaff was efficient but short-handed, which meant that she spent some time hauling dirty dishes into the back kitchen.

"Here you go." Isaac Andrews handed her a plate filled with his lemon chicken dish, along with a smaller plate with a slice of cheese-cake. "Brent informed me that you haven't eaten anything tonight. Sit, eat." His dark eyes narrowed at her, daring her to turn him down.

Smiling, she sat down next to him at the bar area and started eating. Talking the celebrity chef into working at the camp had been one of her greatest achievements. Especially knowing that he was one of her father's oldest friends and one of his biggest critics. Not that her father had a lot of critics, or friends for that matter, but there were a few of them spread out, and she tried to make them *her* friends. She figured if she couldn't have the upper hand with her parents, at least she could influence his friends and business partners. She'd found out early on that half of them couldn't stand her father personally, which ended up benefiting her in the long run.

"Have you heard from your folks?" He sipped his water as he watched her.

"Not today, thankfully." She enjoyed the zest of the chicken sauce and wondered why she hadn't realized she was hungry until tasting the food.

"Your mother called me," he admitted with a grin. "She wants to know why you're choosing to stay here for the holidays and the name of the man you're seeing."

She set her fork down. "You didn't tell her anything, did you?"

"No." He rested his hand over hers. "You have your secrets, and, besides, you're my boss. I didn't want to do anything that would jeop-ardize my position here. I rather like having command of my own kitchen."

"Isaac, we both know you could be anywhere. The fact that you are sticking around here is . . ." She groaned. "Pathetic?"

"It's where I want to be," he assured her. "Besides, if I wanted the fast life of running my own restaurant, I wouldn't enjoy all the other things that come with just being in the kitchen. I'm not one for running my own show. I like handling a kitchen, not a business."

It was one of the things he'd said to her when he'd first agreed to come on as head chef. She'd believed him back then, and she did again now. She knew a lot of people who preferred to stay in the background. She'd been one of them until she'd gotten a taste of running the show herself. Even now, if it wasn't for her four best friends splitting the obligations, she wouldn't be able to tough it out.

"So are you going to tell me who your special man is?" Isaac asked, nudging her shoulder. She'd known the man most of her life. He'd started out working in her family's kitchen. The fact that her mother had never cooked a meal in her life meant Hannah's homemade meals and nightly formal dinners came from a team of kitchen professionals located in the basement of their brownstone.

Her parents' six-thousand-square-foot brownstone on the Upper East Side also included a gorgeous private garden, an indoor pool, and an underground drive-in garage, not to mention the rooftop terrace with views. Still, the lower-level kitchen had been one of the places her mother and father had never entered. Actually, the entire fifth floor, where Hannah's room had been, was another space her parents had never trodden. Thankfully.

She finally answered Isaac with a bit of humor. "I would have thought that it was common knowledge around here."

"I thought so." He nodded while he watched her from the corner of his eye. "I just had to get confirmation from you. The brothers sure made a splash around here. What with Dylan and Zoey and then Elle and Liam all getting together." He pushed the plate with the cheesecake toward her. "Finish this off before I do." He rubbed his flat belly.

She laughed. "You need it as much as I do." She reached over and grabbed another fork just as Zoey and Scarlett walked into the kitchen area.

"Oh, there's more cheesecake left?" Zoey asked, taking up her own fork. Her sister wasn't far behind her.

"This one is for Hannah; there's more for you two over there." Isaac pointed at the dessert counter.

"You spoil her," Zoey added with a slight frown.

"She is the one who got me my dream job," Isaac said with a wink.

"True." Zoey set a plate down in front of her sister and then one for herself. "She still hasn't mentioned to us how you two know each other." Zoey's eyes narrowed. "You two weren't a . . ." She waved her fork between them.

"No," Hannah and Isaac said at the same time.

"I'm almost twenty years older than you three," Isaac added.

"Age isn't an issue." Scarlett's comment surprised them all. "What? Working here has shown me that more than anything," she said between bites.

It was true. Some of the snowbirds who came down here to visit had younger partners and were happier than most of the others.

"Actually, I've learned a lot about love while working here," Scarlett said with a chuckle, adding, "like, how not to sneak around on your spouse. Do you know I caught the guy from cabin two crawling out of the lady in cabin three's window the other morning?" She rolled her eyes. "It wouldn't have been so bad, but he was bare-ass naked."

"Isn't cabin two a couple?"

"Yeah, and it just so happened that the lady in cabin two, Riley, was walking back from the pool with me at the time." She shook her head. "At first I thought . . . swingers. Then I watched Riley's face turn beet red. I've never seen a naked man run so fast."

"Is that why they checked out today?" Hannah asked. "I thought they were dissatisfied with having to move to the smaller cabin instead of staying at Bear-Foot Bungalow, as they had planned."

"No." Scarlett finished off her cheesecake. "I'm pretty sure there's a divorce in their future."

"Maybe our camp T-shirts should say, 'I got caught at River Camp'?" Hannah added with a chuckle.

"T-shirts?" Isaac asked.

"Another way for us to make more money," she reassured him.

"You know, I could always pull a few strings. Have you thought about opening up the outside dining hall and bringing other diners from outside the camp for one night a week?"

"That's a great idea," Zoey said, sitting up a little straighter. "How many tables could we hold? Do you think you could swing it if we got, say, a few more staff members?"

"My kitchen staff can handle it," he assured them. "We would need a few more waitstaff."

"How many?" Hannah asked.

"Four?" Isaac tapped a finger against his lips. "Maybe five."

"How much more do you think it would bring in?" Hannah asked, already calculating the costs of opening the dining hall up to noncampers. She'd have to confirm with the city and make sure that their business license was valid for such adventures. Not to mention that every staff member would have to be on hand for the evening.

"I can run some numbers and get them to you tomorrow," Isaac answered.

"Let's do it." Scarlett smiled. "Something tells me that the more diners we can bring in here, the more rooms we'll have booked down the road. I mean, letting the locals see this place might just be the ticket we need. After all, they have friends who come down here for vacation, right?"

"Right," Zoey added with a nod.

"Elle and I talked about having an open house day once a month. You know, showing off the amenities to the locals. Maybe even let them enjoy one of Isaac's wonderful dinners. But having outside diners come in once a week—that's pure genius." She touched Isaac's arm. "Thanks."

"Anything to keep this place open. I've never worked somewhere like it before, and I don't plan on leaving anytime soon."

She felt the same way and wondered how anyone could ever walk away from the wonderful place. Then her mind turned to Owen, and she remembered how easily he'd left before. Did he still feel the same way? Would he walk away again so easily?

CHAPTER SIX

There was yet another note on his desk the following morning. This one, however, had a little more detail than the last.

> *You have until the end of the week to step down from the board or pay the consequences. I'd hate to drag one of your brothers into this mess. Someone might get hurt.*

He felt his blood grow cold at the thought of someone threatening his brothers. It was one thing when this was all about him, but bringing Dylan and Liam into the mix sent him over the edge.

After pulling out the envelope filled with some of the other notes, he tucked them under his arm and marched out of his office just as Joel rushed past Nora's desk.

"Did you see this?" Joel waved a newspaper in front of him.

"No." He frowned at the cover. A picture of his father shoving a man at an airport filled the main page. "What the . . ." He took the paper and quickly scanned the article.

"Leo Costa, head of Paradise Investments of Destin, Florida, was seen assaulting Robert Mitchell of Panama City Beach. The entire incident was caught in front of this newspaper's crew as we took an interview from Mitchell while he announced his candidacy for mayor of PCB."

The article didn't say if his father had been arrested or what the outcome was. Nor did it mention why his father had pushed the man in the first place.

"Shit." He sighed and put the paper down. "Have you found out anything else about this mess?"

"No." Joel shook his head. "I've tried calling the paper for more details, but I just got their answering machine. The cops won't talk either."

"Let me know if you find anything. I have . . . an errand to run." He glanced down at the envelope. "Mind if I take this copy with me?" He waved the paper.

"No, go ahead," Joel said, looking at the envelope Owen held. "Anything I can help with?"

"No, thanks. I'll be out of the office for the next hour. Then I'm heading out for a meeting. I'll be gone for the rest of the day." He made his way toward the elevators.

"Sure thing," Joel called after him, his tone a little flat.

He thought about the notes all the way to his first stop—the local police station. Having an old high school friend on the force meant that he could possibly get some answers about the incident with his dad in PCB. But Brett Jewel wasn't in the office that day, so he ended up turning over the threatening notes to Brett's partner, Bill, who took his statement and suggested he hire a security detail.

"After all, aren't you part of one of the richest families around?" the man said with a little attitude.

When Owen asked him if he knew anything about his father's incident in PCB, the man just shrugged and smiled. "We can't talk about an open case with anyone."

"Open?" He narrowed his eyes. "Can't or won't?"

"As I said, can't." The man leaned back in his chair and watched him as if waiting for him to give up.

"He's my father, and he's been missing for the past few months."

"Well, now, did you file a missing person report on him?"

"No." He sighed.

"I met your father once, shortly after he fired my son from that fancy office of yours about a year back." The man shook his head, and Owen understood where the hostility was coming from. "He's a hard worker, my Colin. Always looked up to men like your father. To men like you. Wanting expensive cars, big homes, fast women. Now he's stuck working down at the local burger joint making minimum wage and driving a beat-up Toyota."

Owen swallowed his anger. "I'm sorry," he said. "I have no control over who is hired or fired; it's not really my field. What has this got to do with my dad going missing and your job here?"

Bill leaned forward slowly, then tapped the paper that Owen had laid on the man's desk. "He doesn't look like he's missing to me. PCB is only half an hour away from here."

The man was an ass. But Owen knew better than to lose his temper. "And this was taken yesterday, which means my father could be in Europe by now."

"Missing persons really isn't my field," Bill said, throwing Owen's words back at him sarcastically. "Now, unless you want to file another report, I have real work to do." He tucked the notes Owen had given him and shoved them all back into the envelope, as if they no longer mattered.

"Right." Owen stood up. "Have Brett call me when he gets back in the office."

"Will do." Just the way the man said it sounded like a fuck you.

He left the police station and drove the ten minutes to the small town of Pelican Point. It was across one of the two bridges crossing the huge bay that separated the mainland from the strip of resort and beach towns.

Here on the other side of the bay, everything seemed to slow down. Instead of tourists rushing around trying to squeeze as much vacation fun time out of their short stays as possible, there were more locals just going about their everyday lives.

He supposed the low-key attitude was one reason he had really enjoyed working across the bay. He wasn't due to meet with the land-owner for another hour, so he spent his time driving around the small town and refamiliarizing himself with the area.

They had lived in Pelican Point for a few years, back before his father had moved them all to Destin to be closer to the business. Owen had nothing but fond memories of the small town. Like spending his summers riding his bike through the empty streets into town to pick up candy with the change he'd saved up doing chores around the house. All the good times he and his brothers had had with their father at the massive house across the way from the camp. Not that he'd ever really thought about the camp housing young girls just a short rowboat trip across the water—at least he hadn't until he'd hit puberty, but by then, they were moving into the city.

Now, he could tell that the town had changed; it was struggling. The camp had been one of its main draws back in the day, but after Elle's grandfather had shut the place down, everything had sort of dried up around it.

He was hoping his newest scheme would breathe new life into the town as well as help River Camp out.

After he'd finally met the owner of the six-thousand-acre property, he was pretty excited about starting his very first project. He'd already talked to a master developer, but he wanted the opinion of someone he trusted about the development. So, after his first meeting, he drove to the campgrounds and hunted down Aiden Stark—one of the main men who had helped in turning River Camp into the beauty it was today.

"Good afternoon." He shook the man's hand.

"I heard you wanted to meet with me," Aiden said as they stepped into his office just down the hall from Hannah's; it had taken all his willpower not to go hunt her down first. He really wanted to see her and clue her in on the new details, but he figured he needed to lock in all the moving parts first.

"Yes, I have a possible project I'll be heading in the next few months that I wanted your opinion on." He set the large binder down on Aiden's desk. "If you could take a look at this and get back to me with your opinion, I'd appreciate it. Not to mention, I would like to add you on to the project as a consultant, if you're interested." He sat when Aiden motioned to the chair.

"Jumping right in." Aiden chuckled and reached for the binder. "Hammock Cove?" He glanced down at the flyer Owen had created.

"Yeah, it would be a fifteen-hundred-home site. At least to begin with. We'd have all the basic amenities of a new housing development."

"Why Pelican Point?" Aiden asked, looking over the information.

"I think the town is ripe for a comeback. Don't you?" He waited as Aiden examined everything.

"This looks pretty amazing," Aiden finally said as he set the paperwork back down. "I didn't know Paradise Investments did anything like this. I thought you guys just owned high-rise beach rentals."

"We do," Owen agreed. "This would be our first. I'm hoping to make the leap and expand into housing developments."

"It's a tricky market. Especially around here." Aiden looked thoughtful for a moment. "But I would agree. If you're going to take the risk, Pelican Point is the place to do it. It has strong bones, as far as little towns go. The mayor is an honest man who is eager to see the town jump back into greatness."

"Do you think it will work?" Owen asked, just as someone knocked on Aiden's door.

"Come in," Aiden said instead of answering him.

When Hannah walked in, Owen stilled and felt his heart skip at just seeing her again. She looked amazing in her simple camp shirt and jean shorts. Her long hair was tied back, and the new camp hat she wore shielded her blue eyes from him.

"Aiden, Aubrey wanted to . . ." Her words fell away when she spotted him across the room. "Oh, I didn't know you were here already."

"Yes, I needed to ask Aiden something first before hunting you down." He stood and tucked all the papers back into the large binder. He could feel Hannah's gaze on him but was thankful she didn't ask any questions.

"I'll get back to you on this matter," he told Aiden as he started on his way out of the office.

"Oh." Hannah snapped her fingers and turned back to Aiden. "Aubrey needs that thing she asked you about the other day."

Aiden chuckled. "Right, I'll go deliver it to her now."

They left Aiden's office, and she wrapped her arm through Owen's. He heard her breath hitch when their skin touched.

"You're early." She smiled up at him, and their eyes locked for a split second. "I wasn't expecting you for another hour."

"I had a few meetings," he answered as he focused on her face and thought about how beautiful she was in her camp clothing. Even sexier than some of the fancier dresses she'd worn for the dinner parties. When she blinked and seemed to shake herself free of the attraction, she started walking them toward the stairs.

"I can see." She glanced down at the binder. "Want to tell me about them?"

"Over dinner," he said, not wanting to further delay starting their evening. "Did you get the evening off?"

"Yes." She sighed. "I'm all yours tonight." He liked the sound of that.

He stopped her at the foot of the stairs and drew her closer. "If only." He watched in amazement as her face turned a little pink.

"I need to go change," she said, pulling back.

Instantly, he thought of tugging those shorts off her narrow hips, of pulling that T-shirt slowly over her head, and . . . he tried to clear his mind, but he heard himself asking, "Can I come up and wait for you?"

"Yes." She tugged on his hand. "But you have to tell me where we're going first. I need to narrow down my outfit choices."

He glanced down at her shorts and T-shirt with a grin. "What you're wearing is perfect."

She rolled her eyes as if it was the most ridiculous thing he'd ever said. So he followed her up the stairs and sat on the old sofa while she disappeared into her room down the hall. Seeing a book on the new coffee table his brother Liam had built for them, he opened it up and lost himself in the pages for a few minutes. Among his best memories as a child were all the trips to the library his father had taken him and his brothers on.

He didn't hear the front door open, but when Scarlett sat across from him, he glanced up from the pages.

"I didn't know you read." She smiled over at him as she leaned down and pulled off her tennis shoes.

"A lot of people can read." He set the book down.

"True—you just didn't seem like the type." She glanced at the book. "To enjoy horror."

"Who doesn't?" He shrugged. "Obviously someone here does." He motioned to the bookcase full of books by the same author.

"Grandpa Joe," she said, as if that explained everything. "This used to be his place." She glanced around, and he could see the sadness behind her eyes.

"Elle's grandfather," he said, remembering the images he'd seen of the man. "He was the one who initially opened the camp."

"Right." She leaned back on the sofa, looking tired. "He was a father figure to us all."

"He left you five this place?" he asked. He knew the story, or at least what they had talked about in all the interviews they had given, but he had yet to hear it firsthand.

"Yes," she answered as she wiggled her toes. "I don't know what some of us would have done if we hadn't been given this opportunity. I mean, take Hannah for example . . ."

He sat up a little. "What about her?" he prodded.

"Well," Scarlett started, and he could tell that she was too tired to see the interest he was showing in the story, "she was stuck working for her father." The way she said the word *father* hinted that she couldn't stand the man. "I mean, she was basically an errand girl. She has far too much talent to be running around like that. Oh, and don't get me started on the fact that he was setting her up with rich men more than double her age."

He stiffened at that bit of information. But before he could ask what she meant, Hannah stepped into the room.

"Ready?" she asked, twisting to make the skirt of her soft sundress flare out. She'd braided her long hair to one side, causing it to fall over her left shoulder.

"Yes," he said, jumping up from the sofa.

"You two have fun," Scarlett said with a yawn. "I'm going to . . ." She shifted to pull her feet up on the sofa, then closed her eyes.

"You have dinner, remember?" Hannah chuckled when Scarlett groaned.

"Five minutes," she said, waving the two away from her prone position.

"Thanks." Hannah rushed across the room and hugged her friend. "I owe you."

"Yes, you do, but go, have fun." Scarlett got back up and pulled on her shoes. "And for god's sake, do something wild and crazy so my suffering will be worth it."

Hannah giggled as they walked out the door.

"So." She stopped just outside the apartment door. "What wild and crazy stuff do you have planned for us?"

Taking her hand, he started pulling her down the stairs. "It's a surprise." The sundress and sandals she was wearing would be perfect for his evening plans.

He had packed a beach blanket and a bottle of wine, along with a few other beach necessities. When he parked in front of the local fish restaurant, he turned to her.

"What do you think about getting this to go and making our way over to the beach?" he asked before she could get out of his car.

"That actually sounds way better than sitting inside a restaurant filled with people."

He convinced her to stay in the car while he ran inside for their to-go dinners. He grabbed some snacks as well as the two different kinds of desserts they had. When he came back out, weighed down with several bags of food, she jumped out and helped him by opening the back door of his car.

She chuckled. "Wow, did you buy every item on their menu?"

"I got so busy that I skipped lunch," he joked. "Besides, I didn't know what was good here, so I got a variety of things." He helped her back into the car, then jogged around and got in himself.

"You know the area. Where's a good beach we can go to?" he asked, starting up his car.

"Well, we have this private beach of sorts." She leaned forward. "Head to the outskirts of town."

He followed her directions and ended up parking along the side of a dirt road.

"Elle owns this too?" he asked.

"Yeah, it was her grandfather's land. He had always planned on building on the property, but . . ." She sighed.

He thought about his own plans to build near town. But he wanted to stay focused on her grandfather.

"From what I've heard, he was a really great guy," he said, pulling out bags filled with the containers of food.

"Here, let me . . ." She started to reach for them, but he shook his head.

"I've got all this. You just lead the way." He shifted the bags so he could grab the rest of the stuff.

She skirted him and grabbed up the beach blanket from the trunk, then started walking down the sandy pathway. He followed her until the pathway opened up to a private white sandy beach.

"Wow, this all belongs to Elle?" he asked again.

"Yes," she said with a shrug; then she took her time opening up the blanket and laying it down in the soft sand. "We're just in time for the sunset." She motioned to the right, and he glanced up after setting the food on the blanket.

"It never gets old," he said as he took a moment to appreciate the view. It was true: he had lived in this part of Florida all his life, and so far, he hadn't seen a sunset that didn't make him appreciate where he was. He'd seen plenty of sunsets on other beaches, but this part of the world was his favorite. He knew it was one of the reasons he never thought about leaving.

"No," she agreed. "It's funny, in New York, the sunsets aren't even appreciated."

"Or the sunrises," he said. "I've been there. It's like someone just flips a switch, and suddenly it's dark."

"Yes." She chuckled. "Just an inconvenience to the eyes."

He finished setting out the food, then reached for the wine. Instead of sitting, she toed off her sandals and walked toward the water.

After pouring them each some wine into paper cups he'd gotten from the restaurant, he followed her to the water's edge. She was holding up the skirt of her sundress while the water lapped at her feet.

"This feels so good. I haven't had time to get to the beach for a long time." She sighed and rested her head back.

"You should be able to take as many days off as you want. You're the boss, after all," he joked as he handed her a cup. He knew that the five friends had stakes in the camp, each one using her own talents to make the business flow smoothly. What would it be like to have his brothers run his family's business like that? Could the three of them come together and make it work as effortlessly as Hannah and her friends did? He doubted it, since Dylan and Liam had their own life goals that didn't really revolve around Paradise Investments.

"One of the bosses at least," she said, then took a sip. "I bet you don't get too many days off now either." She glanced over at him.

The last time he'd had a day off was before the board had put him in charge. Not that it had been that long ago, but he was missing the lazier days at the camp. Shrugging, he replied, "No, but I suppose we both love what we do. You just have the added benefit of working outside most days."

"True. It's not like it feels like work either." She smiled. "Which helps."

"Scarlett mentioned you had worked for your father before opening the camp back up?" he asked as they started walking back to the blanket and the food. "This has to be a great deal better than that."

"Yes," she said after he'd helped her sit down on the blanket. "He had me doing a bunch of odd jobs." She sipped her wine some more.

"Scarlett seemed to think the job was beneath you." He started opening the containers of food and then handed her a paper plate.

"No, nothing is beneath me. It was just . . . wrong for me," she corrected. "I mean, surely your dad didn't start you out at the business where you are now?"

"No," he said. "I started in the filing room."

"See?" she said with a smile. "I bet you hated it."

"No, not really." He laughed. "Then again, Lisa"—he leaned closer—"on whom I'd had a huge crush, worked there."

"Oh." She laughed. "Whatever happened with Lisa?"

He shrugged. "We dated for a summer; then she went back to college, and I got moved up to the accounting department."

"Were you heartbroken?" she asked, balancing her own plate on her knees.

"No." He sobered a little, thinking of how all his past relationships differed from how he felt about Hannah. "I don't think that I've ever had a woman leave me heartbroken before. I thought I had, but looking back . . ." He glanced over at her and couldn't stop himself from asking out of curiosity, "How about you?"

CHAPTER SEVEN

Hannah avoided Owen's eyes. How could she tell him that he'd been the only one who had made her feel like her heart had broken a little? It had been different with Joel: he'd broken her ability to trust in some ways, but never her heart. She hadn't been in love with him. Infatuated, yes, but love, no. But when Owen had left her and the camp a month ago, she'd believed that it would take years for her to recover. Now he was back and, to some degree, toying with her emotions.

"No," she lied, and she took a bite of the burger he'd purchased. She didn't think at this point that he deserved the truth. She didn't even know how deep her emotions for him were. She was still too raw to explore them truthfully.

"Why do I get the feeling you're not telling me the truth?" he asked, nudging her knee with his.

"What about you?" She deflected the point. "You can't tell me that out of all of the Lisas in your life, not one of them held your heart?"

"Oh, they held it." He winked. "I just took it back before they stomped on it."

"You don't have to do that, you know," she said, taking up a french fry. She'd seen him act this way before: putting his emotions behind a shield, using humor as a way to protect his true feelings.

"Do what?" he asked her as he bit into his own burger.

"Play the macho guy role." When he remained silent, she continued. "You know, it's a new age. Men are allowed to be sensitive."

"I get it." He set his half-eaten burger down. "The closest I've ever come to being heartbroken was when my girlfriend of three months took a minivacation and came back pregnant."

"Ouch." She winced. Knowing some of the things he had said about his father, she wondered if having a role model who jumped from woman to woman had played a part in Owen's caution when it came to relationships.

"We hadn't been together that long, but the deceit still causes some issues with me."

"I can see why." She shook her head, thinking about all her own trust issues. Most of them thanks to her parents. What kind of person could do that to someone else? Even after all she'd been through with the guys she'd dated in the past, she couldn't imagine doing that to any one of them. "Have you dated anyone since then?"

"No." He sighed, and he reached to pour her some more wine. "What about you? Did Joel break your heart?" He watched her from the corner of his eye.

"A little, but it wasn't because of . . ." She shook her head—brevity was easier than explaining her past to him. "A little. I didn't know you two were related."

She knew the story but figured she could play dumb and maybe get a little more information from Owen than she had from his brothers.

"We technically aren't. At least not that we know for sure." He glanced out over the water. The sun had sunk lower in the sky, leaving dull hues of pinks and purples everywhere.

"Oh?" she asked, turning her own face upward and spotting the first glimmer of stars above them. It was strange: if they were brothers, they were like night and day emotionally. At least from what little she remembered about Joel and how he'd acted and treated her back in the day.

She watched as he started putting all the food in the containers and stacking them back in the bags. Then he leaned back on his elbows, and she joined him to watch the sunset.

"We think Joel is my father's son, but Dad has yet to confess anything to any of us. If he is our half brother, it would have happened shortly before our parents met. Which wouldn't be such a terrible thing. After all, Dad has said that Mom was the only woman he's ever loved. It wasn't as if he'd cheated on her. But for some reason, he refuses to say anything."

"Have you asked him?" She crooked her neck to watch his face. His dark eyes were scanning the horizon as if he was looking for answers there.

"Lots of times. Each time we do, he grows very sad and says he doesn't want to talk about it." He turned his head toward her. When she'd known Joel, it was long before he'd met Owen's father, so he'd had no clue about any family connections. "More secrets he keeps from us." He reached up and brushed a strand of her hair away from her eyes. The move was soft, and she couldn't stop her heart from fluttering when his fingertip brushed against her cheek.

"You have a few of those yourself," he murmured.

"We all do." She sighed and looked back over the dark waters. When his hand reached out this time, she closed her eyes and leaned in to his touch.

"Hannah, I don't know what caused you to wait around this long; hell, there is no way I'm worthy of even touching you . . ."

She stopped him by bending over and placing her lips over his. "Owen." She waited until his eyes focused on hers. "Shut up."

She'd told him the truth almost a month ago. She'd never wanted a man as she'd wanted him. She'd been willing that evening to give him something she'd offered no other man before. Herself.

She was even prepared to try again tonight, since she knew he already held her heart. But knew that he would probably stop her. So she'd have as much fun as she could, while she could.

Thankfully, his hands were already moving over her shoulders and arms as her mouth covered his again. He fell backward on the blanket, and she knew that he was allowing her to take control of the situation.

After pulling his shirt buttons open, she ran her fingertips over his chest as she kept him busy playing her tongue over his lips. He tasted better than the burger had moments before.

"I could just spend all night kissing you," she said against his chin, then nibbled on it and had him groaning.

"You're killing me," he said, his fingers digging lightly into her hips.

"So? Nothing in life is fair," she said, using this opportunity to run her mouth down his neck. When she licked his flat nipple, he surprised her by flipping her over and pinning her to the soft sand. She laughed up at him as he looked down at her.

"You're doing this on purpose!" he accused her.

"Wouldn't you?" she said, challenging him by throwing her chin up, then slowly licking her lips. Her desire for him led her on, making her act on her impulses. "I can still taste you on my lips."

She felt his fingers tighten on her skin for just a moment before he leaned down and started kissing her again. This time, he took charge, and she marveled at the difference in how he responded to her. It was as if he'd lost all restraint.

"Yes," she cried out when his hand roamed up her leg, pushing her sundress higher over her thigh. "Please," she begged when he cupped her breasts and ran his mouth over the spot a moment later.

But when she reached for the zipper on his pants, he pulled away suddenly.

"Hannah." He shook his head. "I . . . not yet." He rested his forehead against hers.

"Why not? Owen, I'm ready. I've *been* ready," she admitted, trying to pull him back down to her.

Hearing his chuckle sent tension through her spine. "Hannah, there's nothing more I'd like to do right now than make love to you all night on this beach, but . . ."

"You won't." She sighed when he nodded in agreement. "Why not?"

"Your first time should be . . . special."

"And making love in a private cabin isn't?" she asked. He'd pulled back that night when she'd told him she was inexperienced. Was he trying to protect her? Did her lack of experience with men turn him away?

"No, let's just say your first time should be really special," he finally answered.

Her eyes narrowed at him, and suddenly she realized that he probably had a point. "You know this because . . ."

He laughed and leaned down to kiss her once more.

"Trust me," he said, then sat up and pulled her into his arms. "Now, I brought us some dessert." He reached for the bag and pulled out two small containers.

"Chocolate?" she asked.

"It wouldn't be dessert if it wasn't chocolate," he confirmed with a laugh.

She supposed she could forgive him, since he'd gotten her chocolate, but still, the entire drive back toward the camp she felt her sexual frustration grow. He'd gotten her all hot and then had left her wanting. The least she could do was leave him the same way. So, when he stopped in the parking lot, she shifted and pulled him close before he could jump out of the car.

She may not have all the experience he had, but at least she knew that she could turn the little things he had done to drive her nuts back on him.

This time, she just ran her hand over the hardness underneath instead of reaching for his zipper. Stroking him until she felt his hips jerk as he moved under her touch.

"Okay," he said, his voice breaking. "Your point has been made."

"Has it?" she asked, looking at him through narrowed eyes.

"Yes, and to prove it . . ." He reached for her. His hand slid up her thigh slowly while he kissed her. When he touched her outside her panties, she sucked in a breath. "Do you like that?" he asked, his breath against the skin under her ear causing goose bumps.

"Yes," she moaned, and she moved slightly, giving him more access.

"What about . . ." He ran a fingertip over the soft material covering her sex, then slowly pushed it aside and did it again, this time without the barrier.

Closing her eyes, she tossed her head back and waited, her breath held as he moved his finger closer to where she wanted him. When he finally dipped a finger into her, she cried out his name. His lips covered hers, taking her breath away even more as he moved in and out of her slickness. She felt herself building, burning for his touch deeper, harder; then, when she felt her own hips jerking against him, he slipped another finger in and sent her into her own release.

"You are amazing," he murmured.

"Come upstairs and we can do that some more," she said, feeling herself floating back down to earth. She'd meant to turn him on, to work him up, but instead, she was the one panting and left wanting more.

Owen chuckled. "As I said, there's nothing I'd like to do more . . ."

Her groan of frustration stopped him. "You're an ass," she said, sitting up and jerking her skirt back down. He was toying with her, making her yearn for him, then taking a giant step backward.

He laughed again at the face she gave him, spiking her frustration.

She knew it was childish, but she crossed her arms over her chest and pouted.

"Soon." He used a fingertip to nudge her chin until she was looking at him. "I don't think I could wait much longer."

"No," she agreed. Suddenly, she could hear noises around her and realized that the parking lot wasn't empty. A rush of embarrassment flooded her.

"Don't worry, they weren't around when . . . earlier," he said, motioning to the car that had pulled in. "Shit, I think that's my brother. Think we can go unnoticed?"

But it was too late. Zoey and Dylan walked by the car at that moment, and Hannah and Owen emerged at their wave, hopefully not looking as rumpled as she felt.

"Oh, I'm not ready for bed." Zoey grabbed Dylan's arm. "Did you know"—she turned to Hannah—"that it's our anniversary?"

"Oh?" Hannah smiled. "How long has it been?"

"Six months." She sighed and leaned against Dylan. "Since I hired him." She poked him in the chest, causing Dylan to laugh.

"You two are an old couple now," Hannah joked.

"Right?" Dylan laughed.

"You guys should come and hang . . ." Zoey started to say, but Dylan was already pulling her down the pathway.

"Maybe next time," he called out to them as he hoisted Zoey up in his arms when she stumbled. Hearing her friend's laughter continue down the pathway sent Hannah into peals of laughter as well.

"That was . . . less embarrassing than I thought," Owen said as he held out his arm for her to take.

"Yes," she agreed with a chuckle. "When Zoey starts drinking before she's eaten, you get that." She motioned to the empty pathway.

"You seem to handle your wine pretty well," he said as they headed toward the main building.

"I've had more practice," she said, remembering all the dinner parties her parents had dragged her to. "My mother is French; well, half-French anyway. She raised me on wine." She shrugged.

"French?" he asked. "Est-ce que tu parles français?"

"Oui." She smiled. "Et toi?"

"No, just enough to keep me near the bars and bathrooms."

She laughed and started climbing the stairs outside the building, thankful for the interruption, since she still didn't know how to handle the heat Owen's gaze was generating. "Want to come up for a drink?"

His eyes ran to the third floor, where all the lights were currently on.

"No, I'd better not," he said. "Besides, I have an early-morning meeting again. You know . . ." He pulled her to a stop before she could finish climbing the stairs. "I do miss working here. The simplicity of the job, the enjoyment of meeting new people."

"Simplicity?" She chuckled. "Maybe we didn't utilize you as much as we should have."

His smile caused her heart to skip. "Baby, you have no idea the things I'm capable of."

She felt her knees go weak as he pulled her closer. "You have yet to prove anything to me," she reminded him, still a little frustrated that he was leaving her wanting, though she understood his need to make things special for her.

"Soon," he said before laying his lips softly on hers. "But for now, dream of me."

When she finally climbed the stairs and entered her apartment, there was nothing anyone could do to stop her from dreaming of him. Or so she thought. But upon seeing her mother and father sitting on the old brown sofa in her living room, everything changed.

CHAPTER EIGHT

The drive back to Destin wasn't as bad as it normally was during the day—the streets were practically empty.

When Owen pulled into his parking spot at his complex, he sat in his car for a moment and enjoyed the view. Even from the parking garage he could see the moonlight hitting the gulf waters. Still, the view couldn't compare to the one he'd had of Hannah underneath him, her hair fanned out on the beach blanket. Her cheeks rosy and her lips swollen from his kisses.

Damn, he really was going to have a hard time waiting for her. But he'd been correct. Her first time should be something special. Something . . . better than he could give her.

After riding the elevator up to the top floor, he opened his apartment door and froze.

"Shit." He stood back, pulled out his phone, and called his buddy Brett. He then stood outside his apartment and waited for the police to arrive as he thought about all the destruction inside.

"Someone toss your place?" Brett asked when he finally arrived with his partner, Bill.

"From the looks of it. I haven't checked anything. I was waiting for you." He glanced over at Bill. "I'm hoping your partner told you about the notes."

By the way his friend's eyebrows shot up, he guessed the older man hadn't passed on the information. Owen turned to Bill.

"The folder I gave your partner a few days ago contained a stack of threatening notes I've been receiving at the office over the past few weeks," Owen said.

"Well, shit." Brett turned to Bill and raised a brow.

"Must have slipped my mind." Bill shrugged.

"Do you think this has something to do with your father's disappearing act?" Brett asked, walking around Owen's destroyed living room. Owen glanced down at his sofa cushions, which had been shredded. He had liked that sofa. He'd just worn it in to the point that the leather was finally soft enough to enjoy.

"Could be." Disappointment laced his tone. "Or it could be someone doesn't like me taking over for him?" In the last few days he'd thought about all the possibilities.

"Well, we'll need a list of any items missing." Brett handed Owen a small notepad and pen.

"Yeah." He ran his free hand through his hair. Just what he wanted to be doing for the rest of the night. Going through his destroyed stuff and trying to see if anything he owned was gone. Glancing up at the massive flat-screen television still hanging above the fireplace, he said, "Something tells me nothing is gone, but everything is destroyed."

The television screen was shattered, and one of his pool cues from his pool table in the next room was sticking out of it.

The mess had been too big for him to handle, so he'd called his cleaning service and had them send over a team of people to help him haul everything out to the dumpster. They were done almost three hours later. The list he'd written for Brett was short. Actually, there was only one thing on it. A family photo that normally sat on his mantel. The picture was one of the last photos that had been taken before their mother, Grace, had passed away. Owen had been four years old and could only vaguely remember the woman who clasped him in the picture.

Was the person who was tormenting him only interested in gaining control of the family business, or was something deeper about his family going on? He'd made a list of suspects and reasons behind each name. Still, nothing weighed heavily enough to zero in on any one person, and the reasons were sketchy at best.

From the way their father talked his entire life, their mother had been a saint. Of course, he counted himself lucky that he did have a few foggy memories of his mother, where Dylan and Liam didn't have any at all.

The sun was just coming up when he stepped out of the shower and pulled on one of his remaining suits. Since he didn't want to trust any of the food left in his house, he had the crew dispose of it all and headed down to the coffee shop in the lobby of the building to get a muffin and a cup of coffee.

Driving into the office that morning, he thought about who to tell. If he let it slip out that his place had been broken into last night, maybe he could see some sort of pleasure on an unexpected face. Then again, if he didn't mention anything, that person might get upset and slip up. At this point, he was pretty sure that it was someone from the board of directors. After all, why would the threats demand he step down from his position? His first guess was that someone else wanted to step into that spot. It was the most logical.

Deciding to keep last night's disaster to himself, he walked into the office with a tray of coffee and a box of freshly baked muffins for his immediate crew. After all, if it appeared as if he was in a good mood, it would only piss off that person even more.

"Morning, Nora." He smiled at his father's faithful secretary.

"Morning, Mr. Costa." She stood up and handed him a few messages as she rattled off their importance.

"Coffee?" he asked when she took a break.

Her blonde eyebrows shot up. "Yes, thank you." She took a cup with her name on it.

"Cinnamon macchiato. Correct?"

"Yes." She scooted the coffee over to open the box of muffins.

"Thanks for all of this," she said. "You're in a good mood today." She set her muffin down and took a sip of her drink.

"There isn't a cloud in the sky. And we live and work in paradise." He turned when the elevator doors opened. "Joel, coffee and muffins?" he asked the man as he stepped out of the elevator holding a stack of binders.

He looked a little surprised but quickly recovered. "Someone had a good time on his date last night," he joked as he took the coffee with his name on it and then set the binders down on Nora's desk and took a chocolate muffin.

"Oh," Nora chuckled. "That's what this is all about. A girl." She'd seen most of his dating life—after all, she'd been there back in the days of Lisa and the filing room.

"This may or may not have anything to do with a woman," he corrected, which had Nora smiling.

"I hate to cut your happiness short, but we have less than ten minutes before the meeting . . ." Joel prompted him as he nodded toward the stacks of binders.

"Right." He shifted, then turned back to Nora. "There are more coffee and muffins to hand out. Would you—"

"Yes." She waved him off. "Go, be a boss." She took the box of muffins and the two remaining cups of coffee for his immediate crew.

He knew that most of the board members worked in other parts of the building, but he was betting that by noon, word would have gotten around that he was in a good mood today. Despite having his place destroyed last night.

His meeting was with a few building managers—upon his last inspection of their buildings, he had been unsatisfied with two of them.

Paradise Investments had a reputation for high quality, and the buildings in question were lacking. They owned more than thirty high-rise condo rentals up and down the Emerald Coast, from Orange Beach all the way down to the tip of Panama City's Lower Grand Lagoon area. Most of the buildings were in Destin and the Panama City Beach area. The two buildings in question were in Pensacola Beach.

After putting the two property managers on notice and discussing the improvements that would be needed in the following weeks to get them back on track, he left the meeting and made his way around to chat with the board members. He made mental notes as he watched each of them closely. Looking for any signs of angst against him or his position.

By the time he'd made it back to his office, he was exhausted. He'd gotten less than an hour's worth of sleep on his guest bed, since his memory foam was in pieces in multiple trash bags.

Which reminded him: the moment he was locked alone in his office, he made a call to an interior decorator he knew and was promised that by the end of the day, his place would have the basics once again. When he took a break for lunch, he ordered delivery and locked his office door to get a quick nap in on the sofa there.

After a half hour's rest, he decided to spend some time with the board's work files. There were eight members altogether. Most of them Owen had known from his childhood—long before they'd worked together.

Kevin O'Brien was his godfather and one of his father's best friends, so he started there and ran through Kevin's history with the company. Then it was on to Mark Smith, another man Owen had known all his life. By the time he'd made it to Julie Shields, he had grown frustrated.

Not one of the eight other members had anything in their past with Paradise that raised a red flag. Actually, just the opposite. His two detractors aside, most of them were content with Owen being in charge. Or so they appeared. When he'd walked around and chatted with them earlier in the day, each one had seemed pleased to take a few minutes to talk to him.

It was about an hour before he was going to clock out for the day when Dylan called him.

He answered his cell. "Hey."

"Hey, Brett called and told me what happened. Are you okay?" His brother's concerned tone reminded him that he should have called them the first thing that morning with an update.

"Yes." He glanced toward the open door, then stood up and walked over to shut it. "I'm fine. I wasn't there."

"Brett says your place was trashed," Dylan said.

"Yes." He held in a sigh when he thought about all his destroyed things. "They are just things," he reminded himself more than his brother.

"Right, but this, tied together with the notes that someone has been leaving you . . ." His brother trailed off.

"Yeah, I'm thinking they're connected as well." He sat back down behind his desk.

"What are you going to do about it?" Dylan asked.

"What can I do?" he asked, scanning over the employee database. "I'm trying to figure out who would profit from me stepping down."

"Have you come up with anything?" Dylan asked.

He chuckled. "So far . . . you and Liam are about it. Besides Dad. Even those two jerks on the board are clean."

"Right." Dylan sighed. "I can assure you, brother, that I do not want to be in your shoes. I like where I'm at, and I think I can speak for Liam on that front as well."

"Yeah, I got that." He smiled, knowing that his brothers had found happiness at River Camp. "It just doesn't make sense. I mean, we've known most of the board members since we were kids. I just can't see any of them doing something like this."

He shut down his computer—as a boss, he should be able to clock off an hour early. Especially since he was having a hard time keeping his eyes open.

"How did they get into your apartment, anyway? We have security there," Dylan asked.

Owen stood up and looked out the windows and watched the beachgoers frolicking in the surf. "About that, it appears there was a power flux last night. For almost an hour, all of the cameras in the complex were constantly being rebooted."

"They didn't catch anything?" Dylan asked.

"No." He glanced over at the sound of his door opening. Joel stepped in. "Listen, I have to go. I'll call you later."

"Okay. Have you talked to Hannah yet?" Dylan asked.

"No, I'll call her . . . soon." He said his goodbyes and turned to Joel. "Yes?"

"I've got the new budgets for both units in Pensacola." He set the papers down on Owen's desk.

"That was fast," he said as he picked up the papers.

"We've been working on them for a few weeks," he reminded him.

"Right. I'm going to take these home and look them over tonight." He tucked the papers into his briefcase. "I'm heading out early."

Joel followed him out of his office. "Want to grab a drink?"

"No," Owen answered, thinking of sinking into the new bed he imagined was waiting for him at his place. "Not tonight, but thanks." He locked his office doors behind them.

"Night." He waved to Nora as he passed her desk.

"Have a good weekend," she called after him.

He'd forgotten it was Friday night. Just knowing that he had the full weekend to himself made him want to drive out to the camps and spend it with Hannah. But he was too tired to drive across the bay, so he drove to his place instead.

Even though nice new stuff greeted him as he entered, it was stiff and uncomfortable. He tried out the sofa and chairs and felt like a stranger in his own home.

Walking into the bedroom, he smiled in relief at the new king-size bed—the mattress was the same one he'd had before. Even the sheets and the comforter were the same. After tugging off his shoes, he lay down on the bed fully clothed and enjoyed being still for a few minutes.

When his phone rang, he pulled it out of his pocket and answered, half-asleep.

"Zoey told me what happened. Are you okay?" Hannah's concerned voice had him smiling.

"Yes." He rolled his shoulders and thought about holding her. "I'm fine. I was with you when they broke in."

"How bad was it?" she asked, her tone a little stiff, and he wondered if she was okay herself.

"I'm sleeping in my new bed," he replied. "The decorator was already here and gone. I have all-new stuff," he added with a yawn. "Gosh, I wish you were here with me." His mind was too foggy to care what he was saying any longer. She was silent for a moment, then responded, ignoring his last statement at first.

"That was fast," she said, sounding surprised. "I wish I could see it too."

"She works for the company and owed me a favor," he said, slipping further into relaxation.

"Oh?" Hannah's voice was soothing him to sleep. "I'll bet she did." She chuckled.

"No, not like that. She's at least twenty years older than I am. Besides, I'm starting to have a type." He sat to remove his jacket and tie.

"Oh?" she prompted.

"Yeah." He smiled. "I seem to be enjoying the princess type."

"I'm not a princess." The tone of her voice changed, and he could hear the annoyance there.

"Perhaps, but you should be treated as such."

She went silent for a while. "I have a few days off—Saturday and Sunday are my days this week." He would have responded if he hadn't been so foggy minded. "I could always come and . . . visit? Spend a few days at the beach?"

"Hell yes," he blurted out, feeling a little more energetic. "When can you be here?"

"Tomorrow morning," she answered.

"Perfect. I'll text you my address. Hannah . . ." He heard her moving around. "I can't wait to see you again."

"Me too," she said, then seemed to have shifted the phone, and he caught the edges of her conversation with someone. "I have to go. I'll see you tomorrow. Good night."

"Night." He dropped his phone next to him on his new bed and quickly fell into dreams of holding her.

CHAPTER NINE

What was Hannah thinking? Offering to spend the entire weekend with Owen at his place in Destin. When Zoey had mentioned that Owen's place had been broken into, she'd been so concerned she'd broken the girl code and called him. She'd never been that bold before, but hearing his sleepy tone, she knew that she could convince him to let her come over.

What did that say about him that he'd agreed? Did that mean he was ready to be with her now? Or had she just taken advantage of him?

But she needed the time away, especially after the dance she'd done to get rid of her parents.

As far as she knew, they had ended up spending only one night in Florida. Thankfully. Of course they never did include her in their plans, so she wasn't sure they had left yet. What she did know was that she wanted to be unreachable to them if they did stick around.

It wasn't their first trip to the camp, nor, unfortunately, would it be their last. Since the camp was "filthy," as they put it, they stayed at a rental place just outside Destin when they visited.

Still, the shock of seeing them was enough to have her on edge for days.

Her mother had raked her with her gaze, then had quickly given her a disapproving look at her outfit choice. Her father had been oblivious to any of the assessment and instantly asked why she continued to torment them by dragging them across the States to deal with the heat. As if it had been her fault that they had traveled all the way to Florida unannounced.

At times, her parents acted more like children than the monied elites they played in front of their friends and business partners. Or basically anyone they wanted to show off to.

Her parents had prodded and poked her and her friends with intrusive questions about her life, all of their dating lives, and the finances of the camp, but thankfully, her sisters weren't ones to gossip.

That next morning during their normal breakfast meeting, she'd told her friends that she was going to spend the weekend with Owen. Which had been a little awkward. After all, two of her friends were currently involved with his brothers. She didn't know yet if that made it weird or just . . . perfect.

"You *are* sleeping together!" Zoey had shouted.

"No." It was a gut reaction to deny it, which had Zoey's eyebrows shooting up in question.

"No as in . . . not yet?" she asked.

Hannah rolled her eyes. "No, I mean . . ." She became embarrassed, which caused all her friends to give her grief. In the end, it was Scarlett who got everyone off her back.

"Don't mind them. They just think that since they're annoyingly happy, everyone else has to be as well," Scarlett teased. "Go, have fun this weekend. If you need anything, you know where to find us."

"We've got this," Elle added. "We'll handle your parents if they come around again."

She hugged each one of them.

Before opening the camp's doors, they had all picked two days a week to be off from work. Which meant that between the five of them, every three days a week, two of them were gone. Normally, their schedules were easy enough to move around and account for the time, but with Zoey and Elle both wanting more time off to spend with Dylan and Liam, things had been a little strained.

But they had made it work, and now that they had officially hired the five new staff members, she knew that the heavy load they had been feeling would lighten up a lot. Most of the new employees were already on site, with only two due to start the following week. She'd interviewed or met most of them and had liked all of them.

The way everyone respected her and tiptoed around her and her friends was one thing about running a business that Hannah hadn't gotten used to yet. She didn't think they were bosses to be feared, but after the entire mess with Ryan, they figured they couldn't get too comfortable with the employees. Especially since the memory of Zoey and Elle dating employees was still fresh in everyone's minds. Even though the Wildflowers no longer looked at Dylan and Liam as employees. Just knowing that the two guys normally made more each month than they could pay them working at the camp in a year had turned the brothers into a sort of volunteer workforce. Besides, both of them had admitted that they were gladly donating their River Camp paychecks to a local foundation, Spring Haven, which helped kids without families.

But if the books didn't level out soon, Hannah was willing to bring up one option: the five friends cutting their paychecks to make the place work. Not to mention that the men had already suggested they waive their paychecks completely until things got back to normal.

The first year of any business was always the hardest. Not that her gofer experience in her father's company had given her any useful experience. Having sunk everything they had into fixing up the camp to make it what it was now, she and her friends knew that their own income had to be skimmed in order to make everything level out.

After all, they were all living on the campgrounds and didn't really have any bills of their own. She had a few credit cards she'd maxed out when living in New York, as well as a car payment now, since she'd needed something to get around in. When she'd lived in New York, her biggest expense had been her loft apartment. Most of her income from her job at her father's corporation was eaten up by that. She'd barely had enough to scrape together some of her other necessities when she'd lived under her parents' thumb. She believed that her father had kept her like that: desperate.

Even though she was still living pretty desperately now, it was on her terms. Besides, she had felt more freedom in the past year and a half than she had her entire life. Well, except for her time each summer that she'd spent at the camp when she'd been younger.

It was funny, looking back at her life. When her mother had told her that they had enrolled her in summer camp in Florida, she'd argued with them and had even cried over having to spend a summer away from her school friends. Then she'd met her new friends—the Wildflowers. Elle, Zoey, Scarlett, and Aubrey had become closer than family; they had become sisters. She couldn't have made it through high school or life with her parents without any of them.

After using her car's GPS, she pulled into the gate at the massive condo complex. The sign read **WINDSWEPT CONDOS: A PARADISE INVESTMENTS PROPERTY**. She hadn't known what to expect—she'd kind of known he'd be living at one of his company's properties. She'd seen plenty of them around town. You didn't live near Destin without having heard of Paradise Investments before. But this building was one of the newer ones, built within the last five years. When she pulled up to the security guard, she explained that she was there to visit Owen Costa.

"Yes, Ms. Rodgers, you're expected." He handed her a bright-yellow card. "Leave this on your dash. You'll want to park on the eleventh-floor garage in spot number two."

"Thank you." She glanced up to the tall building and thought about driving her car up eleven floors. She'd just watched a movie the other night where a woman drove her car off a high-rise parking garage in the city. Sudden images of her car plunging off the tall building into the beach below played over and over in her mind as she started slowly up the incline. By the time she'd parked in the spot marked for her, her knuckles were white, and she was a little breathless from the fear. She sat in her car for a moment while she tried to steady her heart down again.

At a knock on her window, she jumped and squealed. Owen was standing outside her car window, smiling at her.

"Everything okay?" he asked through the glass.

"How do you do this?" She slowly opened her door. "Park up here every day?" He chuckled and pulled her into his arms.

"You aren't afraid of heights, are you?" he asked.

"Who isn't?" she retorted, and she relaxed into his embrace.

"Then you're really not going to enjoy staying at my place," he said, stepping back. "I'm on the top floor."

She felt her shoulders sag. "I'm not afraid of heights as far as being in buildings—just driving up to them in a car."

He nodded. "Need help with the bags?" He pointed to the two bags that took up most of her back seat.

"Yes, thank you." She opened the door and took the smaller one, while he took her large rolling case.

She was thankful he didn't mention the weight or the size of the thing. After all, she was only spending two nights at his place. But she needed a few things to be comfortable; besides, she wasn't quite sure what he had in mind for the weekend and liked to be prepared.

They rode the elevators to the top floor, and when they stepped out into a private entryway, she realized that his condo was one of only three up there.

"Do your brothers live here too?" she asked, nodding to the other condos.

"No, Dylan had a place down the beach a ways, and Liam had one across the way. Before . . ."

"They moved to the camp," she finished.

"Right." He smiled. "Dylan and Zoey are having a place built."

"Yes, I know. I've seen the plans Aiden has drawn up for them. It's going to be wonderful."

"I had a security system installed this morning," he said. After setting her bag down just inside the doorway, he started punching a code into the beeping security screen. "I'm still getting used to it." He sighed and tried the code again. "There." He relaxed when the sound finally stopped. "Let me show you around first; then we can hit the pool or beach and have some lunch."

The place was scarce of furnishings, but since he'd just had to replace everything, she'd imagined it would be. Still, the white tiled floors were gleaming, and a soft blue-and-white rug covered the living area, with a new cream-colored leather sofa and two teal chairs facing it. A brand-new television hung over the fireplace.

Her mind flashed to the time when her mother had gotten their home redecorated. One day she'd walked in after school and everything in the house had changed, including her own bedroom. She stiffened at the memory. She knew he had the excuse of having had his things destroyed, but still, her parents' ease in destroying her valued things nagged at her.

"It still has its tag on it." She motioned to the screen.

"Oh." He glanced up and chuckled. "I haven't had a chance to turn it on yet." He walked over and took the sticker off it.

"They broke your TV?" she asked.

"Put one of my pool cues through it." He glanced over to where a new glass dining table and chairs sat in the corner. "I used to have a pool table there. I guess the table and chairs will have to do for now. I'm going to miss the table, though, and my old furniture."

She could hear the pain in his voice—he'd suffered through the destruction just like she had with her parents. "I like these new ones. The place looks really good. Nice and comfortable." She glanced out the wall of windows down at the teal waters and white sands below. A huge balcony ran the entire length of the room and beyond.

The kitchen sat near the back of the room. Its softwood cabinets and white countertops didn't hold any small appliances.

"Did you have to buy all new kitchen stuff too?" she asked, curious.

"You can tell I don't cook, huh? Thankfully, they only destroyed my coffee maker." He frowned. "Maybe you can help me get a new one this weekend?"

"Sure," she said with a smile. He picked up her bags and carried them into a room as she followed him down the hallway.

The fact that it was obviously the master bedroom sent prickles along her nerve endings. A king-size bed on a blue cushioned frame sat in the middle of the room. Two white nightstands sat on either side with matching blue lamps.

"Your decorator has good taste," she said as he set her bags inside a massive closet. Seeing that he only had a few items hanging in the empty space, she followed him in there. "They got your clothes?" she gasped.

"Yeah." He sighed and motioned to his two remaining suits. "This one was at the cleaners, and I was wearing the other one."

"That's just . . . wrong." She shook her head. "We'll have to spend some time shopping for you this weekend." She noticed that he only had three pairs of shoes as well. Turning to him, she narrowed her eyes. "Are you sure it wasn't an ex-girlfriend?"

He frowned at her. "I'm pretty sure."

"Oh?" Her eyebrows shot up. "This kind of damage seems personal. I mean, I could totally see an ex doing all this damage." She leaned closer to him. "Especially if she caught you cheating . . ."

He laughed. "I don't cheat, and besides, I haven't seen anyone seriously in the past year."

She followed him back out into the living room.

"I miss my old sofa, though." He sat down and frowned at the leather. "It took me five years to break the old one in."

She chuckled. "You could always get a secondhand one."

He shrugged, then patted the spot next to him "So, what do you want to do while you're here?"

"Shopping is always fun," she suggested, settling in beside him. "The beach, the pool." She leaned closer to him. "And other things." She liked the way his eyes roamed over her face, causing a quick desire for his touch to surface.

He reached up and touched her shoulder. "Hannah, you caught me off guard last night."

She straightened, hurt surfacing quickly at being rejected once again by him. "You're not trying to back out now, are you?"

"No." He rubbed her shoulder slightly. "I want to do things right with you—not just having sex in what looks like a temporary apartment."

"Okay." She stood up suddenly. "I'll let you. I deserve you. However you want this to play out." She glanced out the window, realizing she could be patient; after all, her own nerves were on high alert. She'd never wanted to sleep with a man as much as she did with Owen and didn't know how to process her feelings for him while her body was vibrating for his touch. "You mentioned something about lunch and the water?"

"Yes, we have a great poolside service."

"Sold." She walked toward his room and her bags. "I'll just change into my swimsuit."

She'd packed all of her sexiest clothes, including her new French-cut bikini and cover-up, as well as a silky white sundress that basically was nothing but straps on the top. Not to mention the underwear she'd purchased months ago, shortly after believing Owen and she would get together soon. Her excitement at finally using the sexy panties had bubbled up the entire drive into town.

After shutting the closet door behind her, she took her time hanging up her items in the empty closet next to his. Then she pulled on her swimsuit and cover-up, slipped on a pair of heeled sandals, and, after braiding her hair to the side, threw on an oversize sun hat to top the outfit off. She took her sunglasses and stepped out into the bedroom just as Owen was coming out of the bathroom in a pair of swim trunks and a tank top.

He saw her and stopped in midstep. "Wow," he said, his eyes running up and down her.

"Thanks." She ran her eyes over him. "You don't look too shabby yourself."

He chuckled as he moved closer to her. "There is a large part of me that wants to convince you to stay up here and spend the day breaking in my new bed." His hands wrapped around her waist.

She laughed. "I might just let you." She rested her arms on his shoulders and enjoyed the feeling of him next to her bare skin. When he touched her, all her nerves seemed to disappear. As she rubbed her body against his, she was practically purring when he finally dipped down and placed a soft kiss on her lips.

"You taste even better than you look," he said between kisses.

When she started to back him toward the bed, she let out a nervous chuckle. He looked into her eyes and then sidestepped away from her.

"Something tells me I'm the one who needs to prepare for being with you." He walked over and pulled out a beach towel from a drawer, then handed it to her. She took the towel from him, knowing she could use some time to get used to the idea of being with him. "Lead the way," he said. Before heading out, he walked over and kissed her once more. "Later."

"Yes." She smiled up at him and relaxed a little. Even though she wanted him desperately, she was still very nervous. After all, she'd waited twenty-two years already; what were a few more hours?

He surprised her by heading toward a doorway on his floor instead of getting in the elevator. After he used a key code to open the door, they took a set of wide stairs down a level and stepped out onto a sundeck. The pool was the size of the smaller one at the campgrounds. Tan chairs, tables, and sun chairs surrounded the gleaming pool. There was a handful of other people around the pool area.

"This pool is for owners. The one downstairs is for renters. We can go to the one downstairs later if you want. It's bigger and just off the beach. That pool has a tiki bar and a lazy river—"

"This is perfect," she interrupted him as she set her towel down on a sun chair while he took the one beside her.

After getting settled, she turned to him. "What would you have been doing this weekend? I mean, if I hadn't come along?"

He shrugged. "Probably working. Trying to figure out who broke in and left me the notes."

"Notes?" She frowned. "What notes?" Instant worry flooded her. Having his place broken into was one thing, but if someone had left him notes, that meant it was personal and not just a random break-in.

He looked at her. "I thought Dylan told you?"

She shook her head. "He mentioned that someone threatened you, and then your place was broken into. Nothing about notes."

He turned a little toward her. "Someone's been leaving notes for me to find. They all pretty much tell me to step down from the board."

"Have you contacted the police?" she asked.

"Yes. What little good that did. I have an old friend on the force, Brett."

"Brett Jewel?" she asked, visibly shocking him.

"Yes." He frowned. "How do you know Brett?"

"He and his partner are the ones who helped out when Ryan Kinsley—"

"Right," he broke in with a nod. "I'd forgotten."

She smiled. "I wish I could forget about that woman."

"Have you heard anything more from the lawyers?" he asked.

"Nothing new. I've given them everything they needed. From here, they claim it's just a legal battle that they'll handle until the judge decides if Ryan has enough evidence against us to go to court."

"When will they know something?" he asked.

"Soon, I hope." She rested her head back. "Let's not talk work this weekend." She turned to him suddenly. "Tell me about you. What were you like as a child?"

He laughed, but after a moment, he started telling her a story of him and his brothers convincing their father that they each needed four-wheelers.

"So, we kept leaving magazines and photos of the four-wheelers around the house everywhere, then ran around making motorcycle noises and pretending like we were riding them through the house. We even staged a few great crashes a few times, complete with bandages and cardboard-box ambulance rides."

She never laughed as much as she did when he talked about his past.

"Still, Dad wasn't convinced, and, in the end, we lost interest in the game and moved on to try to get new bikes instead." He joined her in laughter.

When they both grew too hot, they jumped into the cool waters and splashed around.

"I'm surprised," he said instantly. "Most women don't like to get their hair and face wet when swimming with me."

She'd removed most of her makeup, since she had every intention of enjoying the water and not just looking at it. "I'm not most women."

He pulled her close and kissed her.

"I'm beginning to realize that," he said and then pulled them both under the water.

They ordered food when a waiter came around, and by the time it arrived, she was pretty hungry. After getting a table and chair, they sat under the umbrella and ate their sandwiches, and she enjoyed a frozen margarita.

After lunch, he took her downstairs to the main pool area. They had a short walk on the beach followed by more drinks at the poolside bar. When he asked her about her childhood, she talked mostly about her time at the camp with her friends.

It was strange, but she believed he knew that she didn't want to talk about all the other times when she wasn't with the Wildflowers. It was as if, in her mind, those times didn't really exist. Sure, she had blocked out a lot of her bad memories. After all, having her parents control her so much that her life wasn't her own wasn't something she liked to discuss. Even with her friends, she didn't bring up some of the past.

They were floating around the lazy river when the sun started to sink lower. Owen was holding on to her inner tube, so they floated together.

"I noticed that when you bring up the past, it's always your time at the camp or with your friends. You've never mentioned your parents."

She held in a groan. So he *couldn't* tell she wanted to avoid it. "I try not to talk about them."

"That bad?" he asked, turning her float around until they faced one another.

"It wasn't good," she said.

"So, I take it you won't be going home for the holidays?" he asked.

She narrowed her eyes. "They haven't called you and paid you to nag me, have they?"

He chuckled. "No, just asking."

She shook her head. "No. I have too much to do around here."

"I take it that bit of news didn't go over well?" he asked, standing up and swinging them toward the exit.

"No," she said on a sigh. "So far they've pulled all of their strings to convince me otherwise."

"Nothing has worked?" he asked.

"No, like I said, I have my commitments here. Besides, last time I went home . . ." She shivered.

"Bad?" he asked.

"You have no idea." She took a deep breath and tried to release the tension that just talking about her family built up in her body.

"How about dinner?" he asked. "I know this great place just down the street."

"I could eat." She smiled, pleased that he had changed the subject.

"Then," he said with a wink, "you can tell me all about your parents."

She splashed water in his direction and had him laughing. "Or not."

CHAPTER TEN

It had been far too long since Owen had taken time off and just lounged around. Since his father's disappearance, he'd been so busy that he hadn't had any time to enjoy himself. Even when he'd been working at the camp, the subterfuge had kept him mentally drained.

Being with Hannah allowed his mind to focus on other things, such as her. When they made it back to his place, once again he had to reset the alarm twice. "I'm just not getting this," he complained.

"Here." She nudged him aside. "What's your code?"

He rattled off the numbers. "My birthday."

She raised a brow. "That's not hard to crack." She shifted and, after punching in the code, did a few more things to the screen. "There. Now it's the day you were hired on at the camp." She turned to him as her eyes narrowed. "You do remember that day?"

He chuckled. "Yes, show me how to work this thing."

"My parents have the same system. Well, sort of the same one." She shrugged, and for the next ten minutes she proceeded to show him the basics of his new security system.

"I'll take the guest shower, and you can have mine." He took a few items of clothing from the dresser and disappeared quickly down the hallway.

He didn't want to give her any time to tempt him, because to be honest, after flirting with her and having her body rub up against his all day long, it wouldn't have taken much to persuade him to spend the rest of the night in bed with her and forget about dinner altogether.

As he locked himself in the guest bathroom and showered, he was able to control his libido again, at least until she stepped out of the bedroom.

The soft white dress top was nothing more than straps of material barely covering those perfect breasts of hers. Her long blonde hair flowed around her shoulders in curls, as if she had just let it air dry. The day in the sun had darkened her skin a little more, making her glow as if lit from within.

"Well?" she finally asked, and he realized he had yet to say anything.

"You look . . ." He took a deep breath. "Like trouble."

She laughed out loud. "I am." She moved across the room toward him.

"Yes, you are," he agreed, his hands going to the material—so soft he could barely tell where it ended and her skin began.

"I'm also starving," she admitted. "Where is this place you know?"

"Fatty's," he blurted out, then laughed at the face she made. "It's Italian." He glanced down at her dress and winced. "They have white sauce too."

She smiled. "I'm sure it's going to be perfect." She started walking toward the door. "Coming?"

"Yes." *Hell yes*, he thought. It was going to be even harder keeping his mind off getting her back here and in his bed. Especially after seeing the back of that sundress. Her entire back was exposed, down to the slight curve above her perfect ass.

He wanted to laugh as she closed her eyes while he drove out of the parking garage. "You know," he said once they were safely on the main road, "no one has ever driven off the parking garage before."

"That doesn't matter. Just because it hasn't happened doesn't mean it won't."

"True, but the engineers that we hired to build the place made sure that the cement walls holding the entire garage building together were strong enough to stop a semi."

She glanced over at him. "Again, you can't guard against everything."

Suddenly he thought about his father for some reason. "That's true. I guess I never imagined taking over my father's business due to his disappearance."

She chuckled. "I bet you never thought you'd get hired on at a summer camp either."

He laughed along with her. "Nope, that hadn't been in my scope for life. But I'm thankful for it," he said as he parked in front of Fatty's.

When they walked in, he was greeted by Carla, one of the hostesses.

"Owen." She walked over and planted a kiss on his cheek. "And who is this beauty you have brought us tonight?"

"Hannah, this is Carla." He smiled at the older woman, who gave Hannah a kiss as well.

"Welcome. I have your table ready." She waved them inside. "Go, sit. I'll grab you your wine."

"Thanks." He took Hannah's hand and pulled her to his favorite booth.

"Do you eat here often?" she joked as he slid into the booth next to her.

"Every chance I can get." He didn't bother picking up the menu, since he knew it by heart. "Everything's good, and I do mean everything. I've tried it all."

"Good, then pick something for me." She set down her menu just as Carla came over with a bottle of his favorite wine. After showing it to Hannah, she opened it and poured them each a glass before leaving the bottle on the table.

"Your usual?" Carla asked him.

"Of course." He turned to Hannah. "I get the beef brasato. I think you'll like the spinach ricotta."

After Carla left to put the order in, Hannah sipped her wine. "This is delicious."

"It's a small winery we visited on one of our trips to Italy." He remembered the summer when he'd been sixteen. "Have you ever been to Italy?"

"Several times." He noted an unpleasant look cross her face.

"I take it you didn't have much fun?" he asked, sipping his own wine.

She shrugged. "They weren't really trips designed for pleasure."

"What were they?" he asked, turning slightly toward her. He wanted to wrap his arm around her as she talked but leaned back in the booth instead, fearing the slight contact would distract him from listening to her story too much.

"More like family business trips," she answered, her eyes traveling to the windows as the sky grew darker outside. "When your father drags you along in hopes that his daughter and eye-candy wife will help him seal a deal."

The tone in which she said it spoke louder than any details she could have given him.

"He did that often?" he asked. Not that his father was perfect, but family vacations had been their time for their father to get away from his work, not run to it. Besides, his dad hadn't really needed three crazy boys to help close any deals. Actually, he and his brothers would have probably hurt any deals instead of helping.

"Yes," she answered with a sigh.

"Did you at least have any real family vacations?"

She narrowed her eyes as she thought about it. "Family ones, no. I consider my time at River Camp the only real vacations I've ever had."

He was taken aback by that a little. "Which your parents sent you away to alone?"

She cocked her head. "After that first year, I was never alone. I had my sisters. My Wildflowers."

He had heard the term a few times, mentioned by either her or one of her other friends. She must have seen his questioning look, because she continued.

"The first year we met, Elle pulled us all into staying with her in her cabin. One of our first tasks for the summer was to name ourselves—to create a cabin name."

"You chose Wildflowers?"

"It's what we were." She chuckled, and he noticed that the slight agitation she'd had when talking about her family had disappeared, replaced by happiness and joy instead as she talked about her friends. "You should have seen us back then." She turned in her seat a little. "Zoey and Scarlett were all legs and frizzy hair. Elle was more of a tomboy than Zoey at that point, and Aubrey . . ." She tilted her head with a laugh. "Well, Aubrey has always been perfect."

By the time she was done talking, he was smiling along with her. "You love them," he said easily.

"Of course," she said. "They saved me." Her smile slipped a little.

"From?" he asked.

She closed her eyes and took a deep breath. But Carla's delivery of salads and breadsticks interrupted them. When they were alone again, Hannah took a breadstick and nibbled on it.

"Oh my god." She sighed and closed her eyes. "These are amazing."

"Carla refuses to tell me how she makes them. Not that I could reproduce it, but still." He sighed as he bit into the hot breadstick. "You were saying?"

She shrugged, and he could tell she was trying to avoid answering.

"Hey." He touched her arm. "I'm a great listener."

She smiled. "Right. I've learned that about you from day one." She tilted her head. "Which is why I find myself spilling more than I ever have to my sisters."

"Sisters?" he asked.

"It's the best way to describe what we are. We're all way more than just friends." She shrugged.

The bit about her being more open with him came as a surprise. Sure, from the moment they had bumped into one another at the camp, they'd had an easy friendship despite his and his brothers' subterfuge. Yet he'd never believed that she'd opened up more to him than to her closest friends.

"So, what did your sisters save you from?" he asked, desperate to know now.

She closed her eyes once more for just a moment and took a deep breath before answering. "Myself."

"You were how old?" he asked after a moment of silence.

"Eleven." Her eyes searched his. "And yet I felt like life was pretty much over for me. There was nothing really that living offered me. Back then. My parents were so controlling I couldn't even sit down without being corrected that I had sat down too hard in the chair or I hadn't crossed my legs properly." He could hear the tension in her voice and reached over to take her hand in his. Instantly, he felt her relax a little.

"When I arrived at River Camp"—she turned her eyes toward him—"that first year, I wasn't planning on leaving."

He stilled. His entire body froze; his breath caught in his lungs. "You . . ." He swallowed the bile that had risen to his throat. "You were only eleven."

She nodded. "And had been unhappy for as long as I could remember. I didn't think I could take much more. I didn't want to." He watched her shrug and felt his stomach roll. "I figured a life on the street or . . . whatever . . . had to be better than life with them."

He quickly gathered her in his arms. "I can't imagine what you've gone through."

"They're here," she said against his chest. "In town right now. It's one of the reasons I wanted to be with you this weekend. I'm such a coward. I haven't been able to stand up to them."

He allowed her to lean back and look up into his eyes. "Stay as long as you want," he said, then bent his head and kissed her softly.

Just then, Carla delivered their main dishes, and the subject turned toward their food for a while. Hannah suggested that she have Isaac add a few more Italian dishes to the camp's menu.

He wanted to dig deeper into her life with her parents but knew that the mood had changed. Besides, he could tell that just by talking about them, she was reliving some of her past, which must be painful.

He couldn't imagine being so young and so hurt. At eleven, he'd been playing football and basketball, he'd had more friends than he could name, and he'd spent the summer realizing that girls were more fun to look at than his comic books. There hadn't been a shred of depression in his life at that point. It was strange to think about how much of that had changed now. The worry for his family now outweighed his day-to-day enjoyments.

After dessert, they left the restaurant and headed back to his place. They pulled into his normal parking spot in the high-rise garage and entered the elevator. He didn't want the night to end yet, so he punched the down button for the lobby. "How about a walk on the beach?" he asked as they got in.

"That sounds nice." She leaned in to his chest, since he had wrapped his arms around her as they walked from his parking spot. She fit beside him perfectly.

"Whatever the reason," he said once they had stepped out of the building and were on the boardwalk to the beach, "I'm so thankful you agreed to spend the weekend with me."

Her hand had found his almost instinctively as they walked. Feeling her long thin fingers wrap around his was like feeling the soft white sand between his toes.

"I am too," she said as they stepped onto the beach.

He waited as she pulled off her sandals, and he toed off his own as well. They tucked their shoes into the cubbies provided by his building.

Then he took her hand in his again as they started walking down the soft sand.

"I love the beach at night," she admitted when they made it to the wet sand. "Most of the tourists have gone back to their rentals, sleeping off the sun and food they've enjoyed. The beach is so quiet."

He looked up and down the dark sand and noticed that they were pretty much alone. Pulling her closer, he paused and leaned down to kiss her.

"There." He sighed when he finally leaned back. She had melted against him. "I've wanted to do that since dinner."

"Why the long wait?" she teased.

"Too many eyes," he pointed out.

"Not one for PDA?" She chuckled.

"I worked at your camp. I know what it's like to be on the outside of any PDA." He laughed and ran his hands through her hair, enjoying the softness of it. She'd worn it up all day in a braid, but for the evening, she'd left it flowing over her shoulders.

"Who would have guessed that older people like to have sex so much in public places." She smiled. "We're actually thinking of selling sex toys in the lobby."

"Jesus." He laughed. "You'll make a killing." They started walking again, hand in hand. A thought struck him. "You don't . . . by chance . . . have any?"

"Sex toys?" she asked, a serious look on her face. "I may not have slept with a man, but I am still a woman."

"That doesn't really answer my question," he said after a moment, causing her to laugh.

"Don't worry, I didn't bring any with me." She stopped and wrapped her arms around his shoulders. "You're the only toy I want to play with this weekend."

"Jesus," he said again, before she kissed him and made him forget all about trying to go slow with her. "I'm trying to make your first time special," he said after he'd pulled back to try to get himself under control again.

"Don't," she said softly. "I've waited too long, and I want you too much."

"God." He rested his forehead against hers.

When she took his hand and started pulling them back toward the walkway, he let her pull him along. He almost forgot their shoes and had to backtrack to gather them.

"You make me forget everything," he admitted in the elevator, pulling her closer to his side while he held their shoes under his arm.

"Same here," she said, smiling up at him.

"God, you're so beautiful," he blurted out. "And I'm past the point of being smooth."

"Good," she said as the doors opened. "I don't need smooth right now."

The way she was looking at him, and the way her body felt pressed up against his, he'd be lucky if he didn't take her in the hallway.

He fumbled with the lock and, once inside, dropped their shoes and pinned her against the door as he took her mouth. His hands pulled up her dress and found her wet and ready for him.

"Owen," she said, nudging him slightly, "the alarm."

"Right." He took a quick step back and, with shaky hands, punched in the code. "Damn," he said when it took him three tries this time.

She gently urged him back. "Here. Let me." She entered the new code and then turned to him. "Now, where were we?"

There was a moment of silence, then he was kissing her again. He moved until he'd pressed her up against the wall, his hands going back under her skirt to find her once more. She cried out when he pushed slowly into her heat with his fingers. Her nails dug into his shoulders, and he realized at one point that she'd unbuttoned his shirt and pulled it off him.

When she reached for his shorts this time, he let her slide them off his hips. They hit the floor with a thud, reminding him that his wallet and condoms were in the pockets.

Hoisting her up, he carried her into the bedroom, where he had more condoms in the drawers of his new nightstands. He kicked open the bedroom door, almost stumbling over the new rug on the floor. She giggled and held on to him tighter.

"That would have been a perfect start to this," he said with a sigh. "Landing on the floor. I'm not used to the rug yet." He moved to the side of the bed, and conversation vanished as he started kissing her again. He covered her body with his, only to realize she was still wearing the white sundress. The primal part of him wanted to rip the material off her so he could see her under him, naked. But his practical side had him asking, "How do you take this thing off?"

She chuckled. "Here." She sat up and, reaching behind her, pulled one of the strings on her back, which made the entire front of the dress fall around her waist.

"Jesus," he blurted out, his eyes going to her perfect breasts. "If I had known it was that easy to do that, we would have been back here sooner."

She smiled as she scooted up and kicked off the rest of the dress. All that remained was her soft white silky panties.

His hands shook when he reached out and touched her hip. "I think you might get your wish," he said in a shaky voice.

"Oh?" The soft sound was nothing more than a whisper.

"I don't think I could go slow now," he said, moving back over her. When his mouth covered one of her peaked nipples, her fingers held on to his hair, pulling him closer to her.

He rubbed himself outside her panties until he could feel her wetness soaking the material. Her legs wrapped around his hips, and she ground against him.

When he nudged the silk aside and ran a fingertip over her swollen flesh, he imagined what it would be like pushing into her, taking her over and over. He reached for a condom and slipped it on as she leaned up to help him. Just having her hand wrap around his cock urged him on faster.

"Owen," she said as he moved back over her. He could see the desire in her eyes but could also see something close to fear.

"Easy." He leaned down and kissed her. "I'm right here. I'll go slow for this part." He mentally pulled the reins until he could move slower. Kissing her again, he waited while she tensed for a moment, and when he felt her relax under him once more, he slowly slid farther into her tightness.

CHAPTER ELEVEN

Hannah had never felt anything as wonderful as Owen filling her completely—stretching her until he was fully embedded in her pussy. Her legs tightened around his hips, and her nails dug into his shoulders. She bit her lip, waiting for the pain that everyone had said would come, but when it didn't, she relaxed. Then he started to move his hips, and she lost herself in the feeling of letting someone else take control of her pleasure.

His hands roamed over her, causing fires to be ignited over every part of her skin. She arched her back when he wrapped his strong arm around her waist so that he could hold her tighter, closer to him as he moved over her.

When he kissed her, she felt herself building and knew that her release was close. She'd never really thought about how to provide him with what he needed and for a split second questioned if she should do something more, but then stars exploded behind her eyes, and she lost herself and heard the moment when he joined her.

Feeling his body pinning her to the mattress was one of the best feelings in her life. Her hands and legs went completely lax. She didn't even care that she had to take shallow breaths due to his muscular frame.

"So?" he said against her neck as he moved slightly, allowing her to breathe easier.

"So," she said with a smile.

"Was it everything you've dreamed of?" he asked, his hand resting easily on her belly.

"More." She sighed and glanced over at him. "Tell me we can do that again."

He chuckled. "As often as you want," he admitted as his hand cupped her breast. "You aren't hurting?"

She shook her head. "No, but I've read that the older a woman is . . . the less likely there is to be pain or"—she gasped and sat up, looking down at his new white comforter—"blood." She relaxed. "Okay, lucked out. I'll just . . ." She could feel her own juices on her thighs as she got up from the bed, and embarrassment surged.

He was watching her with a smile. "Go." He motioned to the bathroom. "I'll be here waiting." He leaned on his elbow and watched as she backed out of the room, just in case there was a mess she didn't want him to see it.

Taking a few minutes in his bathroom, she washed and was thankful that she'd done enough research over the years to know that her chances of a messy first time were slim. Still, she took a moment to look at herself in the mirror. She didn't really feel different, but by the look in her eyes and the way her skin was glowing, she knew that it would be impossible to hide the fact from her friends, or anyone else for that matter, that she'd finally had sex. Honestly, she didn't even care anymore.

When she walked back into the bedroom, she'd pulled on her tank top and sleeping shorts. He'd pulled the comforter off and was sitting under the sheets of the bed, looking down at his phone. As she stepped in, he set the phone back on the nightstand.

"Is there a problem?" she asked after seeing the frown on his face when he was looking at the phone.

"No." He sighed. "The board needs me to go to New York in a few weeks." He shook his head. "I'll figure it all out on Monday."

"Does the board usually make demands like that?" she asked, walking over and getting under the blankets on the other side of the bed. Instantly, he pulled her across the bed and into his arms. She relaxed against him, enjoying the feeling of his chest against her face. Playing with his soft chest hairs with her fingertips.

"No, it's the first demand they've made of me. Dad used to go on all sorts of trips," he admitted. "I knew it was possible but had hoped . . ." He shook his head. "No, we weren't going to talk about work this weekend, remember?"

"Right." She glanced up at him, smothering a grin.

"Are you okay?" he asked, his eyes flooded with concern.

"Perfect." She leaned up and kissed him. "If I had known it was going to be like this . . . I would have done it years ago."

"Is it bad that part of me is thankful you hadn't?" His hand was running over her shoulder, and she could feel her body responding and wanting more of his touch.

"No." She swallowed. "Owen, I . . ." She wanted to tell him how he'd made her feel. How much she appreciated him being so gentle with her, but there was a lump in her throat.

He shook his head once more and then kissed her. "You don't have to say anything. I feel like a cad, because all I can think about is peeling that sexy outfit off of you and doing it all again."

She smiled and moved until she was straddling him. She could feel that he'd grown hard against her and instantly started rubbing herself against him. "It's all I can think about," she said between kisses. "It's all I want." She leaned up and allowed him to pull off the tank top. He tossed it off the bed and then leaned up and covered her breast with his lips, sucking on her until her nipples peaked and ached for more.

Instead of pulling off her soft shorts, he nudged them aside and started rubbing his fingers over her swollen flesh as she continued to move over him.

She could tell that he was allowing her to set the pace this time. When she wrapped her hand around him, he leaned his head back on the padded headboard and watched her.

"Tell me if I do something you don't like."

"I like it all," he said, his voice a little gruff.

Given his words, she took her time exploring him, trying new things. She could tell when he really enjoyed something, because his hips would move with her and his eyes would slide closed on a moan.

His hands continued to run over her, and when he pushed his fingers inside her again, she stopped her own exploring and focused on what he was doing to her.

"Yes," he said softly. "Ride my fingers." She moved up on her knees and did as he asked. "Just like that." Then, suddenly, he reached for another condom in his nightstand, and she leaned back, this time helping him slide it over himself.

"Now, do that same thing to me." He put his hands on her hips and helped hoist her up over himself.

When she was positioned just right, he released his hold on her and allowed her to slowly sink down on his length. It was the most erotic thing she'd ever done. Letting her body slip over his. Allowing his dark gaze to fill her with power. She could tell that his entire body was tense, poised for something, but he was so patient as he waited for her to make the next move.

When she had fully sunk onto him, she held still as she felt herself being stretched; then, when she felt comfortable, she started to move over him. Losing herself in the pleasure, she closed her eyes as he leaned up and rained kisses over her chest and neck. When he took her lips, she was on the edge already and felt herself explode once more.

This time when her body went lax, he quickly moved, reversing their positions as he kept their bodies connected. Then, taking her thighs in his hands, he spread her legs wide and tucked them between their bodies as he started moving while he watched her.

"Owen," she said when she felt herself building up once more. His moves were strong and sure, and she couldn't stop her body from reacting to his.

"Yes, that's it," he said, his eyes burning into hers. "Let go. Give me what I want."

"Anything," she said, and she felt her shoulders jerk off the mattress as she felt herself once more falling. This time, she heard his shout of joy as he followed her.

She must have fallen asleep. When her eyes opened again, the room was flooded with light. He'd pulled the blankets over them sometime during the night. Her body felt lax and sated.

"Morning," Owen said from beside her.

The fact that she was practically lying over his chest had her smiling. Glancing up, she looked into his sleepy eyes.

"Morning." She rested her chin on her hands over his chest.

"You look happy." He reached up and brushed her hair away from her face.

"I am. How about you?" she asked.

"Very. So, was it everything you've dreamed of?" he asked again. He planted a kiss on her forehead.

She chuckled. "Fishing for a compliment?" She felt his chest rumble with laughter.

"No." His hands began to run over her back, and she arched into the feeling of them on her skin. "Just making sure I lived up to your dreams."

"Well, since I don't have anyone to compare last night to . . ." She bit her lip and waited; when he pinched her backside lightly, she laughed. "Yes. Last night lived up to my expectations, and more. How about you?" She leaned down and kissed him, suddenly worried. "How do you feel?"

"Hungry, but happy." His arms tightened around her for a moment.

She laughed. "I could eat. What do you have around?"

He frowned. "Nothing. I had all of my food tossed out, since I didn't trust it."

"Smart idea."

"I haven't hit the store yet," he admitted. "How about we shower and head downstairs, and then you can help me replace a few things around here?"

She leaned up, letting the sheets fall off her body. "That's a plan." She watched his eyes move to her breasts and smiled even bigger. "Or we could"—she reached and found him already hard, which caused her eyebrows to shoot up—"add a few distractions between here and the shower . . ." She licked her lips slowly, his eyes heating as he watched.

By the time they finally made it into the shower, they were both covered in a light sheen of sweat. Afterward, instead of taking her time to get ready, she quickly threw on a blouse and shorts, then piled her hair into a messy bun and applied her makeup quickly. She was starving and wanted to get something to eat quickly.

"You look like a woman who spent the night getting pleased," he teased while they rode the elevator down to the lobby.

"I am. You look pretty relaxed yourself," she said, and she stood up on her toes to kiss him.

As the elevator doors opened, she was laughing and smiling, thinking about the wonderful day they were about to have together. The last thing she'd expected was to see her parents.

Her entire body tensed, causing Owen to quickly shield her with his body.

"Mom? Dad?" She frowned at them.

She felt Owen relax a little in front of her, and then he took her hand and stepped out of the elevator before the doors shut on them.

"Hannah," her parents said at the same time. Her mother evaluated her, and her lip curled. Hannah replayed Owen's words from moments earlier. Knowing that she did indeed probably look like a woman who had spent the entire night getting pleased sexually by the man standing beside her, she watched her mother's eyes narrow.

Then Hannah realized that her parents were standing in one of the best beach resorts along the Emerald Coast, dressed as if they were heading to brunch at the country club. Which should have made her laugh, but instead, it was just a normal thing with her family.

"What are you doing here?" She frowned and watched a family with three kids racing across the lobby, all dressed in swimwear and holding towels and pool toys.

"We're staying here during our visit. We were just on our way to your work to try to convince you . . ." her mother started to say, her gaze running up and down Owen as if he was the help and she was trying to figure out why he was still standing there during a private family conversation. "Who is this?" she interrupted herself.

"You're staying *here*?" Hannah asked, ignoring her mother's question.

"Of course. We always stay here. Everyone knows that property owned by Paradise Investments is the only decent place to stay around here."

"I'm Andrew Rodgers." Her father held out his hand toward Owen.

Owen glanced down at her first. When she gave him a quick nod, he extended his hand. "Owen Costa," he said, and he shook her father's hand.

Hannah knew the moment her father paused that he had linked that name to the very resort he was standing in. Her dad's eyebrows shot up quickly, but he composed his expression just as quickly.

"Nice to meet you. We've been hearing all about you."

"You have?" Owen asked, looking surprised as he glanced down at her. Hannah shook her head quickly.

"Not from me." She knew that Owen understood why she hadn't been telling her parents about him.

"No, we . . ." her mother started to say, but after a slight nudge from her father, she shut her mouth.

Hannah raised a brow, and she moved a step closer to her parents as she lowered her voice. "Tell me you didn't have me followed," she almost hissed.

When her father's chin rose slightly, she growled. "Again?"

Owen stepped forward. "This might be a better conversation for a private time." He motioned to the front desk.

"Yes, Mr. Costa?" a woman said from behind the counter.

"Beth, is the conference room available right now?"

"Of course." With a broad smile, she motioned to a hallway. "It's available for the next hour, and just let me know if you need me to clear the schedule," she added as Owen reached for Hannah's hand and started walking in that direction, not waiting to see if her parents would follow. At that moment, she felt nothing for them.

Owen stood back as her parents stepped into the conference room; then he shut the door behind him and waited for her to speak. Instead of talking to her parents, she watched him and felt the need to explain.

"My parents have this nasty habit of always checking up on me. They have a firm that . . . spies on me." Her stomach rolled, and she was thankful that she hadn't eaten anything yet.

Owen glanced over at her parents.

"We have a right to protect our daughter. It's a simple background-checking firm. Everyone uses it," her father explained.

"We wouldn't have to if our daughter simply talked to us," her mother added, with the perfect hint of hurt in her tone.

Her parents were really good at playing the victim.

"Why are you still here?" she asked again.

"We've told you. We were here to visit . . ." her mother started, but when Hannah crossed her arms over her chest, she stopped. "I don't know why you're so upset. You can't blame us, after the last call we had about the holidays. You're so secretive lately."

Hannah swallowed the pain that was bubbling in her chest.

"I think we got off to a rough start." Owen stepped forward after a long silence. "We were just heading in for some breakfast. Would you care to join us?"

Her father met his gaze. "We would be honored," he said quickly.

Hannah remained silent.

"If you'll head into the café and give us a moment . . ." Owen suggested as he opened the conference room door. Her parents looked between them and then stepped outside. Owen shut the door again and gathered her in his arms.

"I'm sorry," he said into her hair as she closed her eyes and rested against his chest.

"I don't want them to spoil this," she said. "They have a tendency to ruin everything good for me."

He nudged her back until she was looking up at him. "I'm not the kind of man who bails on a relationship, once I've committed, because there are a few bumps in the road." He used his thumb to wipe a tear that had slipped down her cheek. She didn't realize she'd been crying and dashed the rest of the tears away herself quickly with the back of her hand.

"You've committed?" she asked, causing him to chuckle. "They hired someone to spy on us," she groaned. "That scares me. It's got to terrify you."

"For the last few months, I've had my own PI looking for my dad." He shrugged. "Families are messed up. Mine is no exception."

She relaxed and took a deep cleansing breath. "You're right."

"Good." He took her hand in his; she enjoyed the warmth and the strength that emanated from it. "Now, let's head in and try to make it through breakfast together."

She nodded, but she tugged on his hand before he could leave. "I'm sorry about all this. Just know, beforehand, that I'm sorry."

He leaned down and kissed her until she forgot everything except for the feeling of his lips on hers. By the time they'd walked into the café, she was ready to handle anything that her parents threw at them.

CHAPTER TWELVE

Owen had sat through his fair share of business meetings. Breakfast with the Rodgers was nothing new and different. The more he thought of her parents as business relations, the more he could tolerate them. The fact that the only emotion he'd seen from them was the little pout her mother had done when she'd mentioned Hannah being secretive had been very telling and had allowed him to set the flow of the conversation.

He kept them on her father's businesses and the travel they had planned for the coming year. They asked him a few questions about his family's business, which he answered while remaining vague.

He could tell that the main reason they were in Florida was to convince their daughter that this wasn't the place for her. The number of times they mentioned how "backwoods" the area was and how she was better off coming back to New York was beginning to be ridiculous.

They had just finished breakfast when the subject of his father came up.

"We've heard your father has been MIA for a while," her father stated after their table had been cleared.

Owen had been prepared for the topic, as it wasn't the first time since returning that he'd been asked about it.

"He's currently taking care of some other business. I've been made chair by the board."

"So I've heard," her father said. He added, "I wouldn't mind sitting down with you and discussing doing business together sometime."

He felt Hannah tense beside him, but he knew how to handle situations like this.

"I'd be honored. I'll have my secretary contact you, if you will give me your . . ." Her father's card appeared like a playing card in a magician's hand. Something told Owen that her parents' visit had nothing to do with them wanting to check up on their daughter but was more about getting a foot in his doorway.

Still, Owen knew that her parents weren't exactly hurting as far as businesses go. Leslie Rodgers was heir to the McCaw fortune, a multimillion-dollar investment firm on the East Coast. The small family-owned business had started out in the South, but shortly after Hannah's parents were married, Hannah's father moved the corporate offices to New York, bought up a bunch of defunct businesses, and, after tearing them down, turned them into high-rise apartment complexes, which pushed the business into a totally different bracket.

"I'd like that." Her father stood and shook his hand. "Well, Leslie and I are going to go enjoy some time while we're here." He helped his wife up. "We'll leave you two to enjoy the rest of your day."

"It was nice meeting you, Owen," Hannah's mother chimed in before following her husband out of the room.

"They didn't even say goodbye to you," Owen said when they were alone.

"No." She sighed. "You're the important one here. Not me."

He gathered her in his arms and held on to her. "I know it sucks, but hopefully you're the kind of woman who likes grocery shopping. Or would you prefer to go somewhere and smash things?"

The fact that she thought about it for a moment had him laughing. "How about I promise to buy you something we can smash later?" she teased.

The sight of her smile was so mesmerizing that he had to lean down and kiss her. "God, I'm so sorry they put you through that." He helped her up from the table.

"Me?" she asked. "They stuck you with the bill."

He laughed and took her hand in his. "Small price to pay." They stepped into the elevators to head to the parking garage.

After helping her into his car, he asked, "Tell me they will at least see you one more time before they head home?"

She thought about it, then shook her head. "No. I'm pretty sure I'll get a call next week. They'll want to invite you up there for the holidays, and when I remind them that I won't even be going home for the holidays, they'll start guilt-tripping me about the entire thing."

"Okay. I thought my dad was bad, but your parents bring 'bad parent' to a whole new level," he said as they drove out of the complex and started heading toward the outlet shops.

She glanced over at him. "Out of the five of us—the Wildflowers—I'd like to take credit for the worst parents, but I think Aubrey wins that award."

"Oh?" he asked.

"Her father is Harold Smith." She waited, and when the name finally dawned on him, she nodded. "Yeah."

"But isn't that man like a hundred years old?" he asked, remembering one of the wealthiest men alive.

"Yes, and Aubrey is the illegitimate daughter of him and a woman barely legal at the time of Aubrey's birth. After her mother died when Aubrey was eight, Harold took over her life." She turned to him. "My friends saved me and Aubrey that summer."

He reached over and took her hand in his, then raised it to his lips and placed a kiss on her knuckles. "You're lucky you found them."

She nodded in agreement. "Just talking about it helps. I mean, I was all ready to smash something . . ."

"Hannah smash," he joked in his best Hulk voice, causing her to laugh.

She sighed. "I was, but now, not so much. It's not like it would change anything in that relationship."

He squeezed her hand as he pulled into the shopping center. "Good, then I can safely take you in here." He motioned to the furniture store he had parked in front of.

She laughed. "Yes, I'd say you're safe. What is it you need for your place?"

"I'm not sure, but when I find it, I'll know." He helped her out of the car and, before she could walk away, pulled her into another hug. "Thank you," he said, and he kissed her.

"For?" she prompted.

"Sleeping with me, for starters." She laughed again. "For spending the weekend with me and for helping me find junk to fill my place with."

"You may be sorry for that later. I have a very eclectic taste."

He laughed and took her hand in his. "So do I."

Four hours later, they broke for lunch, stopping at one of the tourist traps that faced the water. The place was packed, and they ended up having to wait almost a full hour before they were finally seated, looking out at the beach and watching families play in the clear waters as kids played volleyball on the white sand. She had a frozen orange drink, and he had a cold beer.

"You weren't joking about your taste." He toasted her with his beer. "Every time I look down at my frog doormat, I'll think of you."

She sipped her drink. "I believe you should be able to express yourself freely. Who doesn't want a welcome mat that says, 'Welcome to my pad'?"

He laughed. "Apparently I couldn't resist having one."

He could tell all day long she'd struggled with trying to get over her parents' visit. Now, as she looked out over the water, he knew the thoughts were creeping back.

"Fuck them," he said.

Her eyes returned to his, and when she smiled, he knew she'd gotten who he was talking about.

"Would you say that about your dad?" she asked, surprising him.

"If he'd treated me the way your parents had treated you during breakfast, yes. They didn't even really talk to you," he said after thinking about it. "Actually, did they even say anything directly to you?"

"No, not after you introduced yourself."

"I thought not," he said grimly.

"Your dad *has* left you in a bad position—think about it. Would you say the same about him now?" she asked.

"Only at times, but yes," he said honestly, knowing that he'd grown even more frustrated with his father in the past few months. "But there appears to be more to his story than just another crazy trip."

"Is it true that you thought it was possible that one of us was having an affair with your dad?" she asked, leaning forward.

"Yes." He smiled when he remembered first arriving at the camp. "Elle's name was on Dad's calendar."

Her eyebrows shot up. "You thought Elle and your dad . . . you know?"

"It had crossed all of our minds, until we got to know her."

"It's funny. We can't figure out why we're not all very upset with you three for lying to us," she said between sips of her drink. "I mean, you got jobs at the camp under fake names and spent the next few months sneaking around the place." She shrugged. "I suppose it was because after Dylan explained that your dad was missing . . . I guess we all decided to help out instead of being mad."

"Zoey was mad for a while." He nudged her.

"Yeah, and then Ryan pulled a gun on Dylan," she added, and he frowned.

"Don't remind me." Just thinking back at how close he'd come to losing his younger brother had him on edge. "It's one of the reasons our lawyers are working on your case."

"Thank you, by the way. I don't think I ever said that before."

He shrugged. "It's the least we can do. The woman went after all three of us when we were at the camp."

Hannah's eyebrows shot up. "She went after you?"

He chuckled. "Yeah, not with a gun. She just backed us all into dark corners. Not my type."

"Dylan said that she claimed to have been with your dad. Do you think it's true?"

"I could see it," he said. "But my dad can spot crazy pretty easily. I'm sure they weren't together long."

She sighed and again looked out the window as if deep in thought. "I wish there was a crazy meter. We would never have hired her. Do you know that Brent actually feels bad about hiring her? He thinks it's all his fault."

"No one could have guessed."

"No, I suppose not." She went quiet for a while after they ordered their sandwiches. "I think my parents are partially crazy."

"What makes you say that?" he asked.

"They act like people out of *The Stepford Wives*," she said when he waited.

He moved his drink away from the edge of the table. "Right—showing no emotion."

"That, and being perfect. I've never seen my mother with a hair out of place. She's always wearing heels and a dress, along with pearls or diamonds. I mean, you saw her—she even wore that to a beach resort! My father is nearly always in a suit. Not to mention they are both in great shape, but I've never seen them working out."

"Not even when you were a kid?" he asked.

"No." She shook her head. "Even with the gym in our townhouse, I never even saw them in sweat clothes." She giggled. "I used to believe my mother worked out in heels and a dress."

"Okay, now you're creeping me out, and I want to watch that movie again. I can't remember how it ended."

"The old one or the new one?" she asked.

"Either, both." He shrugged.

She laughed. "Looks like we have something more to do tonight."

Just then, his phone rang; seeing Brett's name on the screen, he quickly answered it.

"Hey, Brett," he answered. "Did you find out anything new?"

"We have something. Your security place forwarded me a copy of the last videos they had at your place; we have a still shot of a car that parked in your spot shortly before the cameras went out. Do you have a few minutes to stop by and see if you recognize the vehicle? I could email it . . ."

"No, that's okay. I'm just down the street." He glanced down at his watch, noticing Hannah's intent gaze. "I can swing by."

"Sounds good; see you then." Brett hung up.

CHAPTER THIRTEEN

Hannah sat at the police station while the officer showed Owen a few grainy pictures from the security cameras in the parking garage at his building. It was obvious by the way the two men interacted that they were close friends. Owen had mentioned that they had attended the same school in Pelican Point back when his family had lived in the big house across from the campgrounds. Currently, the owner of the place, Reed Cooper, was seeing Kimberly, Zoey and Scarlett's mother, who lived in the old cabin the girls used to inhabit every summer.

The place had been fixed up specifically for their mother—the divorce from their father had drained the woman of everything she'd had and left the girls high and dry. But since their father's sudden death earlier that year, both girls had come into their full inheritance, which had helped out a lot around the camp. Still, the rest of the friends had made them promise not to spend it all on the business, so Zoey was having a house built for her and Dylan on the outskirts of the camp property, while Scarlett had taken to investing.

She found it strange that the five friends had come from some of the wealthiest families, yet as adults, all five of them had been cut off from their family funds. It was almost as if they had become friends because they had known that someday they would need one another to survive.

The fact that they had been able to pool all their savings together to open the camp had been nothing short of a miracle. Every extra dime they had they'd all put back into the camp so they could have more tiny cabins built for more guests.

Currently, there were more than half a dozen new cabins on the grounds, with even more planned.

"Do you recognize this car?" Brett was asking Owen.

"That's my neighbor's car." He leaned forward and pointed. "But this one . . ." He tapped the screen. "No, it looks like a delivery van."

Brett leaned closer. "We've run the plates. It's a rental. We're checking to find out who had it rented at the time, but the company is demanding a warrant." The man leaned back in his chair. "I miss the good old days when everyone liked the cops."

Owen slapped his shoulder. "We weren't around during the good old days."

"Right." Brett glanced at her. "Sorry to drag you down here on your night off. How are things up at the camp?"

"Quiet now," she said with ease. "Thanks to you guys."

He chuckled. "I've been keeping an eye on Ryan. We hope she's not been bothering you?"

"No." Hannah glanced over at Owen. "She hasn't."

"Well . . ." Owen jumped up from his chair suddenly, looking a little guilty as he shook Brett's hand. "Let me know if you find out anything else."

"Will do." Brett waved to them as they walked out.

"Spill," she said the moment they were in the car. A light rain was falling, making the roads appear to be cleaner than normal.

"What?" he asked, avoiding her gaze.

"Are you having your friend keep tabs on Ryan for me?" She poked him in the shoulder.

He sighed. "Not necessarily. After what happened with Dylan . . ."

She should have thought of it first, but she'd been so busy with running the camp she hadn't thought to hire someone to keep tabs on the crazy woman. Then again, it was his brother the woman had almost killed.

"Of course." She smiled and touched his arm.

He pulled into his building and shut off the car. "Your safety and that of everyone else at the camp played a part as well."

"Thank you." She gave his hair a caress. "I should have thought of it myself." She took a deep breath. "After all, I take after my father in some areas."

"No, parents may make us, but they don't define us."

He leaned over and kissed her until she was tugging at his shirt. He pulled back and glanced around. "As we've just seen, there are cameras out here. Let's go inside."

She followed him into the elevator, and before the doors could shut, he was kissing her again.

"We should have spent the day in bed," he said when the elevator started buzzing because he'd forgotten to push a button.

"Agreed." She smiled over at him. "Next time I have days off." She waited at those words, holding her breath.

"It's a date," he said just as the doors opened again. Then he stopped and took her hand. "Joel?"

The man turned away from Owen's front door and held out a case of beer with a smile. When he noticed Hannah, his smile slipped a little.

"Oh, I thought we'd hang out and have a few brews." His eyes narrowed at their joined hands.

"Thanks, but I've got other plans." Owen held up their hands. "Rain check?"

"Sure." Joel backed up a little. "My key wouldn't work." He was holding out a key ring.

"Oh, right. I had the locks changed," Owen said, adding, "I'll have to get you a new one."

"Thanks." Joel glanced at her. "Hey, Hannah."

"Joel." She nodded a greeting and felt a little relieved when he started to walk away.

Joel glanced back over his shoulder, his gaze puzzled. "Have a good night."

"Thanks," Owen said. He added, "See you at work tomorrow."

Joel stepped into the waiting elevator without a word.

"You could have asked him to stay, couldn't you?" she said once Owen had shut the door and reset the alarm; she felt a little unsure but was happy he hadn't.

Instead of answering, he walked over and wrapped his arms around her. "I see him all the time, but I only have a few more hours with you, and I want to make the most of them." He leaned in and kissed her. Relaxing against him, she allowed him to back her into the kitchen's bar top. When he hoisted her up on the countertop, she wrapped her legs around his hips and held on to him as he made her forget about anything else except him for the rest of the night.

The next morning, he helped her carry her bags out to her car and watched as she drove out of the building.

It was strange, but as she pulled out of the parking garage, she realized she hadn't had a problem driving down the inside of the building like she'd had going up it. Maybe it was the few times Owen had driven with her, and she was now used to it, or maybe she was just too preoccupied with all the new and sexy things he'd done to her last night. She'd never imagined a man thrusting into her with a vibrator while his mouth moved over her could cause her to peak so quickly.

Since she wasn't needed around the campgrounds for anything before lunch, she decided to do a little shopping for herself before driving out of Destin. But as she was putting her bags into the trunk of her car, she noticed a note on her windshield. Had someone hit her car?

Not seeing a scratch on it, she pulled out the note and read it several times before calling the police and sending a text to Owen.

On their advice, she locked herself in her car and waited for the police to arrive.

When she saw it was Brett pulling up in the cruiser, she felt instant relief.

"Are you okay?" Brett asked as she held out the note to him. He read it in a moment.

"Yes, just a little shaken," she admitted, tucking her hands into her pockets. Somehow, she was chilled in the heat of the day.

As they talked, she watched Owen park his car next to hers. Just seeing him sent the gut-wrenching fear from her body. Instantly, she felt drained instead.

"Are you okay?" Owen asked. He jumped out and took her in his arms. She melted into his embrace.

"Yes, I was shopping," she said, holding on to him.

"What does it say?" he asked Brett over her head.

Brett turned the paper he'd placed in a plastic bag around so that Owen could scan the hastily scratched note.

Stay away from the Costas. I'd hate for anything bad to happen to that pretty little body of yours.

"It has to be Ryan," she said. She'd sat in her car, scared and in a panicked state, with her mind playing over the words more than a dozen times. The only logical explanation was that Ryan had seen her shopping and had written the note. "Right?" She looked between the two men.

"I can check and see where she was." Brett tucked the note in the front seat of his patrol car and wrote down something in his notepad. "How long were you here?"

She glanced down at her watch and told him the time that she'd arrived.

"I'll follow you back to the camp," Owen said, rubbing her arms. "You're chilled."

"I . . ." She glanced around as she shivered. "I have a jacket." She took it from the car and slipped it on. The rain the night before had chilled the air as well as leaving the sky filled with dark clouds.

"You don't have to follow me back to the camp. I'm sure she just saw me. Could she still be watching?" she whispered. "Maybe this is what she wanted." She sighed.

"If it was her, we'll know soon. I'm still driving you back," he said.

"Now you're driving me?" she asked.

"Sure. Liam has the day off; he can drive me back here to my car."

Knowing that he would gladly stand there and argue the matter with her, she gave in. "Fine."

He held out his hand for her keys. "Are you done here?" he asked Brett.

"Yes." Brett handed her a piece of paper. "Your incident number. The moment I know anything—"

Owen jumped in and said, "Call me." She was too tired to argue with him about taking care of herself. Instead, she leaned on him, thankful that he was there to help her.

"I'll call you both," Brett said with a wink.

"Thanks." She smiled and slipped into her passenger seat.

For the first few blocks, they remained quiet.

"I don't think it was Ryan," he finally said once they'd started across the bridge.

"Why not?" she asked. "Who else would it be?"

He sighed. "The same someone who broke into my place."

"Why?" She thought about it. "Whoever that is wants you to step down from your position. Me seeing you has nothing to do with that."

He nodded slowly. "True," he agreed finally. "Still, it would just be too . . . perfect if it was Ryan."

"Not everything in life is a mystery." She shrugged and glanced out at the water of the bay. "You saw how she acted at the camp."

"Yes," he answered. "She's a scary woman."

"I think she lives around the area somewhere," she said. She pulled out her phone when it chimed.

It was a text from Elle.

Are you okay? Liam says Owen is with you.

Hannah had texted her friends while waiting for the police. They had wanted to drop everything and rush to her side, but she'd convinced them to stay at the camp and keep working, since she was okay. They had quickly asked her if she thought it was Ryan. She'd replied that she wasn't sure, but the woman was on top of her list of suspects.

"Did you tell your brothers?" she asked.

"Yes, I called them on the way over to you. Just to keep an eye out for anything there," he said, and she realized she hadn't thought of the possibility of Ryan going to the camp and doing something to her friends.

"You don't think Ryan would go back to the camp, do you? We have a restraining order . . ."

"No." He reached over and touched her shoulder just as her phone rang.

"It's Elle." She sighed and answered the call.

By the time they had pulled into the camp's parking lot, she had fully explained what had happened twice—once to Elle and another time to Aubrey, who agreed to fill in the other two.

"Looks like Liam is waiting to take me back." He parked next to his brother's car.

"Thanks for driving me out here," she said, reaching over and placing a soft kiss on his lips before grabbing the door handle. She was very thankful he'd been there for her. She'd wanted some time to gather her emotions before seeing her friends.

"I've got another meeting this week. I'm closing on that property I was telling you about," he said, stopping her from exiting the car.

"You're going to go ahead and build the neighborhood?" she asked, the note forgotten as she thought about the new possibilities.

"Yes, the board thought it was a great idea. A 'solid financial plan,'" he said, air quoting.

"That's really great." She leaned across her car and hugged him. "I'm sure once your dad comes back that he's going to be so proud."

"Oh, I'm sure of it." His smile changed a little. "If he comes back."

"Do you really think that he's hiding to protect you?" she asked.

"I'm beginning to have some serious thoughts in that direction. I know you have to get back to work, but I hope you were serious about spending your days off with me next week."

"Yes, I bought some new outfits." She leaned closer and licked her lips. "Some things you can take your time peeling off me."

"My god, do you think we have some time for me to go in—"

Just then his brother knocked on the glass, stopping Owen's wandering hands, and he groaned. "Scratch that. Give us a minute," he barked as he opened the door.

Liam chuckled. "Easy. Don't kill the messenger. Zoey and Elle are waiting for Hannah on the stairs. They have some news."

"Okay." Owen shut the door on his brother, causing her to laugh. "Damn, I don't know if I can wait until then." He pulled her close and kissed her; then, just as quickly as he'd grabbed her up, he released her.

She walked back to the main building on shaky legs.

"So?" she said, stopping in front of Zoey and Elle, who both looked like they were bursting to tell her something.

"Inside." Zoey grabbed her hand and dragged her inside and to Elle's office.

"Okay, I'm here. What is it?"

"The lawyers called. The case has been dropped," Elle blurted out.

"What?" She felt her heart skip. "Ryan's case?"

"Of course Ryan's case." Zoey laughed. "Who else would it be? Gosh, are we being sued by more than one idiot?"

Hannah laughed and jumped up and down as she hugged her friends. "Do Scarlett and Aubrey know yet?"

"Yes, they wanted to be here, but . . . work," Elle said with a shrug.

"Oh my god." She took a deep breath. "What a relief." Then she thought of the note. "It must have been Ryan who left the note. The timing is just too perfect." She glanced at her watch. "I have to be across the campus soon, and I still have to get everything out of my car . . ." She still felt giddy about her time with Owen. Even the terrifying ordeal couldn't dim the glow from what Owen's touch had done to her.

"Go." Elle elbowed her. "It's my day off, and we won't be leaving until Liam gets back from dropping Owen off. I'll put your stuff in your room." She took her keys from her, then nudged her toward the doorway.

"Are you trying to get rid of me?" She looked over her shoulder at her friends.

"No," they both said at the same time.

"We dragged you in here, remember?" Elle said with a chuckle.

"And now you're the ones pushing me out. Why?" She stopped and crossed her arms over her chest. Determined not to move until they told her what was up.

Zoey moved closer to her with a scrutinizing gaze. "You had sex." Her friend changed the subject quickly.

Hannah's chin dropped. "I . . . did spend the weekend with Owen," she reminded her friend.

"No, I mean . . . knock-your-socks-off sex. I've never seen that look"—Zoey pointed at Hannah's eyes—"there before."

"That's because she'd never had sex before," Elle blurted out.

"Shut up; of course she has." Zoey turned to her and, upon seeing Hannah's look, gasped. "Seriously? Why didn't I know this?" She looked between Elle and Hannah.

"Because you were too busy telling us all about the sex you've had," Elle teased. "Go." Elle waved Hannah away. "I'll hold her off so you can escape."

Hannah took the bait and rushed from the room. She was halfway across campus when she realized that she'd fallen into Zoey's trap.

CHAPTER FOURTEEN

Owen sat in his brother's car as they drove back into town, debating with Liam the entire ride about who could be causing problems. By the time they'd pulled into the parking lot where his car was parked, they had narrowed their list of suspects down to just one. Ryan, again. Even though he had dismissed the possibility earlier, she was the only logical choice. He just couldn't think of anyone in the office who would threaten Hannah; after all, no one really knew about her. Liam had clued him in on the fact that Ryan's case had recently been dropped, which put her back in the running for head suspect.

"Has anyone heard from her?" he asked when the car came to a stop next to his own.

"None of us at the camp," Liam said. "We've upped security around the place, just in case. Last time she snuck in without alerting security, so we're hoping with the new measures we've put in place . . ."

"Good. I'll let you know if Brett finds anything." He realized that wouldn't really stop someone who was determined, but at least they were doing something.

"Hey." Liam stopped him from getting out. "You and Hannah . . ."

He waited, but when Liam didn't finish, he said, "Just like you and Elle are none of my business."

"No." Liam shook his head. "I guess what I was trying to say is, you two are good. You know, just like Dylan and Zoey."

Owen smiled. "Who would have thought that we'd be where we are today because Dad took off?"

"I guess in a twisted way, Dad disappearing on us was a good thing," Liam said with a laugh.

Owen exited the car, then leaned his head back in. "I won't tell Dad you said that." He closed the door to the sound of Liam's chuckles.

The air-conditioning hit him full force when he stepped into his building ten minutes later. He desperately wished he wasn't wearing a suit and that he could spend the day with Hannah again on the beach.

When he stepped out of the elevators, he frowned when he realized Nora wasn't at her usual post. Glancing around, he made his way to his office and froze when he noticed the man sitting behind his desk.

"Dad?" He had to blink a few times. Leo Costa was an older version of his sons. Almost down to the last chromosome. However, since his disappearance, Owen noticed a few more silver hairs in his father's longer, thicker beard. He was wearing one of his casual tan dress shirts and khaki suits that he always wore to the office.

His father looked up from a stack of papers and smiled at him. "There you are." He looked down at the papers again. "Good job with this property in Pelican Point." His dad glanced up again at him, and Owen realized that he hadn't moved. After shutting the door behind him, he finally stepped into the office.

"What are you doing here?" he asked once he was finally able to speak.

"This is my office," his father answered him.

"Not anymore." He stood at the end of the desk. "You were voted—"

"Yes, yes." His father waved him away. "I know all about the votes." He stood up and hugged Owen. "The walls have ears," he whispered to him, sending a shiver down Owen's spine.

His father slapped him on the back. "God, it's good to be back. I've had Nora and Joel get the office next door ready for you."

Owen swallowed and glanced around the room. He'd just gotten used to his position there and was actually starting to enjoy it. With his father back, where did he fit in? "Thanks," he said, taking his father's hint. "Maybe we can do lunch, and I can fill you in on where everything stands?"

"Sounds great. I'm proud of you, son, for stepping up and taking over while I was gone." His father sat back down and motioned for Owen to do the same. "Talk to me about this deal you've started."

"Sure." Owen glanced around as if trying to find any hidden wires or bugs in the room. For the next hour he filled his dad in on his plans. When Nora stepped in, she told him that his office was ready next door, but he remained by his father's side. When noon rolled around, in unspoken agreement they headed down to their favorite restaurant across the street.

"What the *shit*, Dad?" He finally asked him when they stepped outside.

"Fuck, I never wanted to drag you boys into this mess." His father finally looked frustrated and tired, and Owen realized that him holding it together all morning had been for show.

"What the hell is going on?" Owen asked as they walked across the street.

"I'm trying to help collect dirt, undercover-like . . . it's a sting operation."

Owen froze midstep. His dad had to reach out and nudge him out of the street. "A sting? As in . . . the feds?"

"Yes." His father ran his hands through his hair. "Not to mention someone's been trying to blackmail me. That's how the whole thing got started, actually," he ended on a sigh, and Owen could see even more weariness behind his eyes.

"Better start at the beginning, but first, let me call Dylan and Liam and tell them you're back."

"Why don't we call them together? Then, I'll want to arrange a meeting with them somewhere other than here. How about we head out to that camp tonight so we can fill them in on everything?"

"That would work," Owen said, but his father caught him by the arm in the vestibule of the restaurant.

He motioned to his chest. "Son, I can't tell you everything, but I've been given permission to tell you some things." Then he shocked Owen by mouthing, "I'm wearing a wire."

"What in the hell?"

He hadn't meant to say it out loud, but his father covered by saying, "You're right—that door does stick. Let me get it. At least I'm back." He sighed and opened the door for him.

They were seated in a back booth near the bar. Owen figured his father had chosen the spot so that the lunch crowd's sounds would drown out most of the conversation, but he couldn't be sure, since he didn't want to ask aloud.

After getting their drinks, his dad started talking.

"I started receiving threatening notes. At first, they were just little threats like that I needed to step down from the board, then they moved up to personal threats. I filed them away as bogus until a picture of you showed up with you in red crosshairs. That's when I called an old buddy in the government. Well, you could have blown me over when he cut me right off and requested a meeting instead of just chatting. I came to find out my company was under investigation."

"For what?" Owen sat up straight.

"Corporate espionage."

"The hell." Owen shook his head. "No way."

"I thought so too, to begin with. When I was able to bring up the threats to him, things started to fall into place. Someone at the company is either setting me up or trying to get us shut down."

"So what? You disappear on us? So that we have to deal with it all?" All his anger from the past months came flooding back.

"No, I went to find answers. Me and my buddy . . ." He shook his head. "Sorry, too many details. Anyway, I had a lot of questions that needed to be answered—not to mention that I hoped if I left, the pressure and threats would stop."

"Back here in the real world, you left your sons scared shitless, caused us to lie and accuse people we didn't know, and forced the board to vote that I take over for you. Which, by the way, turned the heat up on me."

"What do you mean?" His father leaned forward.

"I've been receiving threats." Owen watched as his father's face turned white.

"Shit." He ran his hands through his hair again. "Shit." Leaning back, he closed his eyes. "I never thought the board would vote to replace me."

"No?" Some of Owen's anger dissipated upon seeing his father's worry.

"No." He opened his eyes again. "I still own the majority of shares . . ."

"Which you took off with, along with all of the money you were due to invest in the business. You could have named a proxy, for fuck's sake," he reminded him. They hadn't even talked about the huge chunk of missing funds yet.

His father sighed. "All I can tell you now is that we're close to the end of this mess."

"That's not good enough," he said, pushing his drink away. The fact that he was no longer hungry or thirsty told him that he was too upset to bother.

"It will have to be. We'll go and meet with Dylan and Liam tonight."

"Go." Owen stood up. "I'm done here." He tossed some cash on the table for his drink and walked out. He hadn't expected his father to follow him out, but Leo caught him just as he was stepping into the parking garage.

"Son." He laid a hand on his arm. "I know this is confusing, but I didn't leave you by choice." He stepped closer and whispered, "We need you to come back inside and act like nothing's wrong."

"I don't know if I can do that." He shook his head.

"Ron thinks . . ." He took a deep breath. "That there's more at stake now than before."

"Ron?" He shook his head.

"My buddy. Now that both Dylan and Liam are . . . involved with the camp—"

"Shit," Owen blurted out. "You aren't saying that River Camp is in trouble?"

"No, not the business." His father's eyes pleaded with him, and Owen got the meaning. This was more than business; this was personal. Which meant Zoey, Elle, and now Hannah. They were all in danger because of his father.

"Shit," he said again, running his hands through his hair, much like his father had just done.

"We really need to talk about your language." His father chuckled and started walking him toward the doors to the building. "Thanks, son."

"Fuck off." He shook his hand off. "I'm not doing this for you."

His father sagged at that remark, but the moment they stepped into the building, he had a smile pasted on his face. He was friendly and upbeat as he passed employees, talking with them briefly as they made their way back up to their offices.

For the remainder of the day, Owen locked himself in his new office and tried to resume his normal routine. He didn't ask Nora where Tom, the man who'd had the office yesterday, had been moved, since he didn't have the strength. He did call his brothers, but then he instantly worried that his conversation would be recorded and sent them a text instead.

Can't talk now. Dad's back in the office. Let's meet tonight. Don't call!

His brothers instantly texted back with a bunch of questions, to which he replied simply:

Later.

His next text went out to Hannah to let her know that he would be swinging by the camp that evening, but when she didn't respond right away, he figured she was in one of her classes.

It took her almost an hour to finally get back to him.

Wonderful news about your dad returning. We'll have dinner all ready. Can't wait to see you.

He chuckled and started typing, his foul mood disappearing quickly.

You just saw me a few hours ago. I knew it, you just can't get enough of me.

I must be crazy, right?

If you are, I'm right there with you. I can't wait to see you too.

His mood improved from that point. Until his father stepped into his office just before five o'clock.

"I figured we could head out there together?" His dad leaned on his desk.

"Sure." He thought about going home first and changing, then decided against it, since he didn't want to drag his dad to his place. Not wanting to explain why he'd gotten all-new furniture to him yet. He figured he'd save that conversation for later, after his father had updated him on what the hell was going on. He logged out of his computer and locked up the office.

Instead of heading to Owen's car, his father started walking toward his own parking spot.

"We'll take my car," he said. He used the key remote and unlocked the car from across the garage.

It took a moment for Owen to realize what had happened—after he woke up. He was lying on the cement, looking up at the roof of the parking garage. His head throbbed as if he'd been beaned with a baseball bat. There was a loud high-pitched ringing in his ears, and his vision was acting up. He had to blink a few times for everything to start to come into focus.

Then he remembered his father and jerked to sit up, only to have his head spin.

"Shit," he groaned, and he grabbed his head as invisible spikes drove into it.

"Owen?" He heard his father's voice from somewhere near him.

"Dad?" He glanced around and found his father sitting on the ground a few feet away, a stream of blood flowing from a large cut on his forehead.

"What happened?" he asked.

"Hell if I know." His father wiped at the cut on his forehead. "I think my car blew up."

It was then that Owen realized the ringing in his ears wasn't just from the blast: an ambulance had stopped just outside the entrance of the parking garage.

Muffled voices echoed around him. He thought he heard someone yelling that the area wasn't safe and they had to wait, but he wasn't sure, since everything came into his ears through the ringing sound.

"Are you hurt?" his father asked him, and for the first time since waking up, he looked down at himself. His suit was ruined, and he was missing a shoe, but he couldn't see any blood, except on the back of his hands, which he must have used to shield his face.

"No, you have a cut, though." He motioned to his father's head.

His father pulled off his tie and used it to swipe at the blood.

"Are you hurt anywhere else?" he asked his dad.

"No, just my head. I think we'd better try and get to them." He pointed to the ambulance. "I don't think they're going to come in here until they know it's safe."

"Right." He started to stand more slowly this time and felt everything spin again. "I must have hit my head," he said when he finally was able to make it to his knees.

His dad helped him stand up. Owen leaned on his old man as he half dragged him toward the entrance of the garage.

They were a few feet away from them when two men rushed over and helped Owen the rest of the way out of the garage. Questions were yelled at them, but his head was hurting too much to answer, so he let his dad take over as he was examined.

When they suggested he be moved to the hospital, he declined, but his father stepped in.

"I'll drive him over there myself," his dad suggested.

"Dad," he started to argue, but instead his father laid a hand on his. "Son, you've got a concussion. You'll want to get it checked out. No arguments."

He would have nodded his head, but his vision was dimming. "Sure," he groaned.

"I think your car survived," his father slurred. "You still park in your spot?"

Owen tried to think of where he'd parked that morning, but nothing was coming to him. "I think." He dug in his pockets and pulled out his keys.

"We'll be at the hospital," his father started to say just as Brett rushed over to them.

"What. The. Hell." His friend took in the sight of them both. "Hell," he said again.

"We were going to head to the hospital," Owen said, unsure why he was even talking.

"Yes, go." Brett started to wave to the ambulance to take them away, but Owen stopped him.

"Dad was going to drive—"

"No, neither of you are in a position to get behind the wheel." Brett turned to his dad. "Was that your car?"

"Yeah, I think . . ." His dad looked like he was trying to remember. "Yeah."

"Then, neither of you are driving Owen's car." Brett took the keys from his father. "Not until I get a bomb squad down here."

The rest of the color drained from his father's face. "Shit."

"Yeah." Brett cracked his neck. "Yeah," he repeated. Owen noticed that Bill was standing in the background, looking a little surprised at the destruction. "Take them both down to the hospital to get checked out. I'll make sure you have an officer go with . . ." Brett turned and, after quickly talking to his chief, brought a young officer over. "This is Evan. He's going to be on you until I can get down there to talk to you both."

"Right," his father said, and he allowed the paramedic to strap him into the seat.

The ride to the hospital was quick, since it was less than five miles away, but the waiting once they were there was excruciating. The whole time his mind raced over the fact that someone had tried to kill them. Someone had planted a bomb in his father's car. And perhaps in his too.

He felt like a fool for not taking all those threatening notes more seriously.

His father was shuffled in with him for scans and X-rays, since he had a head wound. Then they were put in a small room, where they waited for a doctor to check them out as an officer stood not too far away. Even when two men in black suits approached him and talked to him, the officer never wavered. The men talked to his father briefly, then took positions alongside the officer.

Shortly after the doctor had come and gone, his brothers rushed in. They all had to pass through the scrutiny of the men in suits.

"What the . . ." Dylan rushed to take Owen up in a hug. Then turned to their father and did the same, followed by Liam.

"Someone blew up Dad's car," Owen said. For some reason, getting knocked on the head had made him revert to using very short sentences.

"Yeah, Brett called," Dylan said, adding, "Zoey and the rest of the ladies are in the waiting room."

"Hannah?" he mumbled. The pain meds they had given him were starting to work, slightly.

"She's here, but they only wanted two of us to come back at a time," Dylan answered.

"I'll go back out to the waiting area so she can come back and see you," Liam suggested, then hugged him lightly again. "You guys scared us."

Owen leaned his head back with a groan and closed his eyes for just a moment.

It must have been longer than that, since when he opened them again, Hannah was sitting on the side of the bed with a worried look.

He reached for her hand, only to realize that she was already holding his. "You're here."

She tried to smile. "Are you okay?"

"Yeah." He shifted, wanting to sit up, but suddenly his entire body felt like a lead weight.

"Here." She helped him move and put a pillow behind his head carefully. "Are you in pain?"

"A little." He realized that they were alone. "Dad?"

"He's talking to Brett and two men in suits that scared me as they looked at my driver's license," she said, sitting beside him again. "Someone blew up your dad's car."

"I can't remember everything, but I think I got that part down." He watched the corner of her mouth curve up and felt his heart skip.

"It's a mess, apparently. They're trying to figure out if there's anything left so that they can determine who did this."

"Someone tried to kill my dad." That much had sunk in over the past few hours.

She squeezed his hand. "Or . . . the both of you."

He hadn't thought about that. They had mentioned previously that they would be going to lunch together. If they hadn't decided to walk across the street, would the car have blown up then?

"Rest." She touched his cheek. "You look as if you're trying to figure it all out now."

He relaxed back on the pillow. "I am, if my brain would only cooperate."

She rubbed a hand over her brow, and his eyes flew to her face. She looked tired, and he realized he didn't know how long he'd been asleep before she'd gotten there.

"What time is it?" The TV didn't have a clock.

"Just past ten," she answered.

It was just past five when they left the office. "Come here"—he scooted over gingerly—"and lay next to me for a while."

155

"They're going to release you soon," she said as she crawled next to him and rested her head on his shoulder. "Your dad and brothers are going to try to convince you to come back and stay at the camp."

"Okay," he said, half-asleep again.

"Promise?" she asked.

"Yes," he replied, enjoying the way her body felt against his as he drifted off.

CHAPTER FIFTEEN

Hannah sat in her front room and watched Owen like a hawk as he slept on her sofa. He'd moved like an old man, as his father had. They were both sporting cuts and bruises all over their hands and faces. However, while Leo had a large white bandage over his left eye, Owen had several smaller butterfly ones over tiny cuts.

By a quarter past midnight, everyone had crowded into the living space and were now waiting for Leo Costa to fill them in on what he'd been up to over the past six months. Even though Owen had instantly fallen asleep upon lying on the sofa, everyone else wanted "the Great Reveal."

"Well?" Dylan said as his father finished off a cup of coffee.

"I already filled Owen in."

Hannah saw a flash of guilt and worry behind the older man's eyes. All three boys took after their father. Their dark hair and eyes were identical, but as far as looks went, Dylan looked the most like Leo, followed by Owen. Liam obviously had only gotten their father's coloring, because it was the only similarity between the two of them.

"Now it's our turn," Liam said, sitting on the chair arm beside Elle.

"I can't tell you everything—only that the company is under federal investigation, and I'm cooperating with them," Leo said. The news went through the room like a shock wave.

"For what?" Dylan stood.

Leo held out his arms and glanced over to make sure Owen was still asleep. "It's a long story—one that I'd prefer to go over after some rest." He rubbed his forehead. "But, the short of it . . . there were threats, which I turned over to the feds, and I found out about the investigation shortly after. I've been working with them to figure out what's going on. Now, if it's not too much to ask . . ." He stood up and looked to Elle, giving his goddaughter a smile. "If you have a place for me?"

Elle jumped up. "Yes, we have a room downstairs waiting for you. I'm guessing Owen can stay with you, Hannah?"

"Yes," she answered, and she noticed Owen's eyes slide open.

"We'll talk more in the morning," Dylan said.

His father agreed and followed Elle out the door.

"I'm not buying it," Liam said, standing up. He began pacing the floor, but the number of people in the small space confined him to two circuits.

"Buy it," Owen answered as he sat up slowly. "He was wearing a wire."

"Who? Dad?" Liam chuckled.

"Yeah, I saw it myself in the office. He mentioned it to me before we left for lunch." Owen stood up, looking like a man who had just run a marathon. "Come on, let's go to bed." He took Hannah's hand.

She followed him back into her room while the others continued to talk quietly.

She shut her door behind her and leaned on it, watching as Owen pulled off his brother's borrowed clothes and then fell face-first into bed in nothing but a pair of boxer briefs.

She walked over and touched his shoulder. "The doctor wants you to sleep with a . . ."

He moved and shoved a pillow under his head after rolling over. "Yeah." He sighed. "Thanks."

"Do you need anything?" she asked, unsure of her next move.

He mumbled something, which she approached to hear. "What was that?"

"Just you." He opened his arms. "Right here."

She smiled and pulled off her shorts, T-shirt, and bra, and after pulling on a tank top, she climbed into bed with him. Just looking at his face had her realizing how close she'd come to losing him and what that would have done to her. She would have been lost. It was past time she realized she'd fallen in love with him, completely in love.

"I'm so glad you didn't explode today," she said, causing him to chuckle, even though she'd been serious.

"Don't make me laugh." He sighed. "It hurts too much."

She tried again. "You scared me."

"I scared myself." One of his eyes slid open as he looked down at her. She reached up and kissed him.

"God, I'd like nothing more than to spend the rest of the night making love to you, but . . . I can't keep my eyes open." He shifted, and she settled in the crook of his arm.

"Go to sleep," she said. "We will have plenty of time for that later."

The doctor had warned her to wake him each hour and check on him, which she had done thanks to setting her phone alarm before she fell asleep. Yet in between, Owen hadn't moved a muscle all night long. Once she awoke, she figured she'd have an hour before her normal routine started, and she rolled easily out of his arms but landed with a thud on the floor of her bedroom when she misjudged the distance.

"Are you okay?" Owen chuckled from above her.

She glanced up at him. He was leaning over the side of the bed, smiling down at her. His left eye was almost swollen shut, a deep purple with green hues around the edges. The side of his lip was a little swollen, and some of the bandages had come off in the middle of the night, exposing the tiny cuts. Still, he looked happy and a whole lot healthier than last night.

"Yes." She rubbed her elbow where she'd banged it against her nightstand. "I . . . misjudged that."

"Smooth," he said. "You were a dancer, right?"

"Shut up," she said, getting up off the floor.

He chuckled, then groaned, and he held his head as he followed her into the bathroom. Halfway through her shower, he scared her by opening the door and stepping under the spray with her.

"This shower isn't big enough for two people," she complained, but instead of him answering, his hands gripped her hips as he pulled her into a kiss.

She plastered her wet soapy body against his and moaned at the contrast. When his hands slid down to cover her butt, she moved slightly, grinding herself against him. It was his turn to moan.

"Tell me you have some condoms . . ." he said between kisses.

She stilled. "No." She thought about buying packages downstairs at the little store. She'd be mortified. "You can't feel well enough to . . ." she started, but when he shushed her, she looked up into his eyes. She could see pain, but the look of desire and determination was more dominant.

"Then we'll just have to have some other kind of fun." His hands started moving over her, and she relaxed. When his fingers found her and slid into her, she forgot all about the need for protection. She wanted him but knew he would hold himself back for her sake.

"Two can play like this," she said, taking him into her hands and using the soap to rub him.

"This is the most fun I've had in a shower in a long time." He groaned as he leaned his shoulders against the tile. His hands stilled on her as she worked the soap into a bubbly lather.

"My god," he whispered, and he pulled her up to cover her mouth.

"Yes," she agreed as he started moving again. "Can't we . . ." She was trying to think of a way but then bit her bottom lip when he brushed his thumb over her clit. He moved them until her shoulders were pinned against the cool tile, then leaned down and covered her breast with his mouth.

Since he hadn't shaved yet, his stubble caused all-new kinds of sensations to surface over her skin, sending goose bumps scattering across her body.

"Owen," she cried out. "Please."

His fingers dipped inside her again, slick with the suds from the soap, while he sucked her nipple into his mouth, nibbling on it gently with his teeth. "Come for me, Hannah," he said against her skin. "I want to feel you tighten around my fingers."

She couldn't have stopped her body from giving in to his demands. It was like he controlled her, completely.

When she felt her knees weaken, he held her under the spray until she came back from her wonderful trip.

"There you are." He chuckled as she started standing under her own accord again.

When she reached for him, he shook his head. "Later." He sighed. "I think all of my energy was just drained." He glanced down at her. "I may need some food and a nap."

"The doctor said . . ." she started; worry filled her mind.

"Hey, I'm okay, just a little weak still. Besides, I want to talk to my family."

"Right." She quickly rinsed off under the spray and stepped out while he finished his own shower.

"Your brother and Zoey left you some clothes," she called out after finding a pile of things sitting on the edge of her bed with a note from Zoey: "Heard you guys up and about. Here are some clothes for Owen for today."

"Thanks," he called back from inside the shower.

She dressed quickly and spent a few minutes braiding her hair and applying her standard daily makeup. By the time she was done, he was dressed in khaki shorts and a camp T-shirt.

"His shoes are too small." Owen held them up. "Liam and I have the same size."

"Wait—Liam left some flip-flops . . ." She ran out of her room to the front door of the apartment, then carried them back to him.

"Thanks," he said again. She watched him walking and could tell he was still sore but well enough to make the short trip.

When they stepped out again, Scarlett greeted them in the kitchen, a fresh cup of coffee in her hands.

"How did you sleep?" Scarlett asked Owen.

"Like a baby," he answered. "Is my dad up yet?"

She shrugged. "I'm just getting up now too. Wanna cup?"

"I'd love one."

"Count me out. I have to go," Hannah said, glancing down at her watch. Then she leaned up on her toes and kissed him. "Will I see you for breakfast?"

"Yes, and apparently, I'll be around after as well," he said.

"We can swing by your place and get you some more clothes?" she suggested.

"I'll have one of my brothers take me to get the rest of my things. It's Liam's day off, remember?"

"Right, gotta go." She waved at them as she rushed out of the room.

She dashed down the stairs, talked to Julie for less than a minute, then rushed out the back door. When she emerged, the sun was shining and the fresh air hit her, causing her to smile.

"Someone's in a good mood," Zoey said as she joined her on the pathway.

"Why shouldn't I be? My boyfriend is alive."

"Boyfriend . . ." Zoey nudged her playfully.

Hannah stopped and frowned at her. "What do you call Dylan?"

"My fiancé." She smiled down at the ring on her finger.

"I mean, before. I mean, what do I call Owen?"

Zoey chuckled. "Boyfriend is just fine."

"Okay." She sighed and started walking again. "I didn't know if the rules had changed since the last time I dated."

"From what I'm guessing—and heard in your bathroom this morning—a lot more has changed in the way you have boyfriends." Zoey actually winked at her, which sent her into peals of laughter.

"Yes," she finally said as they stepped into the dining hall. "This time it's different."

Her first obligation was near the back of the dining hall. She'd started an early-morning tai chi session on the front lawn, but she had to grab a health bar before heading over there. She'd skipped dinner last night when she'd heard what had happened to Owen and his father. Now her stomach was reminding her about it.

After grabbing both the breakfast bar and an orange juice, she stuffed her face as she made her way back out toward the front. Several guests were waiting in the yard for her already, and she smiled and put herself into professional mode. For the next half hour, she went through the basic moves she'd learned as a teenager in this very same spot.

By the time her class was over, she felt more centered and extremely hungry again. Still, she ended up standing around talking to a few guests from the class. This time was one of Hannah's many joys in her day-to-day life. It was difficult to explain, but being around people her parents' age and having them appreciate her and treat her with respect somehow made her feel more . . . worthy.

Even though she knew the camp had had a string of parties, for the most part, the guests were extremely polite. She still had her moments when she'd stumble across a couple trying to get away with having sex on the beach or in the pool area, but after upping their security around the grounds, most of that had died down.

Oh sure, they'd heard about the wild parties held in some of the cabins late at night, mainly from the cleaning crew, but at least they weren't destroying the property anymore.

By the time she'd walked back into the dining hall, a bead of sweat was rolling down her back. Even in October, the heat was in full force. She knew that by ten in the morning, she'd be looking forward to teaching the water-aerobics class.

After getting a tray of food, she found her friends in the back corner where they normally met every morning. Yet the event turned special with Leo's presence next to Elle.

"Hi. Where's Owen?" She sat down and glanced around.

"He should be here soon. I saw him down by the water," Scarlett said, setting her own tray beside Hannah's.

"We normally have a morning meeting," Elle was telling Leo. She touched her godfather's arm. "But for you, we'll meet later today."

"Thanks. I know Joe would be so proud of you. This place is pretty amazing." He placed a hand atop hers and turned to the table. "All of you girls. He loved you all like granddaughters."

"It still gets me," Zoey said between bites, "that you're Elle's godfather. I mean, she's mentioned you before, but—"

"Hey," Dylan broke in. "At least Elle mentioned him. Dad never said a word to us about Elle. There was a time we actually thought that you and she . . ." He let the hint hang in the air.

Leo shook his head. "I was nuts for her mother a very long time ago. Plus, after what happened . . ." He shook his head and turned to Elle. "I loved your mother, and Joe and I were close. After your mother's death, it pained me to be around as often."

"I understand." She touched his arm.

"Did you ever date a woman named Ryan Kinsley?" Aubrey asked, getting everyone's attention.

"Ryan . . ." Leo thought for a moment. "I don't think so."

"Long dark hair, about my height, skinny, beady black eyes," Zoey supplied. "Has a real entitled attitude."

Leo chuckled. "Sounds like a few women I've seen over the last couple years."

"Well, this one pulled a gun on your son," Zoey said.

Leo's gaze flicked to Dylan. "I heard about that. I also know that the girl's lawsuit was dropped."

"So, you did hear about it," Dylan chimed in.

Leo's eyes kept darting around the table, and Hannah could tell he was keeping something from them. "I can't tell you boys everything..."

"Yes, you've said that before," Owen said as he arrived at the table.

Hannah nudged Aubrey over and made room for him. After Owen sat down, his father continued. "But what I can tell you is that from the call I received this morning, we need to step up our security, all of us. Including you girls." He patted Elle's hand.

"This is bull." Liam slapped the table. "Who? Why? Just what the hell is going on?"

"Someone's out to destroy the business," Owen said. His black eye had darkened slightly, giving him a more dangerous look.

"If we knew that, this would all be over," Leo said. He added, "I'm heading back into town."

Owen jumped in. "So am I."

Leo slapped the table this time. "No, you're staying put. We've decided it's the best way—"

"Screw that. Who is this 'we'?" He glanced at his brothers, who quickly shook their heads.

"The feds. They think it will be easier if the three of you and the rest were in one place. Plus, I am not going to put any of you in the line of danger again."

"Should we close the camp?" Elle asked, concerned.

Instantly, Hannah went on guard. She hadn't thought about the possibility of closing the camp. What would that do to their business?

Could they recover from the lack of income? Not to mention the damage to their reputation.

"No, I don't think there is any reason to close the place down," Leo answered quickly.

"What about you?" Dylan asked his father.

"I'll have more security," Leo answered.

"More?" Liam asked. "As in, you had security when someone blew up your car?"

Leo took a deep breath. "We didn't expect a move so quickly."

"But you were expecting a move?" Elle asked. This was getting even scarier. Knowing that someone had been watching over Leo and Owen before the bombing, yet someone else had still been able to get to them. How was she supposed to relax now, when Owen could be in danger still?

Leo chose not to answer but instead stood up from the table. "My ride is going to be here soon." He stopped and glanced down at Owen. "They're going to bring some of your things today." He handed him a card. "Text what you need here, and it will be arranged." Then he glanced around the table. "Until you get the word, all of you will need to stay on the campgrounds."

"What?" Several outcries filled the air. However, Hannah relaxed a little just knowing that Owen would be closer to her.

"I'm just the messenger." Leo shrugged. "Sorry."

"That's bull." Owen stood up and followed his father out of the dining hall.

"Hey, at least you're not cursing," Leo joked as he glanced back over his shoulder at Hannah. She was not letting these two just walk off and hastened to catch up.

"Until things die down," Leo told her, "it's in the best interest for all of you to stay put. Elle's going to be meeting with someone from a security firm that works with the feds. They'll be staying on campus just to keep an eye on things."

"I understand." Hannah touched Owen's arm and felt him tense. She knew he wasn't happy about staying at the camp. Did that mean he didn't want to be stuck with her?

"I won't be a prisoner. I have a closing later this week," he reminded his father. "I have a business to run."

"The board has been made aware that you are taking some time off to heal from your injuries," Leo replied.

"What about you?" he asked.

"As far as they know, I'm fine." Leo sighed. "I need to play this as if it was nothing for me. I need to draw their fire."

"Like hell." Owen shook his head. "No, I'm going—"

"Son." Leo touched Owen's shoulder, his voice going lower. "I need to know that you three are safe. That all of you are safe. I can't do what needs to be done if I fear that somehow you won't be."

Hannah watched Owen's shoulders slump and knew that his father had convinced him to stick around. Of course, she was happy about that, knowing that this was the safest place to be and that he was going to be out of the line of danger. She too couldn't have rested if she'd feared for him every moment they were away from each other.

"I'll keep an eye on him," she assured Leo. "All of them."

"Thanks." He gave her a peck on the cheek, then turned and left.

"He's a fool," Owen said softly, "if he thinks the three of us are going to let him walk into danger by himself." He turned, and she could see that his brothers had the same determined looks on their faces as he did.

She had to act immediately or the three of them would be sneaking off the campgrounds and putting themselves in danger.

After breakfast, she texted Zoey and Elle and told them she had to meet them in the pool house.

"What's this all about?" Elle asked when she finally walked in.

"We have to do something. I'm sure you know by now that Dylan, Liam, and Owen are not planning on sitting around here for too long. Not while Leo is the one risking his life."

"Yes," Zoey said with a groan. "Dylan's already making plans on escaping."

"So is Liam," Elle added. "What can we do to stop them?"

Hannah shrugged. "That's why I called this meeting. We need to come up with something to keep them here and keep them safe, and we need to do it fast."

CHAPTER SIXTEEN

"Why are we doing this?" Liam asked, pacing the floor. "We should be leaving. It's not like there are bars on the windows. Let's just go."

"Where?" Dylan asked as he lounged on the sofa. "You expect us to walk into the office tomorrow morning, and what?" He waited, but as an answer, Liam just threw up his hands.

"You two are perfectly fine to stay here, but I actually have work to do back at the office. My only concern is getting Hannah to stay put and not follow me. Which, I'm sure she would." He was glad they'd met to plan while the women were working, but this was not going the way he'd expected.

"Damn right, she would, which would send the rest of them after you," Dylan said. "So you'd be best not to go and stay here to keep them all safe, like Dad suggested."

"Screw that. Dad's the one who took off on us." Owen almost barked it. "He's the one who left us this mess. I was cleaning everything up just fine until—"

"Yeah?" Dylan's chuckle stopped him. "What do you think that break-in to your place was? I'd say you got lucky you didn't return home while whoever was trashing your place. We'd probably be scraping you off the floor, along with all of your stuff."

Owen felt his gut twist a little. He hadn't thought of it like that. Nor had he thought about someone hurting Hannah until she'd found that note on her car.

"Yeah, I can tell by the way all of the blood just left your face that you're finally thinking." Dylan stood up. "Face it, bro, you're not going anywhere. None of us are, because we have something Dad doesn't have. Something worth protecting and fighting for." He turned to look over at a picture of the five women hugging one another on opening day that sat on a bookshelf.

"Women," Liam added with a groan.

"I was going to say someone we care about, but yeah, women will work." Dylan chuckled and slapped Owen on the back. "Welcome back to River Camp," he said before leaving the apartment.

"I have a class." Liam glanced down at his watch. "I take it you're staying put?" Owen nodded and sank onto the sofa. "Once you're feeling up to it, I'm sure Britt could use some help down at the bar. They hired a new waitress down there but not another bartender yet."

"Sure," he said, rubbing his forehead.

"Get some more rest—you look like shit," Liam said before leaving.

He would have laughed, but the truth was, his head was splitting. When he lay back on the sofa and closed his eyes, he drifted off immediately.

He woke to Scarlett looking down at him. "You snore," she said with a grin.

He cleared his throat and sat up as his eyes ran over her, assessing her quickly. "It's allergies." He knew that it was due to sheer exhaustion as well but didn't want that bit to get back to Hannah.

"It wasn't loud; just thought you ought to know." She sat across from him, and he could tell she was assessing him as well.

"What?" he asked after taking a sip of coffee from the mug she offered him. "Is my hair sticking up too?" He reached up and patted the top of his head, realizing that he was overdue for a haircut.

"Yes, but it's kind of sexy. I'm just making sure you're not going to drop dead on us. Hannah was busy, and I told her I'd give her a full update." She tilted her head. "You don't look like a man who is about to sneak out of the camp and rush back to your dad's side."

He closed his eyes for a moment and remembered what it was he was staying for, then looked her in the eye and said, "I'm not going anywhere."

She waited a heartbeat before nodding her head, as if she believed him. "What made you change your mind?" she asked.

He liked that she was being blunt with him. Shifting slightly, he watched her as his black eye's vision cleared. She was prettier than her sister—not that Zoey wasn't hot, but Zoey had a natural beauty, where Scarlett was just knockout gorgeous. He thought it was the eyes and high cheekbones they both shared, but where Zoey had a tomboy charm, Scarlett had bedroom eyes and lips that most women needed to pay for.

"Trying to figure me out?" she asked, resting her chin on her hands. "I'm not that hard. I stick up for my friends, I speak honestly, and I will gladly kick anyone's butt if they hurt someone I love."

He smiled quickly. "That's what I was just telling myself. It's the reason I think I like you."

"You think?" she asked, sitting up.

He chuckled. "I guess it all depends on if you've decided not to kick my butt."

"I'll let you know when I come to a decision," she said, flexing a bicep. "Are you going to try to leave?"

He sighed heavily. "Not until I'm allowed to by the powers that be."

"Which aaaare?" She dragged the word out.

"Your sister . . . Hannah," he said, causing Scarlett to smile and nod.

"Okay." She jumped up, then took a plate from the counter and held it out. "You've earned a brownie."

The plate was filled with chocolate bars as big as his fist. After taking one, he bit into it and groaned with pure pleasure.

Scarlett chuckled. "They are that good." She sat down again and took one for herself.

"Tell me you made these, and I'll dump Hannah," he said, taking another bite.

She smiled. "No, I wish. It's Isaac's new dessert chef."

"Pastry chef," he corrected.

"Yeah." She waved her hand. "Whatever. Anyway, they're fantastic."

"What's her name?" he asked.

A burst of laughter exploded from her before she answered. "Betty, and she's sixty years old."

"Who cares? Age isn't an issue when you can bake like this." He waved his half-eaten brownie in the air.

"Right." She took another bite of her brownie. "I'm thinking of changing sides myself and asking her out."

He joined her in laughter until the bruises around his eye protested. "I heard you guys could use some more help around here?"

"Nope, strict orders. You are not to lift a finger today."

He slid back on the sofa. "Good, because after this"—he finished off the brownie—"I'm thinking of having a bubble bath and some champagne."

Scarlett chuckled again. "You're funnier than your brothers."

"And sexier," he pointed out, reaching for another brownie, but she pulled the plate away.

"Over my dead body." She shoved the rest of the brownie in her mouth, causing him to laugh.

"Okay." He stood up. "Going to head in for that bath." When she mumbled something, he stopped. "Sorry, what was that?"

She held up a finger as she swallowed down her enormous brownie bite, then grabbed the rest of his coffee to wash it down.

"Hannah's bathroom doesn't have a bath. If you want, use mine." She motioned down the hallway. "I'm heading out to deliver these anyway."

"Thanks. Did they deliver my things?"

"Yes." She waved toward the hallway again while holding on to the plate. "It's all in Hannah's room."

"Just one more?" He turned his most pleading gaze to her. "Please?"

She chuckled and rushed toward the door.

He'd slept through lunch, so before finding the bath, he dug in the refrigerator and made himself a cold turkey sandwich and had a bag of chips. His mind kept wandering to how he was going to protect Hannah and her friends while he was so sore that even lifting a sandwich to his mouth hurt.

He normally didn't take baths, but his entire body ached. What he should have done was pull on some shorts and gone out to sit in the hot tub, but he knew it was probably still over eighty degrees out there, and sitting in a hot tub was the last thing he'd want to do in that kind of heat. But here in the cool air-conditioned apartment, a hot bath sounded perfect.

As he waited for the tub to fill, he found some Epsom salts and added them to the water. Looking at himself in the mirror, he realized how badly he was bruised. Dark spots covered most of his ribs and arms. Then he turned around and gasped at the massive bruise that had spread over his back.

He must have landed pretty hard on the cement floor of the parking garage. Had his father gotten as much bruising?

As he slid into the hot water, he groaned when the briny water hit his aches and open cuts. Closing his eyes, he rested back and played over what he could remember from the explosion.

He reviewed the last minutes in his mind several times. He was pretty sure that his father unlocking the car door while they were still fifteen feet away had saved their lives.

Then he remembered that he hadn't asked about his own car. He reached for his cell phone and sent a text to Brett and got an almost instant reply.

Your car was clean. I've moved it to your building's parking garage, since the one at your office won't be usable for a while. The keys are at the front desk. How are you doing?

I'm sore. Thanks, have you found out anything new?

No, the feds have pretty much taken over. I can't tell you anything new.

He set the phone down and sank deeper into the bath again—letting the heat and the salts soothe away most of the aches. His mind flashed to Hannah and how worried she'd been when he'd woken up at the hospital. If it had been her instead of him . . . he felt his heart skip a beat. He didn't know what he would have done.

His brother was right: the three of them had more to live for than their old man did. It wasn't as if his dad had never been in love before, but, knowing that Dylan had already proposed to Zoey and that it wouldn't be long before Liam did the same with Elle, the brothers had so much more to lose. After all, he and his brothers didn't mess around, as their father had. Even though he knew that his dad had found the only woman he'd ever loved in their mother, Owen had secretly wished that someday Leo would find that kind of love again with another woman.

He wished his father could tell them everything that was going on. The secrecy was killing him. It wasn't as if he could really do anything about it anyway. Not while he was being held captive at the camp. Sitting up, as water cascaded off him, he suddenly saw the one thing he and his brothers could do to help their father.

After pulling on his clothes and taking a few minutes to clean up Scarlett's bathroom, he stepped out and found Scarlett, who'd returned from her errand.

"I have a plan," he said, sitting down in front of her.

"Who doesn't?" She glanced at him over the book she was reading, her dark eyebrows slightly arched upward. "I'm listening."

"It might be a long shot, but how do you think everyone would feel about getting the word out that I'm fighting my father for control of his business?" Of all the plans he'd come up with, it was the smartest one so far. If he could get a little of the heat off his father, then maybe he and his brothers could work together to catch whoever had targeted them.

She set her book down and sat up a little. "Why would you do that?"

"To set a trap." He filled her in on the rest of his plan. He didn't really have a completed plan, he realized, but the outline had sounded good in his head. After saying it out loud, he was beginning to wonder why he'd thought it was a good idea. Of course, he knew they could work out the details with everyone coming together.

Two hours later, after everyone was once again assembled in the room, he explained it once more.

"I don't like it." Hannah shook her head. "You're still recovering from the explosion."

"So is my dad, but he's all alone."

"How do we get this plan rolling?" Dylan asked. "I'm in." His brother reached down and took Zoey's hand in his. "It's the best way."

"I agree," Zoey said. "If it was our mother . . . I wouldn't hesitate."

Scarlett jumped in. "Agreed."

"Let me get this straight." Elle got everyone's attention. "Your father and the FBI have told us we can't leave the campgrounds?"

"Which we plan on abiding by," Owen said quickly.

"Right, but you want to sue your father for his ownership of the company, claiming mental incompetence?"

"It should never go to court, and hopefully we won't have to really go far, but once the word gets out that I'm trying to take control of the company again—"

"There will be an even bigger target painted on you," Hannah said, shaking her head. "No. You're lucky you survived that bomb!"

He remembered what his father had said—about the threats he'd received with the pictures of him in the crosshairs. He quickly filled everyone in on what his father had told him. "We all were targets. Whoever is behind this has proven that they will go to great lengths to get us out of the way. Even as far as murder." The room fell silent. "So, the only question we need to ask ourselves is if we are willing to sit idly by and let someone take what our family has worked hard for?"

"What assurance do we have that you'll be safe? All of you?" Hannah asked, looking around the room.

He glanced over at Reed Cooper. The man had remained silent but observant in the corner of the room. "That's where you come in."

"I'm just a business owner myself," Reed started. "I run a distillery."

Owen guffawed. "This room is filled with people who know your past."

"I still have some connections, from my . . . past excursions." Reed rubbed his jaw.

"Think they would care to help out around here? Maybe fill a few empty roles to blend in?" Owen asked.

"I could arrange it." He nodded.

"We can't afford—" Elle started.

"On my dime," Owen broke in. "This is, after all, my crazy idea."

Elle nodded. "I'm in." Hannah shot her friend a look. "I think it's a good idea. A solid plan."

"Even if it puts Liam in danger?" Hannah asked.

"He's already in danger. They all are." Elle motioned to the brothers. "Owen was there when his father's car exploded. They were lucky they didn't die. I'm not sure they will be so lucky next time."

Hannah's shoulders slumped, and he could tell that she'd come to the same conclusion.

"How soon can you make the arrangements?" he asked Reed.

"End of the week I can have a team in place around here." Reed turned to Elle. "I can work with you about placement."

She thanked him and then stood up, pulling Liam off the sofa with her. "If you're done, we're going to get going. I have an early morning."

"Me too." Zoey jumped up and waited for Dylan. "Let us know what you need from us."

The couples, along with Reed, left, while Scarlett and Aubrey quickly disappeared down the hallway into their rooms.

"I still don't like it," Hannah complained.

"I know." He reached for her and pulled her closer to him, holding on to her until he felt her relax her head against his shoulder. "But it's the least I can do. My dad may be a little off, but he's always been there for us." He loved the way she felt in his arms. He knew he'd moved deeper into their relationship and needed to tell her how he felt, but he wanted to wait for the right moment.

"Right." She sighed. "You were lucky." She glanced up, and he kissed her forehead. "How are you feeling?" she asked, brushing a fingertip over his bruises.

"Better, now that I feel like I'm not just sitting around waiting to hear that my father's been murdered."

"I heard you want to marry our new dessert chef." She tilted her head at him. "Trust me: she's happily married, with grandchildren our age."

He smiled and held on to her. "Tell me you can bake, and I'll stay put."

"I can," she agreed, "but not as well . . ." He stopped her by kissing her.

"It doesn't matter. We can both always learn. Come with me . . ." He took her hand to draw them toward her room.

"Owen," she said after he'd shut the door behind them. "I . . ." She motioned to the bedroom wall. "Scarlett and Aubrey are right next door."

"And that's why god created walls," he teased, moving closer to her—almost stalking her, since she kept moving just outside his reach. Smiling, he finally cornered her and pulled her into his arms.

"Yes, but . . . I don't think I can be quiet."

"Then don't," he suggested before kissing her. "Trust me. They know what we're doing in here regardless of if they hear us or not," he said as he ran kisses down her neck. When he felt her relax and arch into him, he knew that she no longer cared that her friends could hear them.

CHAPTER SEVENTEEN

Falling asleep in Owen's arms was becoming an addiction.

The next few days had been some of Hannah's favorites. Even though they'd had a few stormy days, her mood had remained light and carefree. She spent every morning having breakfast with her friends, with Owen sitting beside her. And if Scarlett and Aubrey knew what they were doing in the bedroom at night, they never mentioned it or even hinted at it.

She sat in her office as she went over the plans to prepare the camp for the large Halloween festival she had planned for the following weekend. The dining hall would be transformed for the masquerade ball this weekend, which would be open to the general public—her idea, to raise some extra cash for the holiday festivities she had planned. Then the hall would be transformed again for the Halloween costume party for the following weekend.

Even if guests weren't staying for the week of Halloween, they would be able to still enjoy the festivities. She had ordered her costumes for both parties from her favorite place in New York, and the dresses were now filling up most of her small closet.

On the other hand, Owen's work had turned more intense as he planned out their next moves. She wondered where he was now. She and the rest of the Wildflowers had had a quick private meeting, without the brothers, where they had talked about emergency plans if anything went wrong. It wasn't as if they had a lot of options, but at least they had come up with bringing a few of their trusted employees into the fold. When Dean's name came up, the five of them questioned if he would be able to keep the knowledge to himself. It wasn't as if they wanted the entire camp to know that they were putting themselves and guests in the direct line of danger. In the end, Dean was left out of the inner circle.

Owen had had several meetings with Reed Cooper and a few other people who showed up at the camp. She was surprised when four of the ten people Reed had brought on board were women—younger women who easily blended in with the rest of the employees.

Most of the men, however, would take up patrol at night in addition to posing as guests.

Aiden had a few cabins that were still under construction, which Reed had determined were perfect places for their men to set up their base.

"The most important item is that we tell no one outside of this room," Reed had stressed during their last meeting. "Even if you trust them"—Reed had glanced at the brothers to punctuate his remark—"it's vital you keep this plan a secret if we're going to pull this off."

Everyone had agreed, and Hannah realized that the only people she would have told were already in the room.

She'd never been one to have a gaggle of friends. When she wasn't at summer camp during her summers, her friends list was almost empty. Sure, she'd had a few acquaintances and one or two school buddies, but for the most part, the rest had been friends her parents had approved of or, worse, friends her parents had invited over themselves for her.

Which meant they were only there so her father could connect with their parents.

Now, as an adult, she didn't mind that her friends consisted of only a handful of people. After all, it wasn't the number of friends, but the quality. She would, at this point, gladly lay down her life for any of them. Even Zoey and Scarlett's mother, Kimberly, had been brought in on the secret. Mainly because she had started dating Reed, and he hadn't wanted to keep her out of the loop about what her daughters were up to.

Kimberly was like her and her friends' den mother. Ever since Kimberly had moved into their old summer camp cabin, River Cabin, she was the one the girls ran to for help or for advice.

When her friends' mother found out that she and Owen were an item, she made a point to join one of her yoga classes.

"So, I hear you're seeing Owen?" Kimberly fell into step with her as they walked toward the gym area.

"Yes." Hannah smiled over at the woman.

Kimberly lay a hand on hers, stopping her on the pathway. "He suits you." Her blue eyes twinkled.

Hannah laughed. "Thanks, I think."

"There's the girl I remember from the first summer I met you. I think you were thirteen . . ." She tilted her head as she thought about it. Kimberly squeezed her shoulder lightly as her smile slipped. "You don't laugh near enough." When Hannah frowned, Kimberly shook her head. "You should smile as often as you can. Take it from someone who had her smiles stolen from her. Laughter is the best medicine."

"I hear you and Reed Cooper are an item?" She tucked her arm in the woman's and started walking again.

Kimberly's smile brightened. "That man makes me feel twenty again." Hannah laughed and enjoyed the yoga class even more with Kimberly in attendance. Glancing out her office window now, she thought about their plan to keep the camp and the Costa brothers safe.

Since the new plan involved a few other key people around the camp, Aiden had been invited to the meeting as well. After all, two of the agents were going to be on his crew, or pretending to be at least.

Hannah had wanted to bring Isaac in on the deal, but Reed had talked her out of it for now. Since Isaac had put Brent in charge of who worked in the dining hall, she agreed that he didn't need to know. After all, she'd given him full rein to choose his kitchen and front-of-house staff, and none of Reed's people would be working in there with him.

By the time the meeting was over, they had decided that two of the women would be working in the dining hall directly under Brent: one was on the cleaning staff, and the other one would work at the pool bar. The six men would be scattered all over—some with Aiden, a few with the grounds crew, and the rest out of sight.

She had met a few of them already and knew that she'd have a hard time maintaining her calm when she saw them around camp—after all, according to Reed, he'd only hired the best team. She wasn't sure what that meant. Were they all killers? Bodyguards?

She wanted to ask the man but didn't want to sound stupid, so she sat back and listened instead. Questions were asked, ideas were thrown around, and by the time she and Owen were lying in her bed together that evening, she was feeling a little dizzy about the plan.

"You seem like you have something on your mind." He ran his hand over her bare shoulder.

"I . . ." She leaned up and looked down at him. "How is this going to work?"

"How is what going to work?" He waited, his eyes capturing her face as if he was trying to memorize everything about her.

"I mean . . ." She scooted up until she was leaning against her hard headboard. Instantly, she thought of his softer one and silently wished for it. "These people are just going to be around the camp for an indefinite amount of time?"

He shrugged and sat up beside her, bringing his strong shoulder to brush against hers.

"No, I mean, not indefinite." He was quiet for a moment. "I would think that things will move quickly after I make the call on Monday."

Did that mean that he would leave again? Could she handle him abandoning her once more? Their relationship had moved beyond what it had been previously, and it had almost broken her when he'd left back then. Should she ask him if he planned on staying with her? Would asking that question make her weak?

"To your father's lawyers?" she asked.

"Yes." He sighed. "As far as the board is concerned, I am in charge. My father has just made it known that I'm taking some medical leave." He rubbed his forehead. "Which, because of the explosion, they will believe, and they'll allow my father to step back in, temporarily."

"Won't they question his fitness?"

"Some will, but for the most part, most of them are glad that he's back."

"What about your new project?" she asked, thinking of another angle to see if he planned on sticking around. "Here in Pelican Point?"

"I've postponed the closing until next week and asked them to bring the documents here so I can close without leaving the campgrounds."

"I hope it won't put you behind in your plans," she said. That meant he was sticking around for at least a short while, she thought. She should just ask him, but she'd never had so much riding on an answer before.

"No." He smiled and wrapped an arm around her, then pulled her back down until she'd settled on his chest. "It's not pushing things behind too much. It will be okay. Sleep," he whispered. "I've got everything under control."

When his arms were wrapped around her, her mind slipped away from all the worry of losing him, of the camp's success, and of the physical threats they were under.

"You'll need a costume," she mumbled before falling asleep. For some reason, she dreamed of Ryan chasing her through the campgrounds with a gun the entire night. When she woke, Owen was already in the shower, and after looking at her phone, she realized she'd slept through her alarm. She rushed around the room, gathering everything she would need for the day, and then headed to the pool for her morning water-aerobics class.

Then, since she hadn't gotten to see Owen before leaving, she was slightly surprised that he wasn't at their normal breakfast meeting. His brothers were missing as well.

"Where are they?" she asked Zoey.

"They're calling the lawyers in Elle's office."

Elle sat down next to Aubrey just as Zoey answered. "I'm so nervous. I know nothing will probably happen soon, but it feels like they're lighting the fuse to a bomb," Elle said. "I thought . . ." she started but then shook her head.

"That they would include us?" Zoey finished for her.

"Yes," Elle said, waving her fork. "I mean, it's a pretty big step."

"It is, but they needed to do this alone," Zoey said.

"I suppose," Hannah said, and she pushed her half-full plate aside. Food didn't matter with this issue on the line.

"They're brothers first," Elle started. "Just like we have a responsibility to each other first, that's the way they roll as well."

"Yes," Hannah said with a groan. "I get it."

"But, having said that, I agree. I was hoping to be in on the call," Elle said as she leaned her chin on her hand.

Scarlett then jumped in. "Stop moping around. The three of you look like someone just shot your granny." She giggled. "They're just making a call."

Hannah nodded and glanced at her watch. "I have ten minutes before I'm needed in another class. We'd better talk about the masquerade party."

"Right!" Elle clapped her hands together and pulled out her iPad.

The mood changed from anxiety to excitement as she filled her friends in on the party plans. By the time she'd rushed to the next event she was in charge of—a soccer game where the players were encased in giant inflatable balls—she was in a better mood.

The rain started halfway through the day, dampening some of the rest of her daily events but not canceling them, since it was just a light mist. She was too busy during lunch to enjoy eating with the rest of the gang and instead grabbed a sandwich and ate it on the run.

Her mind kept running over the list of worries she'd shoved to the back of her mind last night. There were so many of them that, at one point, she actually wrote a list. It wasn't as if she could do anything, really, to alleviate any of the items. But having them down on paper somehow freed her mind of them a little.

Shortly before the dinner hour, she helped the crew finalize the rest of the decorations for the ball tomorrow night in the main dining hall. Since the rain had continued and was now almost flooding the yard, the outside decorations would have to wait until it stopped. If it stopped.

She stood back and admired her handiwork, and that of the crew who had volunteered to help her out. Which had included Owen and his brothers. If they were worried about their well-being, they didn't really show it. The brothers had joked with one another as usual while they helped out. Of course, that didn't stop her from worrying about them. She knew that, just like how she felt about Owen, Zoey and Elle would be crushed if anything happened to the men they loved.

Long sheets of black and white hung from the ceiling, blanketing the entire thing in soft material. A soft black net material covered most of the rest of the ceiling, which would have LED lights on it, making it seem as if it were filled with tiny stars. The bar area had been encased with black net material, letting the blue lights she'd hung over the bar shine through.

"This looks amazing," Owen said, wrapping his arms around her. "But isn't the party tomorrow night?"

"Yes, but the final touches won't be done until then. This is just the basics," she answered.

Owen motioned to the room. "This is the basics?"

"It is—wait until the larger items arrive," she said.

"Wow, remind me to have you throw all my parties in the future," he said with a chuckle.

"It's one of my greatest talents," she said as she rose up on her toes and kissed him. She was pleased that he liked her hard work. It was funny, but she'd always looked for acceptance from her parents, but having it from Owen was more intoxicating than any praise she might ever receive from her mother or father.

"This looks amazing," Elle said, walking into the room. "Your mirrors arrived."

"Oh!" She clapped her hands with excitement. "Where are they?"

"In the back."

Hannah drew Owen toward the back of the room and out the stage door. There, in the narrow hallway, stood the huge thick-framed mirrors she'd rented.

"What are these for?" Owen asked, looking at the six massive frames.

"They'll line the walls of the room, making the entire place look larger," she answered, admiring the frames.

"Isn't the room large enough?" he asked with a chuckle.

"No." She frowned over at him. "We've sold almost a hundred tickets so far. Have you forgotten that this will be the first event open to the public?" If this first event was an enormous success, then she would plan one like it every month.

"So, we drag the mirrors out?" He moved to one.

"No, not until tomorrow." She stopped him, her arm on his. "Now, we go up and get ready for a normal dinner. Tomorrow night . . ." She gasped and turned to him. "Tell me you got a black suit for tomorrow night."

"Yes." He pulled her into his arms. "I had one of my new suits delivered here instead of my place."

"Do you think the agents will blend in well enough?" she asked, worried that somehow the guests would realize that something was going on.

Owen smiled down at her. "I think we have nothing to worry about." He kissed the tip of her nose. "Everything is going to be perfect. Do you always get this jittery before a party?"

She chuckled. "Yes."

"Nothing is going to go wrong. Besides, I'm here." He took her hand and sparked a smile from her again.

"Good." She relaxed a little. "Let's go get ready, then."

His bruises were almost all gone; the only one still remaining filled his entire back. Still, she had helped him by putting ice packs on his back and rubbing his sore muscles when they had time together. The slow massage had turned into a steamy sexual encounter, which she counted as easily one of her favorite experiences with Owen.

As they changed now, she realized that they had settled into the tiny space together pretty well. She had believed that she would constantly be bumping into him, but instead, they moved around one another as if in a well-rehearsed dance.

When they walked into the dining hall, she had on her cream-colored cocktail dress, and he was in his nightly dinner attire—khakis and a polo shirt. As they entered the hall, they immediately were pulled in different directions.

Owen was quickly snagged by Brent and asked to help serve drinks, while Elle pulled Hannah toward the back hallway again. "The pillars are here." Hannah rushed to inspect them and loved the look of the black-and-white-checkered pillars.

"Whoever you use to get this stuff is amazing," Elle added. "I can't believe you can rent all of this." Elle ran a hand over the old frame that Hannah planned on using as an entrance.

"We are only a few hours from New Orleans, you know," Hannah said.

"Four hours, if not more," Elle reminded her.

Hannah shrugged. "It will be worth the extra delivery charges. Trust me." She turned to her friend. Out of the corner of her eye, she saw a reflection in one of the large mirrors and froze. Blinking twice, she gasped and turned around, but since the mirrors were crowded in the tiny space, she got turned around and lost sight of the figure.

"What?" Elle tensed beside her.

"Ryan," Hannah said in a low tone, her nails digging into Elle's arm. "I . . ." She glanced around and realized that they were alone in the small space. She shook her head and swallowed. "I thought I saw—"

"Let's go get the men. We'll have them do a sweep around the grounds, just in case," Elle said, looking around the space as if she expected Ryan to jump out of the shadows.

"No." She rubbed her eyes. "I'm just tired. I had nightmares all last night that she was chasing me around the camp."

"Still," Elle said, pulling her out into the dining hall. "I'll have them look around just in case."

"Thanks." She hugged Elle. "I'm not crazy."

"No." Elle chuckled. "Just tired and worried about too many things. You should have taken the day off instead of rushing around all day."

"No." She shook her head. "I'm too nervous about tomorrow night."

"So am I," Elle said, then waved Dylan over to them. Hannah stood by while her friend explained that Hannah thought she'd seen Ryan in the back hallway. Instant worry filled her, causing her body to shake slightly. How had Ryan gotten on campus? Was Hannah just seeing things? She was tired, true, but so tired she was seeing things?

Dylan disappeared quickly and came back fifteen minutes later with Owen and Liam by his side.

"We've got the team out searching." Owen touched her arm. "Are you okay?"

"Yes, I think I'm just tired and seeing things." The more she thought about it, the more she was sure she'd imagined the entire thing.

"Why don't you head on up and go to bed early?" Dylan suggested.

"Yes, go. We've got things under control around here," Scarlett added.

"No, I . . ." she started to say, but Owen stepped in.

"Thanks, everyone. See you in the morning." He took her hand and walked with her toward the doorway.

"Where are we going?" she asked when they started walking down the pathway instead of toward the main building.

"Fresh air always helps clear the mind," he said as they walked to the beach.

When they stepped out into the clearing, she was surprised to see a beach blanket and a bottle of champagne chilling in a bucket of ice.

"When did you organize this?" she asked him.

"I was in the process of putting it together when Dylan texted me about Ryan. I was going to drag you down here after dinner, but . . ." He shrugged as they sat down. "I moved up the time frame and had my brother suggest it. I could tell you were tired." He touched her face softly. "You didn't get enough sleep last night. I kept you up too late."

She relaxed back on the blanket and giggled. "I let you keep me up."

"True." He chuckled and reached for the bottle. "Now you'll enjoy some champagne and tiny mousse cakes that Betty made us." She sat back and watched him open the bottle easily and then pour them each a glass. She loved watching him move. Seeing the play of muscles in his arms turned her on more than she wanted to admit. Then he pulled out a container and opened it, showing off four of the most perfectly made mousse towers she'd ever seen. There were even little swirls of hard chocolate on top, along with cream and a mint leaf. Instantly, she thought about lapping the mousse off Owen's perfect pecs, and her body started to vibrate. Then she remembered where they were and figured she would have plenty of time later to indulge her fantasies with the man she'd fallen for.

"God, I love that woman," Hannah said as she reached inside and took one out for herself.

"If I wasn't already crazy about you . . ." Owen joked.

"You're crazy about me?" she asked after taking a bite of the dessert. Joy at his admission filled her heart, making her chest warm. She knew a blush must be creeping up her cheeks.

"Madly," he said, his dark eyes meeting hers.

"Me too," she said with a smile.

"Here's to going crazy." He held up the champagne flute.

"Together," she added, and she tapped her glass to his.

CHAPTER EIGHTEEN

The next morning, Hannah woke after a long night's sleep, totally refreshed. When she remembered what the day held for her, she almost jumped out of bed.

"Morning," Owen said groggily, hugging her closer, as if he sensed her intent.

"Morning." She turned in his hold and looked at him. "Your bruises are fading."

He smiled a little. "Some of them, anyway."

She ran her fingers over his face. "I like things this way," she said, surprising herself.

"So do I," he admitted.

"I mean . . ." She moved her shoulder a little so she could get a better look at him. "What is going to happen when you have to go back to work? Back to your own place?"

He sighed slowly. "I'm not sure. I guess we'll have to make it work long distance."

"You know where I'm at." She glanced around the room. "Here, where I want to be."

"And you know where I'll be. But we're both here now," he said, causing her heart to sink, before he added, "What if I come and make a fool out of myself at the tai chi class?" He chuckled. "I hear it's great for getting rid of stress and loosening up sore muscles. Something I seem to have an abundance of lately."

She swallowed her hurt and worry about their future together. "Sure, you're welcome to join me." She pulled on her yoga pants and a tank top while he put on a pair of gym shorts and a T-shirt. At least the class would distract her from the death-by-slow-cuts of a long-distance relationship.

They walked to the front yard together, hand in hand. When they arrived, a bigger crowd was there compared to a few mornings before. It was always hit and miss, with people joining them on the lawn. If the weather was nice, they usually got more of a crowd, like today.

As she took up her position in the front, she noticed that Owen was hanging near the back of the group.

Just going through the moves while the soft music played, her entire body slowly got in tune with the world. Her mind settled and cleared as every worry she had slowly melted away. She was here, she was present, and Owen was with her.

After the session was over, she sat in the grass next to Owen and sipped from her water bottle.

"Wow, that was amazing," he said, rolling his shoulders. "I don't think I've felt relaxed since that hot bath the other night. I should have taken this up years ago."

She giggled. "I learned tai chi when I was thirteen. It was one of the only ways I had to cope with stress from my parents."

He reached over and took her hand in his. "I'm sorry."

She smiled over at him. "Until all the Wildflowers found each other here, which gave me—gave all of us—a new outlook on life."

"True." He glanced around the green grass.

She did the same and watched couples and people moving around them. She could hear the laughter from the pool area and could see a group of people horseback riding through the trees on the pathway. This was where she wanted to be. No matter what happened in life, she wanted to be just here.

Taking a deep breath, she smiled over at him. She would consider herself very lucky as long as he was here with her. But she knew she couldn't allow herself to rely on his presence to make herself happy. She'd believed at one point in her childhood that it was her parents' jobs to fill that role. Which of course they never would have.

"This is where I belong," she said, as if to herself. "It's magic."

"I felt it that first week I was here," he agreed.

She glanced at him from the corner of her eyes. "You did?" She was a little shocked to hear that he liked the place. She'd assumed he did, but until now, he'd remained silent on the subject, at least in front of her.

He smiled and squeezed her hand. "Yeah."

"So it wasn't just me that kept you around?" she teased, causing him to laugh.

"That did play a big part, as well as bringing me back here." He lifted her hand to his lips. "I'm going to have a very hard time leaving again."

"You didn't seem to have an issue with leaving the first time," she pointed out.

"I was a fool." He plucked at the grass, avoiding her gaze.

"*Was?*" Her eyebrows shot up.

He flashed a smile at her then, his perfect teeth shining in the sunlight. The hint of dimples by his mouth sent her body into full sex mode. She wanted him, again, here and now. Would it always be like this? Would the distance hurt the same way?

"I am a fool. Any man would be who walks away from you and this place." He sighed. "I wish I could stay here forever."

"I know. You have your life." Her stomach ached, and she was starting to have a pain in her chest just thinking about him leaving. Knowing that most long-distance relationships never worked out. She wasn't trying to control him, but she knew that if he left again, it would be for good this time.

"Yeah." He sighed. "Speaking of which, I promised Liam I'd help him move a few more benches around."

"He's made so many of those; he's actually thinking we could sell them. Did you know he created an iron brand and is burning the camp logo into the wood?"

"Yeah, I saw them." He shook his head as they collected their things and stood. "I have no idea where he gets his talent."

At the fork in the pathway, they parted ways with a soft kiss. She had to rush up and shower, while he needed to go help Liam.

Afterward, she pulled on her outfit for the day and rushed down to meet everyone at the breakfast table.

This time it was just the five of them as they discussed the details for the party that night. Elle had assured her that Reed's team hadn't spotted Ryan on the grounds the night before. Which just assured Hannah that she had imagined seeing the woman in the back hallway.

"We've sold almost one hundred and twenty tickets," Elle said, filling them in. "So, besides our current sixty-three guests, that's a total of one hundred and eighty-two diners tonight. I've filled Isaac and the crew in on the numbers."

"We're approved for up to two hundred in the main hall, so we should be fine," Hannah said, looking down at her phone and scrolling through her notes. "I have everyone, including the new employees, scheduled on shift tonight."

"My turn," Elle said. "Security will have everyone remove their masks and confirm IDs before letting them in. I've requested the back doors be locked from the outside, as to not allow extra guests inside."

Her eyes flitted around the table. "For emergency purposes, they will remain unlocked from the inside."

"What about the kitchen staff?" Zoey asked. "Have they been warned not to let guests in the back?"

"Yes." Elle nodded. "This isn't a normal night around here; everyone will be updated once more before we open the doors."

Hannah checked off an item on her list. "Good. After lunch, the crew and I will begin moving everything into the hall and prepping for the night."

"Will you still have time to dress?" Aubrey asked.

"Yes." She smiled. "I'll make sure I do. I may have to leave a little early on the prep work, but I think we can get everything done." If only her other list of worries could be so easily marked off. Knowing that, once everything was settled, Owen would be leaving was weighing so heavily on her mind that she was losing sleep, not to mention being so distracted during the days as well.

"I'm so excited," Aubrey shocked them all by saying. Aubrey's moods didn't usually swing too far from the center. "The dress I picked out from your guy in New York arrived yesterday, and . . . wow. He was right about the color too."

"I knew you'd look great in pink," Hannah said, turning her mind away from her worries. Her friends always seemed to smooth out the wrinkles in her life. "How about the rest of you?"

"I'm crazy about my dress." Elle sighed. "I'll feel just like Cinderella."

"Dylan's going to have a hard time recognizing me," Zoey said with a chuckle. "I've never worn anything that fancy before."

Everyone turned to Scarlett. "I think I'm going to feel like a vixen." She shrugged. "I may stay at home."

"No!" everyone said at the same time.

"You can't." Hannah took her hand in hers. "You are a sexy vixen— at least you can be for tonight. You're going to knock everyone down with that dress. I picked it out for you." She smiled, remembering the deep-red color of the female fox costume and knowing that it would be perfect for her friend. "Trust me."

Scarlett shrugged. "I guess for one night I can dress up."

"Okay, so everyone has their tasks for the night?" Elle asked.

Aubrey jumped in. "Yes, I'm on door duty."

"Stage, making sure everything goes smoothly," Zoey said.

"Waitstaff," Elle said.

"I'm running the photo booth." Scarlett had begun to smile a little at the thought of the event.

"And I'll be hanging out at the bar," Hannah finished, then giggled. "Okay, that came out wrong."

Everyone laughed. "Until tonight." Elle placed her hand in the middle of the table. It was funny, but she still enjoyed an old-fashioned cheer.

"Tonight." Everyone put their hands in and then raised them all at the same time.

She filled the next hour running errands for the kitchen staff—making sure the extra deliveries were brought in and put away. Then she checked in with Britt and made sure the woman had everything she needed to tend the bar. When she was done there, she helped out with the lunch crowd. She had to wait until some of the men arrived so they could help move all the heavy mirrors into the room, but the columns were light enough for her to arrange.

When Owen and his brothers, along with Damion and Dean, walked in after the last guests had left, she had just put the final column in place.

"You should have waited," Owen said, giving her a kiss.

"I wanted to play around with the positioning of these." She motioned to the pillars, pleased at where she had ended up putting them.

"Where do you want the mirrors?" Owen asked. Instantly, the memory of seeing Ryan in the reflection surfaced, and she shivered. Shaking the vision from her mind, she glanced around the room.

"Against the walls: here, here, and there. Three on each side," she said, motioning to the spots.

"What about the other one?" Liam asked from the doorway to the back area.

"That one will go in front of the door, so people have to pass through it. The balloons and flowers should be here soon." She checked her watch. They were set to be delivered within the half hour.

A few of the dining crew came out of the kitchen. "Where do you need us?" a crew member named Laura asked her.

For the next hour, she directed everyone. Two hours before the doors were set to open, she placed the last feather in a flower vase and stood back. The crew who had helped out were all standing around.

"I can't believe how wonderful it all looks." Laura sighed. "It's going to be so romantic."

Hannah hoped that the evening would be romantic enough to convince Owen that living here could be a possibility. Hadn't it been why she'd poured so much into this event? If he could just see how wonderful things were here, maybe he'd change his mind and stay.

"You outdid yourself." Owen wrapped his arms around her. "It's hard to believe we're standing in the same room."

She was very pleased. Even though the place was blanketed in light from the main lights (which would later be turned off), she could just imagine how romantic everything would be. Even the champagne waterfall was in place. Britt had outdone herself there: glasses and bottles made up a large tower topped with a hanging chandelier that she had brought herself. It had taken Owen and Liam some work to get it to hang just right, but with the vine of pink LED lights hanging over it, it was easily one of her favorite additions to the decor.

There was even enough room left over to have a small dance floor. The DJ was currently setting up near the stage.

"You'd better go get ready." Owen nudged her toward the door. "I saw that massive bag holding your dress in your closet. It might take you a while to get into it."

She smiled. "Right. I have a mask for you." She kissed him before she moved over and took a smaller box and handed it to him.

"Thanks." He frowned at it. "I've never worn a mask before."

"I can't wait to see you in it." She tilted her head. "I might not even recognize you."

He pulled her closer and kissed her. "I'd know you even if I was blindfolded." He kissed her again. "It doesn't have flowers or feathers on it, does it?"

She laughed and, instead of answering, started walking out the door and then called over her shoulder, "Wear it."

Even though the fear and dread of their future loomed over her, she tried to push those thoughts and worries to the back of her mind as she showered. She then took her dress and other necessities into Scarlett's room so Owen could shower and get ready without seeing her or her seeing him. For some reason, she really wanted him to see her for the first time at the ball. She supposed it was a childhood fantasy that she had: seeing her Prince Charming from across the crowded ball . . .

"Ouch!" She glared over at Scarlett after her friend pinched her. "Why did you do that?"

"You were daydreaming and ignoring me. Help me zip this thing up." She turned her back to Hannah.

The skirt of the deep-red dress that she had chosen for Scarlett filled most of the bathroom. After Hannah zipped it, her friend turned around. "You look even more amazing than I thought you would in that dress."

The tight top of the dress showed off Scarlett's shoulders, and the straps snaked up to make a tight loop around her neck.

"Are you sure about this?" Scarlett looked at herself in the mirror after putting on her red fox mask.

"Go." Hannah nudged her out of the bathroom. "You're going to have all the men begging you for a dance. You'll be the belle of the ball."

Scarlett laughed. "Right. Do you need help putting that on?" She nodded to Hannah's dress.

"No, I don't have any zippers," she teased.

"Or top. That thing is all skirt and no coverage for . . ." Scarlett motioned to her breasts.

Hannah laughed. "Hey, if you've got 'em." She picked up the curling iron and continued to put tiny ringlets in her long hair.

"I'll leave then," Scarlett said. "I'm going to walk over with Aubrey."

"Okay, see you over there." She waved with her free hand.

When her hair was done, she piled the small tiara she'd purchased online on top, pinning a few strands of her hair up to complete the look. Then she stepped into the skirt of her dress. Scarlett was right: there wasn't much of a top to it. Even though the skirt filled the bathroom, the top was only two long pieces of silky material that, thanks to some well-placed double-sided tape, would stay put over her breasts. She wrapped the material around her neck, keeping it in place to act like a choker.

After grabbing her black-cat domino mask, she put it on and finished her look off with the deepest-red lipstick she had.

She arrived just as Zoey and Dylan were walking in. It was almost half an hour before guests were due to start arriving. They had all agreed to be early to make sure everything was in place. Zoey's strapless long blue dress had sparkles on the skirt, making it appear as if it were the night sky filled with diamond stars. She'd piled her long dark hair up in a loose bun and had curled some of the wisps around her face. Her owl mask had white and blue feathers that matched the color and theme of her dress perfectly.

"You look amazing," she said to her friend and then hugged her.

"This is some dress." Zoey chuckled. "I didn't think Dylan was going to let me step out in it."

"Are you kidding? I'm going to have fun taking it off you later." He leaned in and kissed her.

Aubrey opened the door for them. Her light-pink dress showcased her pale skin and red hair so perfectly that Hannah had to do a double take. Aubrey wore a butterfly mask with so many vibrant colors on it that they accented her dress and hair.

"Wow, just . . . wow." Hannah blinked a few times. "You really do have flawless skin."

"Not right now—I have a sunburn." She pointed to her pink shoulders.

"You're perfect," Zoey added, giving her friend a hug.

"Thanks, you two—three, I mean—look great," she corrected herself, and she smiled at Dylan.

"Thanks." He winked at her. "I have a mask somewhere here . . ."

"Over there," she said, pointing to the table with all the extra masks.

Dylan grabbed Zoey's hand and dragged her across the room.

"You outdid yourself this time," Elle said, coming up behind her.

Hannah turned around and gasped. Elle's pale-blue dress was almost a perfect replica of the Cinderella dress. Elle had even tied up her hair with a blue ribbon to match the image. Her mask represented the swan. Its white and gray feathers went with the silver dress perfectly without taking away from the illusion of the Cinderella dress. She did a little turn and set the skirt to swaying. "Have you met my Prince Charming?" She reached for Liam's arm.

"We should do this more often." Aubrey sighed. "I never believed I'd enjoy playing dress-up as much as I am now."

"Ten minutes, everyone." Scarlett got their attention. The women took their places. Hannah was glad they'd walked through their roles earlier.

"There's an actual line out there," Aubrey called from the door. "Should I let them in early?"

"No," Hannah said. But her breath caught when she saw Owen standing in the doorway.

The mask she'd picked out for him concealed his dark eyes. His black suit fit him like a second skin, and she felt her chest constrict. He was everything she'd ever dreamed of in a man. Not only was he handsome, but he was the kindest, most caring man she'd ever met. Even though he'd hurt her by leaving before, she understood his reasons for doing so. Family was important to him. She'd never experienced that but had dreamed of it all her life. Which somehow made him even more appealing.

Owen met her in the middle of the dance floor. The million LED lights hung above their heads as the DJ started playing the first song to welcome guests.

"You look . . ." Owen shook his head. "There are no words," he said, his hand coming to rest on her hip as he stepped closer. Her wide skirt crinkled between them, and he glanced down with a laugh. "How do I . . ."

She leaned over to place a quick kiss on his lips. Noticing the bright-red lipstick she'd left on his mouth, she grinned. "There, now everyone will know you're mine."

"I'll need something to show them the same," he said, pulling her back for another kiss. "That look in your eyes, that's my mark."

But Aubrey's "Places, everyone!" call separated them all to their positions. Hannah felt like she had floated back to her spot, since Owen had accompanied her.

CHAPTER NINETEEN

Owen had never been to a ball before, but he was pretty sure that all the other balls in the history of balls would pale in comparison to this one. Hannah not only knew how to throw a party, but she knew how to bring out festivity in everyone around her.

Not to mention she looked damn good in a long flowing skirt. He'd about swallowed his tongue when he'd seen her standing across the room in that outfit.

"Hey." Dean nudged him. "Watch what you're doing."

"Right." Owen finished pouring the champagne and handed over the glass to a guest. It was amazing how inventive people had gotten with their costumes. There'd be more than a few cabins with . . . after-party events tonight.

About an hour after they'd opened the doors, the entire place was so packed he had a hard time keeping an eye on where Hannah was. He knew that security had their eyes out for Ryan or anyone else who looked out of place, but that didn't have him relaxing too much.

When Brent, the head waiter, pulled him aside and asked him to help deliver food, he lost himself in the work and also lost track of time. When he did catch a glimpse of Hannah, he could tell that she was having a wonderful time. She and her Wildflowers had posed for a group picture at the photo booth. When it was Hannah's turn to take an individual photo, he handed the tray over to someone and rushed across the room. Grabbing her up and bending her back, he kissed her just as the picture was taken. Cheers and catcalls filled the space as she came up laughing.

"You looked busy," she said when he pulled away.

"I was, but I'm never too busy to stop and kiss you." He didn't know what his future held—only that he wanted to be with her, even if it meant driving out to the camp every night.

"I'll remember that next time." She grinned up at him, and he heard a few more pictures being snapped. "I have to . . ." He nodded over his shoulder. "I think I handed my empty tray to a guest."

"Then I guess you made someone else very happy too." She used her thumb to wipe the red lipstick off his lips.

For the rest of the night, he could taste her on his lips and couldn't get the feeling of her in his arms out of his mind. As he worked the room, he wondered just how he fit into her world. She belonged here, with her "sisters," as she called them. It wasn't as if working at the camp hadn't been fun. He'd enjoyed his time there, but the fact was he had a drive to do something bigger, something of his own. Even if it meant setting out and starting from scratch. He didn't know where that put him and Hannah: only that, whatever the future held, he was determined to be with her.

The crowd came in waves. To accommodate everyone, all the hotel guests were scheduled between the hours of six and eight, while the paying guests arrived at eight and stayed until ten. It was a smart plan that allowed for the waitstaff to not feel overwhelmed. Much.

The tables were cleared quickly after the first guests had left and were reset before the next wave came.

The DJ kept the music flowing as the food continued to come out of the kitchen perfectly. He hadn't heard one complaint all night long.

When most of the second guests were done eating, the dance floor filled up, and he stole a moment to pull Hannah out as a slow song played.

"Are you having fun?" he asked as he held her close.

"The most fun I've had in a long time." She sighed against his chest.

"I bet you've attended lots of events like this?" he asked.

"So you know a debutante when you see one?" she teased. "You?"

"No, this is my first," he admitted. "So how soon can we ditch this?"

"Not as soon as I'd like," she answered, nuzzling his cheek just as the song ended. "Elle's waving me over. Duty calls."

"Yeah, I need to go help with the cleanup." He groaned. But before he let her go, he leaned down and kissed her once more. "Later," he promised.

She smiled and disappeared into the crowd.

He was just stepping off the dance floor when he heard a shout and a scream. Jerking around, he saw Hannah sway toward him. A spotlight shone directly overhead, making her blonde hair glow. Her hands were gripping her waist, and when they came away, as she looked down at them, he noticed with horror that they were completely covered in something red.

Everything slowed down as if in a movie—a masked woman in a tight slinky black dress stood next to Hannah, her arms raised as light glimmered off the already-blood-soaked blade while it slowly started to swing down, directly toward Hannah's face and chest.

Hannah's hands came up quickly in a self-defense move as another scream echoed in the room. But just then a bright-pink mass darted quickly across the dance floor and tackled the woman to the floor.

"Bitch!" the woman in the black dress cried out. "All of you. You ruined everything."

Owen rushed to Hannah's side and caught her before she slid to the ground.

"I'm okay," Hannah said several times while her face turned very pale.

"Call—" he started to cry out.

"911!" someone finished for him as the crowd shuffled aside, allowing plenty of space for Elle, Zoey, and the rest of them to gather around them.

Aubrey had the woman in a headlock. The knife lay on the dance floor where it had fallen. Dylan walked over and pulled off the mask. "Ryan," he spat out.

Like shadows, several people swarmed out of the darkness and took over. Reed was there suddenly, sitting beside Owen and putting pressure on Hannah's stomach wound. "Easy," he said in a calm voice. "Help is on the way."

He eased Hannah down until she was prone. Owen removed his jacket and placed it gently under her head, while Reed nudged the thin strap aside, exposing part of her stomach. Blood oozed out of a large gash, and Owen felt the room spin, but he bit his lip and held on, since Hannah's skin was now almost translucent.

"She can't do blood," Zoey cried out as she threw her mask aside.

Hannah's laugh sounded like a gurgle in her throat. "I pass out at the sight of it." Her eyes rolled back in her head with those words, and she lolled to the side.

"Easy." Owen glanced up at his brother, who was standing over him as if unsure what to do next. "Give me your jacket."

"Here." Liam tossed him his.

He used it to cover the majority of her chest, while Reed worked on stopping the bleeding.

"She'll need some stitches," Reed told him.

Just then, Dr. Val rushed in. "Move aside. I'm a doctor," she had to say more than once. The tiny Asian woman was dressed in a bright-green gown and shoved several people away with a force greater than her size.

Owen thought it was funny, but if she'd been a man, he bet most of the people surrounding them would have moved aside easily.

"Looks like just a small laceration. I don't see any signs of an actual puncture," Reed told the doctor.

Owen sat there, now holding the jacket to block the view for Hannah, if she came to, and realized he was blocking his own view as well. He wanted to know how bad it was, but his focus was on keeping Hannah safe.

"Bring her into my offices," Dr. Val said to him. "Mr. Cooper's right: it's not as bad as it looks."

"But there's a lot of blood," Zoey said. The four other ladies were all holding on to one another.

"Yes, and it will continue to bleed until I can close it up. Quickly," the doctor told him.

He didn't hesitate. Picking her up gently into his arms, he saw Hannah's eyelids flutter and then open. The doctor kept pressure over the wound. They walked awkwardly down the hallway and through the last doorway, into her examination room.

"Everyone out," Dr. Val told the others as they tried to shuffle in. "You stay." She pointed at Owen with bloody fingers.

He felt bile rise up in his throat but swallowed it down and held on to Hannah. There was no way he was going to let anyone kick him out.

"Talk to her," the doctor commanded while she started cutting away the dress around the wound. Reed had followed them into the room as well and shut the door to block out all the others.

"I can help. I have medical training," he said quickly.

"Oh yeah? I guess you'll have to do. Hold this while I clean up and prepare everything," she told him, handing him a fresh piece of gauze.

Reed placed his hands over Hannah's ribs, causing her to groan slightly.

"Hey," Owen said, getting Hannah's attention. "I'm right here. I'm not going anywhere." He dashed at the tears sliding down his face. Then he realized he was still wearing his mask and tossed it aside. She'd lost hers somewhere between getting stabbed and him catching her.

"Ryan?" she asked. "I bumped into her . . . I recognized her and said something. She was heading toward you." Hannah closed her eyes.

"Keep her awake and talking," Dr. Val said quickly. "She's in shock. I need to start working on her. I'm giving her a local . . ." She turned away and continued moving around the room as she prepared the shot.

"Hannah!" he called out until her eyes opened again. "Honey, you have to stay awake. Talk to me, sweetie," he begged. Desperation filled his voice. "Please."

"Shh," she said, reaching up to touch his face. "I'm right here. I'm not going anywhere." Her voice was weak, and when her arm fell away from him, he caught it.

"Hold her still," Reed said as the doctor injected her.

"You won't feel a thing after this. It appears to be a clean laceration. You'll have a little scar. How still you hold for me will determine how big your scar will be."

"I've always liked you, Lea," Hannah said to the other woman.

"And I like you." The doctor touched her shoulder with her gloved hand. "Now, hold still."

"Yes, Doctor." Hannah sighed and closed her eyes.

"Hannah?" He touched her shoulder himself, but she opened her eyes.

"I'm here; just trying to hold still. Everything's pretty much numb now."

He could see her color returning to her face as she took slow, deep breaths.

"That's it," the doctor said after ten minutes.

"How many stitches?" Hannah asked, already looking as if she felt better.

"None," the doctor answered. "Since it was a straight cut, I cleaned the area and used ZipStitches. They will pull the skin together, leaving only the cut scar and no stitch marks."

"Really?" Hannah smiled up at Owen. "Cool."

"I'm going to give her some antibiotics, and you'll need to keep the area dry. If they pop off . . ." She gestured to him to look at two rows of what appeared to be zip ties glued to her skin. "If any of these pop off of her skin, bring her to me immediately. If she shows any sign of a fever or redness or swelling around the wound . . ."

"Right." He nodded.

"I'm going to give you another shot. This one's an antibiotic. Then I'll give you a prescription," the doctor said as she worked.

"I hate shots." Hannah sighed. "But since I'm numb . . ."

The doctor chuckled. "This one will be in your arm." That had Hannah groaning.

"Is my dress ruined?" she asked while the doctor moved around her.

"I . . ." Owen frowned. "I would think so. There was a lot of blood."

"It was a rental." She sighed again. "I suppose I won't be getting back my deposit now."

He chuckled and leaned down to kiss her. "I'll pay for it."

"No." She shook her head and winced as the doctor sank the needle into her arm. "I'll pay for it."

He leaned in and kissed her again.

"You should tell everyone I'm okay," she said, motioning to the door. "I'm sure they're all worried."

"I don't want to leave you," he murmured.

"I'll tell them. I'm done in here." Reed walked over and, after washing his hands in the sink, stepped outside.

Owen heard a bunch of voices shouting questions before the entire room grew silent and just Reed's voice could be heard.

"What happened to Ryan?" Hannah asked as the doctor cleaned up all the blood on Hannah's skin.

"Aubrey tackled her. That's the last I saw," Owen admitted. "We'll find out soon enough. There's no way she got away."

Hannah smiled. "Aubrey has a black belt in judo."

"Yeah, I knew instantly not to mess with that one." He smiled down at her and brushed a strand of her hair away. "You lost your tiara somewhere."

She shrugged. "I'll let you buy me another one."

He laughed. "Anything you want."

"I'm all done here. Do you think you can sit up?" the doctor asked.

"Yes," Hannah answered, and with his help, she sat up.

"Amazing." The doctor shook her head. "How did those stay in place?" She motioned to the black straps over Hannah's breasts.

Hannah chuckled. "Double-sided tape." She showed her the strip just under the material.

"I'm going to have to get me some of that." Dr. Val chuckled, and Owen cleared his throat to remind the ladies he was still in the room.

"Right." She sighed. "You're all set. Take it easy—no heavy lifting—and I'll want to see you back here in the morning."

"That's it?" she asked, looking down at the bandages covering the strips of zip ties.

"You were lucky."

"I ducked." She shrugged lightly. "I remember bumping into her as she pushed through the dance floor to follow you."

"Tell us when we're all together. I'm sure you don't want to have to tell the same story a hundred times," he said.

"Right." She nodded, and he helped her stand up. "I lost a shoe." She frowned down at her foot.

He picked her up and carried her to the door, which the doctor opened to her waiting friends.

As they stepped out, everyone gathered around her.

"Easy," he said. "She's fine." Elle held up her shoe.

"Thanks." Hannah took it from her and hugged it to her chest. "But I don't think Owen is going to put me down until we're upstairs."

"Where we will all hear the story." He squeezed her gently and turned to Dylan. "Where is Ryan?"

"Reed's men carted her off and assured me that she was heading to jail," Dylan answered.

"Perfect. Will the crew be okay if we all skip out?"

"Yes," Elle said. "The party was pretty much over, but I do want to step back in. There's a crowd of people waiting out there to hear how she's doing."

"Go." He smiled. "We'll wait for you." He started walking out the door.

Liam and Elle disappeared toward the dining hall, while the rest of them followed them up to the stairs.

"Go change out of those pretty clothes," Hannah said to everyone. "Then meet us upstairs. Bring brownies."

When he moved to set her on the sofa, she stopped him. "I want to put on some clean clothes."

He sat her on the edge of her bed in their room. "What do you want?" He dug into her dresser.

"Those." She pointed to the soft purple pajama bottoms and a tank top.

He helped her out of the dress, making sure that he didn't jostle her too much as he held the giant skirt while she stepped out of it. Two strips of tan tape covered her breasts, and he smiled at her.

"That's a sexy look." He nodded to the tape.

"Later." She sighed, and then she held her breath as she peeled them off. He winced when he realized the pain she must be in as she pulled the tape off her skin.

She tugged on her tank top, and when she shivered he handed her a long cream sweater to throw over it all.

"Thanks." She sighed again, and she hugged the soft material. "I'm chilled."

"The doc said it might happen. How are you feeling other than that?" he asked.

"Tired and numb," she answered. "And hungry, but alive."

He'd been trying to control his emotions, for her sake, but now, as he looked at her, everything burst from him. He gathered her up in his arms and held her as tears rolled down his face. "I don't know what I would have done. I can't stand the thought of losing you."

"You won't." She held on to him.

"I came close tonight." He pulled back, and when she noticed the tears, she reached up and wiped them away. "Don't ever leave me like that." He kissed her, putting all his fears and passion into his movements. He wanted to show her how he felt, to let her know how much she meant to him.

"I won't," she promised, and she held on to him again.

"I love you," he said, pulling back so that he could see her eyes. He knew the kiss had shown her, but he had to say the words. He had to know that she understood how he felt about her.

"Yes." She smiled. "I think I know that now."

He chuckled. "Was it that obvious?" He'd been a fool thinking she wouldn't have seen it.

She laughed. "The same way it's obvious that I'm in love with you too."

"No matter what happens, this means more than anything else in my life." He had to explain. Needed her to know that everything else was second to being with her.

"Same." She reached up and touched his face.

Leaning in, he kissed her once more, letting his feelings take over his movements, and he felt as if he had everything he'd ever wanted in life, finally.

CHAPTER TWENTY

Hannah lay on the sofa while Owen and her friends circled around her. She kept her hand over her rib cage, as if the pressure helped with the pain.

"So," Elle said once she'd settled at Hannah's feet. "What actually happened?"

"Owen and I had finished our dance. You'd waved me over . . ." She paused, as if replaying the scene in her head. "I was walking off the dance floor and bumped into someone. I looked over to say I was sorry and knew instantly that it was Ryan. She was only wearing a small mask that covered her eyes. I don't know what upset me more: the fact that she'd dressed up as if she'd been invited to the party or the fact that she actually sneered at me when I turned toward her. Anyway, I think I said her name . . ." She shook her head. "The next thing I knew, pain exploded. Someone screamed."

"Honey, that was you." Elle squeezed her feet lightly. "I saw what happened. I screamed too when I noticed the knife, but I couldn't stop her from cutting you."

"No." She shook her head. "It was so fast. Then I saw the blood, and I guess I kind of lost it." She looked down at her hands. She sighed and rested her head back. "How did she get in?"

"Apparently, she snuck in through the kitchen, wearing a mask," Zoey added with dismay. "A problem that we've discussed in detail. We think she had help. We're looking into it further. Asking every employee."

"She was chummy with several," Elle added. "I'll interview them myself."

"We can do that together," Zoey agreed.

"How many stitches?" Elle asked, turning to Hannah.

"None. Lea used zip . . ." She glanced over to Owen for help.

"ZipStitches," he answered for her. "Pretty much zip ties holding her skin together, just like it sounds. But the good news is there won't be scars from the stitches."

"How big was the cut?" Zoey asked.

Owen held up his fingers about six inches apart. The room was quiet except for Elle sniffling.

"Hey." Hannah nudged her with her feet. "I'm okay. I'm alive. Lea says I was lucky she didn't plunge that thing into me."

"I don't like it when psychopaths skin my friends." Elle closed her eyes.

"She'll be locked up for good now," Liam said, squeezing Elle's shoulders.

"One would think," Dylan pointed out. "Somehow, after pulling a gun on me, she walked free."

"That was her first offense. They're bound to keep her locked up now," Zoey said.

"I'll call first thing in the morning," Owen said, and he held on to Hannah. "She not only stabbed you, but she broke the restraining order. That's three strikes, if we're counting."

"Does this mean . . ." Elle started, but she shook her head.

"What?" Liam asked.

"You don't think it was Ryan causing your dad all those problems? I mean, she did say she'd known your dad before. What if she'd been the one causing all the drama?"

"It's a possibility." Owen had always assumed that it had been someone on the board who wanted him to step down. Someone who would benefit financially. Ryan didn't own any stock in Paradise Investments that he knew of. What could she gain from his family's business being ruined? Ryan had been out for fame and . . . what? Revenge?

"I think it's worth looking into," Elle said, and the other women nodded agreement.

"Okay," he said. "I'll have Brett check into it."

Just then, there was a knock on the door.

Liam jumped up and looked out the peephole. "It's Reed," he said, and then he opened up the door for the man.

"I thought you'd all gather." He stepped inside. "How are you, Hannah?"

"Fine, thanks to you." She smiled at him.

Reed nodded. "I thought you'd all want an update. Ryan Kinsley has been moved to the county jail. She will go before the judge in the morning for breaking the restraining order, trespassing, and assault with intent to murder. Luckily, your wound is not serious or life threatening. Still, she'll most likely be charged at the felony level, which automatically carries jail time."

"How long?" Hannah asked.

"It depends on the judge. For her first offense, when no one was hurt, she was let off with a slap on the wrist and a fine, but her gun license was revoked, which is why she chose a knife." He shook his head. "I think that pretty much will tell any judge that she was willing to go to great lengths to do harm. Bail has been denied."

"Thank you," Hannah said again. "Your quick thinking saved us tonight."

Reed chuckled. "It was Aubrey." He nodded to her as she sat across the room, her knees tucked up to her chin. "I would have been proud to have you on my team, back in the day." Aubrey smiled and blushed a little. "I'm going to convince Kimberly to take your next judo class. Hell, I might even join her. I could use a refresher."

"Tuesdays and Thursdays at one." Aubrey gave him a wink.

"We'll be there. Well, I'll leave you all to get some rest." He turned to go.

"Thank you!" several people called out. He waved back to them before Liam shut the door.

"You forgot the brownies," Hannah said with a sigh.

Scarlett chuckled and got up from her spot on the chair. "No, we didn't. We just wanted to hear what happened before we dug in."

Hannah sat up a little, and Owen noticed her wince with the movement.

"Hurting?" he asked, worried when he saw pain in her eyes.

"A little," she said. "I'm tired too, but I want chocolate more than sleep."

Scarlett handed her a brownie on a small paper plate, then a glass of milk. "Since you can't have wine with those." She motioned to the bottle of pills.

"Right, thanks," she said.

Owen took one from Scarlett, balancing it so he could keep holding Hannah.

"What happens next?" Liam asked.

"Now, we continue our plan," Owen answered, thinking about putting himself in the spotlight and trying to get the attention of the attacker. If they could get them to make a mistake, to change their plans, then maybe he could figure out who was behind it all. "This changes nothing. We move forward every day."

"Sure it does," Hannah said as she finished off her brownie. "I can't teach my classes for the next few days. Not until I heal."

Zoey jumped in. "I'll take your classes."

"I'll take the swim aerobics," Scarlett said, then looked at Zoey. "You take the yoga, since you're already doing some other ones."

"I'll do your tai chi sessions," Aubrey finished.

"It's settled." Elle stood up. "Let's allow Hannah to get some sleep." She took her brownie with her. "I'm going to go enjoy this under the stars in my—in *our*—tree house." She reached for Liam's hand. "Night." She leaned down and placed a kiss on Hannah's forehead. "I'm glad you're okay."

Once they were alone, Owen finished off his brownie. "Think you can move?"

"Not yet." She sighed and leaned back against him. "If I close my eyes now, I'll just keep playing the scene over and over again."

"How about a movie?" He nodded toward the television.

"No, how about you read to me? My eyes are too tired to focus right now," she suggested instead, and she motioned to a book.

"Sure." He reached down and opened it. An ace of hearts playing card fell out where she'd marked the spot. "What's this?" he asked.

"My lucky bookmark." She shrugged.

"Lucky?" he asked.

"My first summer here." She sighed.

"Okay, tell me the story." He placed the card back in the book and shut it, shifting slightly so he could watch her face.

"My parents were too busy to fly me down here. It was the first time I'd flown by myself. There was supposed to be a town car to pick me up at the airport; instead, a van from the camp showed up."

"What happened?" he asked after she was quiet for a moment.

She closed her eyes. "I was so afraid that the bus driver, a nice old man, talked to me the entire ride. I told him that I didn't want to be here, or anywhere, for that matter." She sighed again. "It was the first time I'd told anyone I was thinking about hurting myself." His arms tightened around her a little. "He parked the van on the side of the road, and we ended up talking for more than an hour. Then he pulled this card from his pocket." She reached for it out of the book, and he marked the spot in the book with his finger while she looked at the tattered thing. "He told me that this card had been the first thing his wife had given him when they'd met in Vegas. I thought the thing was old then." She laughed. "Now look at it. Anyway, he said that he'd kept it all these years to remind himself that his life had changed that day. And that if he handed me the card now and gave it to me, for as long as I had the card, my life would be changed forever. Part of me thinks that the guy just had a playing card in his pocket, and he made up a sob story for an eleven-year-old depressive girl."

"He sounds like an amazing man."

"Grandpa Joe was—Elle's grandfather." She nodded when he tilted his head. "It wasn't just the Wildflowers that saved my life that summer; Joe showed me what parents, or grandparents for that matter, could be like." She wiped a tear from her eyes. "I've never loved an adult like I loved Joe." She fell silent for a moment, then looked up at him. "Read to me—get me out of this slump."

He kissed the tip of her nose and opened the book. "This is a murder mystery. Are you sure you want me to read this?"

"Yes." She chuckled, then winced. "I'm dying to know who did it."

He shook his head and stared at the top of the page. By the end of the third page, he was dying to know who did it as well. But when he felt her body totally relax and knew that she'd fallen asleep, he placed the card in the pages and then pulled the blanket on the back of the sofa over her. Then for the next hour, he tried to get comfortable. When he finally gave up, he was sure that she was fast asleep. After pulling her up into his arms, he walked her back to her room.

"Who did it?" she asked in a sleepy tone.

"I didn't finish the book yet." Even though he'd wanted to know himself, he'd refrained from skipping to the last chapter. He knew the reader's code. One simply didn't scan ahead.

"Oh," she moaned as he set her down gently.

"Are you in pain?" he asked, pulling off the jeans and shirt that he'd changed into after the ball.

She squirmed a little. "Only when I move."

He crawled in beside her and wrapped her in his arms. "Better?"

"Mmm," she mumbled, but since she didn't wince, he took it as a good thing.

"I love you," he said again, and he kissed her hair. He loved the way saying the words made him feel—even more when she said them back to him. He'd never said them to anyone before, but now, he felt like it was the most natural thing in the world to say to her.

"I love you." She sighed, and he could tell that she'd drifted off again.

It still took him a while to fall asleep; he supposed it was the scene of Hannah being stabbed playing over in his mind a million times. He kept telling himself he should have been the one to protect her, but he knew he'd been just too far away.

His dreams were filled with darkness, and when he felt Hannah stirring next to him, he woke with a jolt.

"You okay?" he asked her.

"Yes. I'm ready for something for this pain, though. It burns."

He sat up and flipped on the light quickly, then reached over and lifted her shirt. As he touched her skin, he knew instantly that she was running a fever.

"Damn," he cursed under his breath.

"Is it bad?" she asked, her voice weak.

"Enough that I'm going to get the doc over here." He reached for her phone, since he knew she'd have everyone's number programmed into it.

"No, it's in the middle of the night." She groaned a little when he shifted her.

He ignored her and punched the number on her phone.

"Hello?" The doc sounded already awake.

"Hey, it's Owen. Hannah's running a fever." He felt her forehead again. He'd have to find the ibuprofen.

"I'll be right over." She hung up without a goodbye.

He let her get some more rest while he waited. When he heard the knock on the door for the apartment, he let the doctor in, then went in to carry her out to the living room sofa to be looked at.

"Sorry if I woke you," he said as she sat beside the sleeping Hannah.

"You didn't. I was on my way to the hospital. I work for a few hours there in the morning." She took Hannah's temperature. "One oh one. Not awful, but it's a good thing you called." She lifted Hannah's shirt.

Hannah woke. "Hi, Lea."

"Hi, how are you feeling?"

"Tired and cold."

"Hopefully, I'll be able to fix one of those."

From his position standing over her, he could see the redness of her skin around the wound. "Infection?" he asked.

"Yes. I'll need to give her another shot. Did she take any of the antibiotics I gave her yet?"

"No, you said in the morning."

"Good." She peeled back the bandages, and he watched her reclean the area.

"So?" Hannah asked.

"It's a small infection. As long as you get some rest, this should clear it up. Who knows where that knife was before Ryan used it?" The doctor pulled out what she needed from her bag, and he stood back as she gave Hannah a shot.

When she was done, she replaced the bandages and then stood up. "Let me know if anything changes," she told him, then turned to Hannah. "Get some rest."

"Well?" he said once they were alone again. "I don't think I'm going back to sleep. Do you want anything to eat?"

"I could eat," she said. "But the question is, can you cook?"

"You're looking at the best breakfast chef in the camp."

She chuckled. "I'm not sure about that. We have Isaac, remember?"

"Oh, yeah." He frowned. "Okay, the best one in the apartment."

"I'd probably agree with you on that, after I taste what you can do." She yawned again.

"Rest." He walked over and kissed her forehead. "I'll wake you when it's ready."

She nodded and closed her eyes, and he went into the kitchen to make something for them.

A little under half an hour later, just as the sun was starting to light the apartment, he woke her, a plate in his hands. "Think you can wake up and eat a little?"

Her eyes opened and zoned in on the plate he was holding out for her.

"Is that chocolate?" she asked. "We had chocolate in the apartment?"

He chuckled. "I may have run down to the kitchen and borrowed some. Think you can eat?" he repeated.

"Yes." She reached for his hand to sit up. He noticed that she already looked better. After she took the plate from him, he reached up and touched her forehead. "Well?"

"Fever's gone, but the doc said it might be masked by the shot and to still take it easy," he answered.

"I'm tired, but the chills have gone away." She gave him a weak smile.

"What's all this?" Scarlett walked out of her room still in her sleeping shorts and T-shirt, her dark hair piled on top of her head in a messy bun.

"Breakfast." Hannah smiled. "Owen made me chocolate chip pancakes."

"Yes!" Scarlett raised her arms in victory, and he laughed.

"You're lucky I made more." He got up from the sofa and walked in to get her a plate. "Turkey bacon?"

"Yes, please." She sat at the little bar area.

Aubrey walked out of her room. "Hey, is there some of that for me?"

"Give me a second—I can make some hot ones." He got back to work.

By the time he was done, everyone who had gathered last night was sitting around the apartment eating his pancakes.

"I have yoga this morning," Zoey said, pushing her half-empty plate away. "God, I shouldn't have stopped by, but Scarlett sent me a picture, and I was super jealous." She turned to her sister and stuck her tongue out.

"I'm so evil." Scarlett rubbed her hands together and did a little laugh.

The fact that everyone had also stopped by to see how Hannah was feeling made him even more aware that the five friends were as close as any family could ever be. The unique living environment had drawn them closer and had spread to his brothers as well. Dylan and Liam were back to their old selves—the way they had been when they had all lived under one roof, minus the angst and acne.

He missed those days and was a little jealous at how close his brothers had grown again.

Sitting around with the group was like being part of something bigger—something he hadn't felt in a very long time.

By the time everyone had left, and it was just him and Hannah left in the apartment, he knew the commute into Destin would be worth it every day just to be around Hannah and his brothers.

CHAPTER
TWENTY-ONE

Hannah slept for most of the day. Her body had shut down on her, but when she woke, she felt stronger and almost back to her old self. With the exception of the tug she felt over her ribs every time she moved.

Owen pampered her so much that she felt a little guilty, since he was the one who was still bruised. All she had was a cut over her ribs; he'd been the one who had almost blown up.

After escaping into the bathroom to freshen up, she decided tape and a plastic bag were the best way to cover her bandages and get clean. Owen helped her tape herself up, and after she'd showered, he was there, waiting for her.

"Let me check." He nodded to the area. "Make sure you didn't get anything wet."

She poked his shoulder. "I am capable of washing, you know."

"I know." He looked deep into her eyes and kissed her on the temple. "I'm enjoying pampering you."

"I'm not one to deny a good pampering." She leaned back as he checked her bandages.

"They got a little wet, but not too much. I'll change them." He helped her up on the counter, and she leaned back against the mirror so her skin didn't crinkle as he carefully changed the gauze and taped fresh bandages over her skin. "There." He stood back when he was done. The fact that she was sitting on a towel, her entire body exposed to him, and that his eyes were so focused on her cut, somehow touched her even more. Then his eyes slid up to her breasts, and she chuckled.

"That took longer than I would have thought," she joked.

"What?" He frowned at her and picked up a towel and wrapped it around her.

"You, ogling my breasts."

"I don't ogle," he said, helping her off the counter.

"All men ogle when it comes to naked breasts." She laughed and flashed him for a moment. Instantly, his eyes moved back to her breasts, and she laughed again. "See? Ogle eyes, right there." He cracked up at her comment.

"Can you blame men? You have perfect breasts," he said while she pulled on a pair of clean sweat shorts and a camp T-shirt. "I ogle when you're injured, since I can't touch."

"You can touch," she said. "I'm not made of glass."

"No, but until you're back to at least ten percent, I'll stick to ogling." He leaned in and kissed her.

"I feel great enough that a small walk . . ." she started, and when he started to shake his head, she rushed through the rest of her statement. "I mean, just a short walk, to the docks and back. I won't push myself. I want to see the sunset."

He sighed. "If you get tired, I'll carry you back."

"Deal." She disappeared into her room to grab her shoes. Putting on the shoes was harder than she would have thought. By the time she was done, sweat was dripping down her face. She worried that it would take her longer to heal than she'd imagined. She was hoping that she could be back at work in a day or two, but at this rate, it would take longer.

Owen was on the phone but hung up when she stepped out of the room. "What happened?"

"Nothing." She frowned. "Why?"

"You look like you've just run a marathon." He frowned down at her in return. "The walk is off."

"No," she groaned. "It was my shoes. Bending over to tie the damn things." She should've just slipped on her flip-flops instead of being foot conscious.

"Your body is healing and fighting an infection. It's going to take some time."

"I would really love some fresh air," she complained. "Please." She hated begging, but she needed to feel like she was back to normal. She'd been thinking too much, unable to push the idea of calling her parents out of her mind. Not that they would care too much that she'd been stabbed. Or would they? They would probably use it as an excuse to claim that her job was too dangerous and try to convince her to move back to New York with them. She didn't want to give them more fuel against the camp. Which meant calling them was off limits.

"Okay." He nodded. "But we take it slow."

"Thanks." She smiled and reached for her jacket.

"It's eighty degrees out still," he warned her.

"Just in case I get the chills." She threw it over her arm. "Ready?"

They stepped out of the apartment, and she frowned at the stairs. If she used up all her energy on them, she wouldn't make it to the docks, since she was still panting from tying her shoes.

"I'll carry you down." He reached for her, and she enjoyed feeling his strong arms lifting her up. She held on to him as he easily jogged down the stairs with her in his arms. At the base and before anyone could see, he set her gently back on her feet.

When they walked by the main desk, Kimberly rushed around and gave her a light hug. "I'm so happy that you're okay."

"Thanks." She hugged her back.

"Let me know if you need anything."

"We're just going out for a small walk," Owen said as he started toward the door.

They were stopped more than a dozen times before they hit the docks, each time by an employee or guest, each one telling her how thankful they were that she was okay.

Owen, thankfully, kept the conversations quick and explained that she wanted to watch the sunset at the docks.

By the time they had reached the docks, she was exhausted and was thankful for the new swing bench that Liam had built and then set up at the waterline.

"Are you doing okay?" Owen asked, his arm wrapped around her shoulders. She was grateful she'd brought the jacket. The light mist in the air chilled her.

"Yes." She sighed and rested her head against his shoulder as the sunset lit up the sky. "I may let you carry me back."

He rubbed her arm and held on to her. "It's nice . . ." he started, but when he didn't continue, she glanced up at him. "Having people care for you."

"We've got a good bunch of people here." She thought about all the flowers that now filled the apartment.

"It's like one big happy family here," he said, and she heard a hint of something in his tone. She sat up and turned slightly toward him.

"You miss it?" she accused him.

"Of course. Who wouldn't?" He waved his hand around. "I mean, just look at that." Tonight's sky was filled with bright oranges and deep yellows. It was an amazing view.

"I mean, besides the view—you miss the people. You miss us," she teased him.

"I've missed *you*." He leaned in and kissed her.

"What did your dad say?" she asked after settling back on his shoulder. "I assume that was him on the phone?"

He nodded. "I told him about Ryan attacking you and that it could have been Ryan behind the bigger scheme. But he doesn't think it was her." He shook his head. "Of course, he wouldn't tell me why he thinks that, but . . ."

"Hey." She sat up and looked into his eyes. "I'm sure things will smooth out soon."

He stood up and walked to the edge of the water. Following him, she enjoyed the sounds of the evening coming to life—the buzz of the night bugs as they skimmed the surface of the water and the sound of the frogs and toads hiding somewhere in the darkness, trying to catch an evening meal.

She touched his arm and waited until he turned to look at her. "I know it's hard, treading water, being stuck here . . ."

"I'm not stuck." He pulled her into his arms and kissed the top of her head. "I'm where I want to be." She rubbed his back with long even strokes. "This has nothing to do with this place, but I need to know that things are safe. It's like waiting for the bomb to drop."

"I can understand. At least we have one threat we no longer have to worry about."

"True," he said. "Reed stopped by earlier, when you were asleep. He told us that the judge has denied her bail. It's the first step in keeping her where she belongs."

"That's wonderful." She sighed and felt one of her weights lift from her. "Will we have to testify or something?" She didn't know the process. After all, she had never known anyone who had been arrested before.

"I'm not sure, but if so, we'll do it together." He took her hand. "How about we sneak into the kitchen and see if Isaac has anything left over?"

She thought about how much energy she had left and decided food could boost it enough to get her through the rest of the night.

"I could eat." She took his hand, and they slowly made their way down the well-lit pathways to the back door that led to the kitchen area.

The moment they stepped in, she was greeted and hugged several times. Someone nudged her into a chair, and a plate with a cheeseburger was set in front of her, while Owen stood and ate a burger.

Halfway through the meal, however, she could feel her energy fleeing, and she handed Owen the rest of the plate to finish off.

"How are you holding up?" Elle asked when she walked in and found them there as she was picking up tomorrow's dinner itinerary from Isaac.

"I'm here"—Hannah wrapped her napkin around her cutlery—"but needing a nap."

Elle hugged her. "Go, rest. Let your body fight this off. We've got things around here."

She glanced over toward a row of perfect cupcakes behind a glass case. "Thanks, but I'd feel better if I could take a few of those . . ."

Elle laughed. "I'm sure Betty will let you take as many as you want." She walked across the room and brought back a pink box. "Here."

Hannah picked out two frosted cupcakes, and Owen picked out a couple for himself.

"Let's grab some milk," Owen said before they left. "I used the rest of yours this morning."

Elle whisked herself over to the gleaming chrome fridge and brought back a container. "Now go, before Isaac kicks us out."

Hannah laughed. "He would never kick me out."

"No, he wouldn't." Elle smiled at her. "Night . . ."

"Night," she replied.

"Think you can walk?" Owen asked, his arms full of the pink box and the carton of milk.

She shrugged. "It's not that far."

"What about the stairs?" he asked, causing her to groan.

"I forgot about those."

"I can run up and drop these off, then come back and carry you up," he suggested.

"Good plan." She gave him a peck on the cheek. "I've grown fond of being carried, but only by you."

After they were settled in the living room again, he turned on the television and found an old movie to watch. They sat there enjoying the sugary desserts.

By the time her second cupcake was gone, she knew that she'd used up all her energy, and she snuggled into Owen as the movie played. His hand smoothing her hair and stroking her shoulders further comforted her.

She woke when Scarlett and Aubrey came in. The television had been muted, and Owen was still holding her but was reading a book at the same time.

"I'm sorry," she said, sitting up. "I didn't mean to fall asleep."

He set the book back on the table and gave her a kiss. "I don't think you had a choice. You were exhausted."

"Did you bring us any of those?" Aubrey nodded to the pink box.

"Nope." She sat up and stretched, only remembering the cut after feeling the pull of pain. "Sorry." She knew her friends worried for her, especially after seeing their faces when she winced with pain. They all looked like they wanted to help her but didn't know how.

"It's okay," Aubrey clarified. "I really don't need any sugar before bed. It gives me nightmares." She sat down and toed off her tennis shoes.

"What's new?" she asked after a moment.

Owen filled her in on what he'd found out about Ryan. Then the talk changed to the Halloween party in a few days; Hannah realized that it was going to be hard on her to help decorate.

"We need to discuss security. To step things up from last time, we're requesting that masks not be allowed upon entry. Once inside, people are free to put them on after they've passed through security checks. If they leave, they will have to go through the process again." He waited for her response.

"I can get behind that." She thought about how easy it had been for Ryan to sneak in. "I guess I was too out of it to ask earlier, but how did cleanup go after the party?" she asked.

"Fine. Everything was done by noon the following morning. The mirrors and pillars were shipped back with no problems," Scarlett said.

"That's good." She thought of all the decorations that were about to start surging in for the next party. The time she'd spent with Owen had given her a break from her routine, which she had enjoyed, but it had exhausted her.

"We should just cancel the party," Owen said, sounding a little frustrated.

"No, we need this. We have to get right back on our feet. I will not let what happened, what she did, to set the mood for all future parties." She straightened her shoulders slightly. "We're better than that. This is a way for us to prove that nothing she did or could do can break us."

He took her hand in his and carried it up to his lips. "You're pretty amazing."

She smiled and thought of all the things that needed to be done before the party. Just as she was about to start running through a list with him, her phone rang. Seeing her parents' number, she groaned.

"Want me to answer it?" Owen suggested.

"Oh, they would *love* that." She smiled as she picked up the phone and answered herself. She didn't want to give her parents the pleasure.

"Hi, Mom." She waited.

"Why must we find out through the media that our daughter was stabbed?" Her mother's tone wasn't that of a concerned mother, but instead was one of scolding.

"I'm not sure." Hannah leaned back. "Maybe because I've been recovering from a stab wound and an infection?" She hoped her sarcasm landed—never a sure thing, with her mother's obliviousness.

"Don't take that tone with me. We've been worried about you after finding out this morning," her mother started.

"You found out this morning?" she asked. "Then why are you just getting around to calling me now?"

Hannah wondered what media outlet had done a report on the incident last night and if the camp had been mentioned. Instantly, worry flooded her. After all, if the camp had been depicted in a bad light, it could keep guests from flooding in.

After reaching down and wincing slightly, she pulled open her tablet and did a quick search; meanwhile, her mother backpedaled while still berating Hannah about not calling them and letting them know directly that she'd been attacked.

When she found the report, she snapped her fingers to get Scarlett's and Aubrey's attention. She had all but ignored her mother while she scanned the article, until her mother's voice had become too loud to ignore.

"Mom, I have to go. I'm . . . not feeling well." She hung up.

"Can you believe this?" She motioned to the article.

"I know. It's great, isn't it?" Aubrey smiled. "I mean, even the bit about you getting stabbed wasn't bad."

"Did we know that the local paper would be there last night?" she asked to the room. Even though it had all ended up being positive for the camp, she would prefer to have known about it ahead of time.

"No." Scarlett shook her head. "I didn't. Maybe Elle knew?"

"Text her," Hannah said to Aubrey.

"I'll text them all the link." Aubrey copied the link and shot it out to their group message, getting an almost instant reply from Elle.

Wow! How cool!

Zoey didn't reply for a few minutes.

Sorry, we were in the shower when you sent this. This article looks great!

Gross, I didn't want that picture in my head.

Scarlett sent four eggplant emoji and a donut, making Hannah chuckle.

"What? It's bad enough that we have to listen to you two . . ." she started, only to get a kick from Aubrey.

Hannah felt her face heat, and she covered it with her hands. "My god."

"It's not that bad. I was just . . ." Scarlett got kicked again by Aubrey.

"And on that note, I'm going to bed." Hannah stood up and walked with Owen down the hallway.

"Hey," Owen said once they were snuggled together in her bed. "If it bothers you that much, could we move into a room downstairs?"

"It doesn't bother me enough to give up my own bathroom," she admitted, sending him into laughter.

"We could always take over a cabin, like Dylan and Zoey?"

"No." She sighed. "They're building their own place and will be moving out soon. Besides, I know for a fact that every cabin is booked solid through next summer."

He was quiet for a while. "What about moving into my apartment in town?"

She sat up. "That's a possibility. I'll run it by the others tomorrow."

She settled back down and thought about moving into a house with Owen. Did that mean he planned on staying around after the entire mess with his father was over? If the nightmare ever ended, that is.

CHAPTER
TWENTY-TWO

Over the next few days, Owen helped Hannah get back up to speed physically. The infection had really taken a toll on her, more so than the cut had. He went with her to every doctor's appointment, and when the doctor told her that she could start helping again, he followed her around to make sure she didn't lift anything heavy.

Which meant he spent his afternoons putting together Halloween decorations.

"You don't think this is a little . . . too much?" he asked when he'd set the last of the pumpkins down.

"Halloween needs pumpkins," she said while marking something off on her iPad.

"Yes, a few, not six dozen." He motioned around him. "And not all for just one place."

She laughed at him as if he was being silly. "Now we need to put the ghosts together." She turned and motioned to several large boxes.

"How many . . ." He shook his head. "You know what, never mind. I'm calling for backup." He pulled out his phone and texted his brothers.

Two hours later and with the help of both his brothers and a few other employees, the dining hall was once again transformed. This time, instead of a classy masquerade, the place turned spooky. He asked her why they had planned another event so close to the ball where she'd been stabbed. She looked at him like he'd grown another head.

"Guests expect a good time, and parties are part of that. Besides, I'm not going to cancel everyone's fun because of Ryan. I would never allow her to ruin something this great. Not to mention this could be just what we need to repair the social damage to the camp."

He agreed with the last part. If the camp was going to survive a reputation of parties ending badly, they needed to knock this one out of the park.

"What do the guests think?"

"About?" she asked.

"Won't they be leery to attend a party so soon after someone was stabbed at the last one?"

She shook her head. "We have all-new guests in the camp. And I think we've squelched the gossip about what happened at the last party. We need this one to go smoothly."

They both turned and looked around the room.

"You did it again," he said, and he kissed the top of her head.

"You guys did it. I just stood here." She frowned up at him.

"As soon as Dr. Val gives you the go-ahead to start lifting things, I'll back off."

"I don't want you to back off too far." She wrapped her arms around him.

He smiled and kissed her. "I won't be far."

"Get a room," Dylan groaned, and Owen nodded his head. "Got a minute?" Dylan asked him.

"Sure." Owen glanced down at Hannah.

"Go. I was going to finish a few small things here."

"Don't lift . . ." he started, but when she rolled her eyes at him, he stopped.

"Yes, Mom." She pushed him playfully away.

When Owen and Dylan stepped out on the back steps, Liam was already waiting for them. "We don't think the plan's working," Liam said. "Nothing has happened, short of Hannah's attack, which I doubt had anything to do with whoever is threatening Dad and us."

"We think it would be best if one of us—or all three of us—went back into town," Dylan suggested.

Owen rubbed his forehead with a groan. He'd known his brothers wouldn't be able to wait too long for something to happen. Hell, if Hannah hadn't gotten hurt, he would have needed movement as well. But as it was, he was content just being with her and ignoring the rest of the world.

"I'll do it," he said, knowing that he was the only one who had a legitimate reason to be in town and at the office.

"No," both his brothers said at the same time.

"You almost died already," Liam added.

"So, you expect me to let one of you two take the next turn?" He shook his head and chuckled. "I'm the oldest; besides, I actually work at Paradise. You two don't."

"Okay, but you take Reed with you," Dylan said. "He's agreed—"

"Sure," he said instantly. "I would take Aubrey with me, but . . ." He paused with a grin when both Liam and Dylan laughed. "Seriously, that is one woman I wouldn't want to mess with."

"Who is?" Hannah asked as she stepped out of the doorway.

"Aubrey," Liam answered, which sent Hannah into a smile.

"It's so strange to know that such a small package could be so scary," she said.

"Ready?" he asked Hannah.

"Yes. I need to go change for dinner." She stopped and turned to his brothers. "You two do have costumes for this weekend's party?"

They both looked embarrassed. "Yes," Dylan answered. "It was all arranged."

"Like mine?" Owen nodded to Hannah. "She won't let me know what it is yet."

"I don't want you to have time to back out." She grabbed his arm and started pulling him down the stairs. "Later," she called over her shoulder.

"Just tell me I'm not a pirate, or worse . . ."

"What's worse than a pirate?" she asked. "We'll have to discuss what's bad about a pirate later, but I'm curious."

"Everyone's always a pirate." Owen rolled his eyes. "What's the most common Halloween outfit?"

She thought about it. "A cop?"

"Some sort of superhero," he answered. "But yeah, cops are popular too."

"No, you're not any of those," she promised.

"Okay." He stopped and pulled her into his arms. "I assume we'll be a matching set?"

She smiled. "Yes."

"Then I'm okay with whatever." He kissed her. "As long as security does their jobs and makes everyone remove their masks upon entry."

"They will," she answered. "We have some time," she said between kisses, "before dinner." She ran her hands up his chest.

He'd kept the physical contact between them light since the stabbing. After all, he didn't want to hurt her. But now, he could tell that she was almost back to herself fully.

"I . . ." He'd started to find a reason why it wasn't a good idea, physically, but he couldn't think of anything. Instead, he bent down and kissed her until he wished they were already upstairs or somewhere else private. "Let's go," he said, taking her hand in his.

"We'll never make it upstairs," she warned. "Someone will stop us."

He turned and pulled her into the back entrance of the building instead, and they headed for her office two doors down. "Unlock it."

She punched in her code, and he pulled her into the dark room, not even reaching for the light as he shut and locked the door behind him.

Then he pushed her back up against the door and continued kissing her until their breathing was labored.

"I need you now." She pulled his shirt over his head. She leaned in and ran her fingers over his shoulder.

"God." He jerked her shorts and panties off her hips and found her wet and waiting. "I need to go slow," he warned her, but he knew it was already too late. "Tell me if I hurt you."

She shook her head. "You won't," she said, then ran her tongue over his chest as she reached for his shorts.

Instead, he blocked her and spread her legs a little wider, then knelt and laid his mouth over her sexy pussy, licking at her as her fingers dug into his hair.

"Owen!" She cried out his name over and over until he was pretty sure everyone on the floor could hear her.

After standing up, he jerked off his shorts and slid into her slickness as he covered her cries with his mouth, capturing them and causing more of his own.

"Tell me you love me," she said as she held on to him. "I need to hear it again."

He smiled and felt his control slipping a little more. "I love you. Now, let go. I want to feel you come for me. Only for me."

"Yes, only for you," she whispered next to his ear, which caused him to slide over the edge. "I can't move."

She sighed as he held her pinned against the wall.

"Good." He sighed in return. "Neither can I." He chuckled.

"Do you think they would notice if we didn't show up for dinner?" she asked.

He groaned. "Considering it's Zoey's and Dylan's nights off, probably. I'm supposed to be working at the pool bar right now."

She sighed. "Yeah, I'm hosting. I need to shower and change." She glanced at her watch. "And only have half an hour to get there."

"Okay." He started moving again. "Then we'll need to make this time quick."

Her gasp followed by groans of pleasure had him smiling.

When he walked into the pool bar area, Britt ran her eyes over him and grunted.

"What?" he asked with a smile.

"I know a man who just got lucky when I see him. There it is." She pointed to his face. "That smile of, 'Yeah, I just had sex.' Animals." She shook her head.

"And you've never had a look like this before?" he teased.

"Oh, plenty of times." She leaned on the counter. "I just never go out in public after. I wait until the glow dies down."

"Well, I could have chosen to wait until this feeling dies down, but then I'd be leaving you alone here to work all by yourself." He tossed a few empty beer cans into the trash.

"True. Thanks for that." She nodded.

"You're welcome," he said with a laugh.

"Now get to work." She nudged him out from behind the bar. "People aren't going to serve themselves."

He laughed again and headed out to the pool area to take orders.

Just after the sun had set, he was surprised to see Joel stroll up and chat with Britt at the bar.

"What are you doing here?" he asked after setting down the tray of dirty glasses.

"Owen, hey." Joel turned to him with a smile. "I was just talking to Britt."

Owen motioned to Britt that they would like to be alone. "No, what are you doing *here*?"

"Your dad said you guys were out here. I thought I'd come out and check this place out. No one told me how cool it is." He glanced around. "Pretty great setup out here."

Most of the guests were inside having dinner, but there were a few stragglers still enjoying the pool. "Glad you could come out to see it." Owen didn't know how he felt about a new friendship push from Joel.

"I came out here for this." Joel handed him a folder. "I thought you'd need it for the closing tomorrow."

With everything that had happened with Hannah, he'd forgotten about closing on the land in the morning. "Thanks," he said after opening it and seeing the legal documents he'd need for the closing. "I was going to send for these, but I forgot . . ."

Joel slapped him on the back. "No problem. That's what I'm here for."

Just then, Hannah walked toward them, a flowered sundress flowing in the evening breeze as her curly hair blew softly around her face. Owen's breath hitched at the sight. The sun was setting, and the bright colors hit her skin, causing it to almost glow.

Joel caught Owen's glance. "Now I know what's really keeping you here." He nudged his shoulder. "I'll get out of your hair. Don't forget—the closing company will be here around nine."

"Right." He waved the folder at Joel. "Got it. Thanks."

"Sure thing." Joel chuckled, and he disappeared down the pathway.

"What did Joel want?" Hannah asked when she'd finally come to a stop in front of him.

His hands automatically wrapped around her waist. "You look amazing."

"Thanks." She chuckled. "Joel?"

"Oh, he was bringing papers." He'd set the folder down, all but forgotten now, since he was more focused on kissing her. "You look amazing."

"You already said that once. I snuck out early." She nodded toward the dining hall. "Want to take a walk?"

Britt waved them off, having overheard. "Go. You'll be no use to me anyway."

"Thanks, Britt." He grabbed the folder and Hannah's hand, but she stopped him.

"Why don't we put those in my office until the morning?" she suggested.

Instantly, his mind filled with images of taking her again against the wall, and his step quickened. By the time she'd opened her office doors, she was a little breathless, and he felt guilty for dragging her along so quickly.

After setting the papers down, he turned to her and pulled her into his arms. "Want to go for that walk now?" he asked, leaning against the edge of her desk.

"Not really." She snuggled into him. "What I want is right here." She kissed him and he melted.

"I didn't get to go slow earlier," he said, pulling her up until she was almost straddling him. She was even more beautiful when she was looking at him like she was now. After hoisting her skirt up, he gripped her butt and pulled her up until her knees were on the desk on either side of him.

"I'll forgive you . . . this time," she said as she ran her mouth over his. His hands moved farther up her thighs, enjoying her softness as she ground against him.

"I'll try to go slow . . ."

"You don't have to." Her eyes met his, and he felt himself growing harder. "I like it any way, as long as I'm with you."

When he reached the top of her thighs, he pulled back. "No underwear?" Her firm ass met the touch of his hands.

She smiled. "No time—I had to take a five-minute shower and rush out the door with my hair wet."

He swapped their positions fast to position her on the edge of the desk. "My god." He lifted her skirt and just looked down at her. "That is so damn sexy." Then he spread her thighs wider as she leaned back, and he enjoyed the blush that had started to spread on her face.

"Owen . . ." She tried to cover herself, but he stopped her.

"Tell me you're at least wearing a bra?" he asked, his eyes moving to her top.

She bit her bottom lip and then shook her head. "As I said, there wasn't any time, and I couldn't find . . ." She gasped when he reached up and nudged the thin straps off her shoulders. The light material fell, and he stopped her from reaching up so that the entire top fell around her waist.

"My god." His eyes soaked in the sight of her sitting on her desk, almost naked. "You are the most beautiful . . ." He leaned in and placed his mouth over her breast, taking her nipple into his mouth while he stepped between her thighs, spreading them even wider. His fingers found her, running over her slick skin until her hips started to move along with the motion. When he slid one finger into her, she moaned his name.

"I don't think I can wait," she said. "Please, Owen." She reached for his pants, but he stopped her by kneeling once more. This time, her legs were wrapped around his shoulders, and he encouraged her to ride his mouth as he used his tongue until he tasted her come in his mouth.

When he'd settled between her legs once more, he didn't hesitate to slide into her, moving her closer to the edge of the desk as he slid in and out of her, trying to make the feeling of being inside her last as long as he could.

Her nails dug into his hips, urging him on. When he felt her tighten around him this time, he allowed himself to follow her, telling her how he felt as he emptied everything he was into her.

CHAPTER
TWENTY-THREE

Hannah was floating the next morning. Spending an entire night making love with the man she loved should have made her so tired she couldn't move or think; instead, she was energized.

Owen was meeting with the closing company in her office, so she was camped out in Elle's office going over a few last-minute details for the Halloween party. They were working on how to keep new guests from hearing about what had happened during the previous party. Ensuring the guests' safety was their highest priority. Not to mention ensuring their own.

Dr. Val had removed those zip things from her skin, and even Hannah was surprised at the tiny line that was left. Still, it might be a while before she put on a two-piece swimsuit, but by next summer, she was pretty sure the scar would almost be invisible.

When Elle's phone rang, Hannah tried to ignore the conversation, until she heard Owen's name. Hannah glanced up, and Elle looked at her.

"Right," Elle was saying. "Okay, thanks." She hung up.

"Who was that?" she asked.

"Leo." Elle sighed. "Why he chooses to call me instead of . . ." She shook her head. "I think he knows that his sons won't obey his wishes unless they're positioned as requests from me."

"What does he want from Owen now?" Hannah asked.

"He needs to make sure that the guys stay put all next week. Things have taken a turn . . ." Elle frowned over at her. "Apparently, they found out who rented the van used to break into Owen's place."

Hannah sat up. "Who was it?"

"They aren't sure, but the bill was paid on a Paradise Investments corporate card."

She leaned back. "Which means it couldn't have been Ryan."

"Right." Elle twirled a piece of her hair. "That means someone at his office is trying to kill him and his father, and they probably won't stop there."

"Right, so what does he want us to do about it?" she asked.

"He wants to see if I can stop the plan they have about suing him for control of the business." Elle bit her lip.

"Yeah, right." She shook her head. "I don't think we can talk them out of it at this point."

"I know, but Leo says it's vital." She picked up her phone. "We need a Wildflower meeting."

"Oh, I'll go get the wine." She frowned. "Damn. It's only ten in the morning."

"Mimosas." Elle smiled. "Run and get champagne and orange juice and then meet back here in"—she glanced down at her watch—"ten minutes."

"Deal." Hannah jumped up and rushed out, still wincing a little from the quick motion. She bumped into Aubrey in the hallway and relayed the message before disappearing into the kitchen to get what she needed.

After grabbing a bottle of champagne and a carafe of orange juice, she balanced everything in her arms, along with five plastic glasses.

When she opened the office door again, everyone was already gathered around, talking.

"You open and pour," she said, sitting down. She handed the bottle to Aubrey.

Aubrey poured the first glass and handed it to her while Elle filled everyone in on what was going on.

Half an hour later, they each had their assignments to ensure that the Costa men would stay put at River Camp until the end of next week. Hannah seriously doubted she could go through with her plans. After all, first thing Monday morning, she had two scheduled days off.

Spending the night in bed with a man was one thing, but spending a whole two days in a cabin, alone with him, was a different matter.

"It will be perfect. Hannah and Owen will take Monday and Tuesday at the new cabin, then Elle and Liam will get the next two days, while Dylan and I will take the following. That way, they will be apart and not able to talk to one another. But everything depends on us sneaking their cell phones out of their bags. Along with getting rid of our own." Zoey went over the plan once more.

"Elle, without her cell?" Aubrey chuckled.

"Shut up! I can do it if it means Liam and his brothers will stay safe," Elle said. With a large smile on her face, she flipped Aubrey off.

"Yeah, anytime."

Elle laughed. "I'm not into—"

"Enough flirting, you two," Zoey broke in. "I'm late for my next event. Are we all up to date on the plan?"

"Yes," the women chorused.

Zoey started for the door but stopped. "Remember: don't bring your cell phones or any smart devices, not even your iPads or Apple Watches."

"Right," Elle said when everyone in the room looked at her. "Why does everyone have to pick on me?"

"Because you can't go five seconds without . . ." As Zoey spoke, Elle's phone chimed, and she glanced down at it. "See?"

Hannah chuckled.

"What?" Elle frowned up at her.

"Never mind." Hannah shook her head. "How you and Liam ever do it is beyond me."

Elle smiled and sighed wistfully. "He's a great distraction."

"Good. Use that for when you pack for your two nights."

"I won't forget. See?" She turned her phone toward her. "I set a reminder."

"Perfect." Hannah laughed as she carried her iPad back to her office.

Owen was sitting there, alone, going over some figures.

"Did everything go okay?" she asked as she opened the door.

"Yes." He smiled as he looked up from the paperwork. "I'm now the proud owner of six thousand acres." He stood up and kissed her quickly.

"You are? Not Paradise?" she asked, a little confused.

"I am. It was one of my stipulations with the board. This new venture will be my risk, with them earning fifteen percent of the profits."

"Why would you give them anything, if it's all your risk?" she asked.

"Simple. In order to use the Paradise Investments name and connections, I had to give them something." He shrugged. "I talked them down from thirty percent."

"What did your dad think of all that?" she asked.

"He was proud. I think he was even happier knowing that I wasn't trying to zero in on his job and had set out to do something different." He leaned back in the chair, and she watched as his eyes moved to the window behind her.

"I thought the board put you in charge of Paradise Investments?" she asked.

"They did, but now that Dad's back and proving himself . . ." He sighed. "He's promised them the money he took off with by the end of the month. Apparently he shoved it in some bank overseas."

"Oh," she said slowly.

"And we all know money can fix anything." Owen closed his eyes, and she could tell that it pained him. "All it took was a few days with me out of the way . . ."

"You know, I would never bring it up, normally, and I really can't believe I'm going to say this, but we should get our dads together." She bit her lip.

Owen surprised her by laughing. "Oh, that would be just the payback my dad deserves."

She grinned. "At least it would get my dad off my back, trying to convince you to work with him."

"Have they called you again?" he asked.

"Three times since . . . Ryan," she admitted.

"In any of those calls, did they ask how you were or if Ryan is locked up?" His eyes scanned her face as she thought about it.

"Not really." She'd learned long ago not to be too upset about her parents' lack of concern for her welfare. "They asked if you had any food allergies." A nervous chuckle escaped her lips. When he shook his head in question, she sighed. "They still think we're going up there for the holidays, and the other time it was to get your address at the office so they could send you flowers after I mentioned that you and your father had almost been blown up."

"Oh." He frowned. "I'm so sorry."

She shrugged it off. "I'm used to them. If you expect nothing, you won't be upset when you get it."

"That's a terrible way to look at your parents," he said.

"But it's worked for me." Her phone alarm sounded, and she stood up. "I have to go coach a beach ball soccer game on the beach. I love my life." She leaned in for a kiss before jogging outside.

She was in a great mood the rest of the day, enjoying her classes and the guests she ran into. The following day was much of the same. Each class went smoothly—each event had her laughing and enjoying herself even more. She really did love her job and where she was in life. Just knowing that in four days she would have a wonderful getaway with Owen had her almost dancing on air. One where they wouldn't be disturbed at all. Just like Elle, she was connected to her phone and smart devices. But most of her connections were circled around River Camp. If she had a day or two away from them, she was pretty sure she could live. Except for pictures.

She put a note on her phone to pack her old Canon camera so she could capture some of the beauty of the surrounding area. And maybe they could even use a couple of her pictures for the website. Most of the images that were up there were hers.

The Hideaway Cabin, as it had been christened, was on the outskirts of the campgrounds and only accessible now by horseback. Which meant that once Carter dropped them off there first thing Monday morning, they would be stuck there until he picked them up on Wednesday morning. That is, unless they wanted to hike out, but she would convince Owen to wait it out.

Two full days alone with him—she was both excited and nervous at the same time.

She was really good at keeping secrets. Actually, Zoey was the worst out of the bunch, but still, if she knew that Dylan's life was in danger, Zoey wouldn't break. Besides, she was the one who'd come up with the plan of getting the brothers out there and apart for the week anyway.

The cabin wasn't 100 percent ready for guests yet—Aiden's men were scheduled to finish up that week—but after some convincing, he put his men off till the next week. It was going to be perfect, since the few things that still had to be done were the phone system and the internet connection, along with some paint touch-ups.

Now all she had to do was convince Owen to head up there with her in a few days. She figured she'd wait until the last minute, since he was the kind of guy who packed days in advance. She was too, but for this trip she would refrain.

The entire camp was festively decorated. Pumpkins and bales of hay sat at every trailhead, along with a rather scary-looking scarecrow at the main trailhead that gave her the heebie-jeebies every time she passed it.

The rest of the main hall's decorations were arriving later today, and tomorrow was setup day for tomorrow night's main event. She was as excited about this party as she had been for the masquerade.

The first news article had caused more reporters to call in to the camp, but so far, she'd only talked to a few local ones. They had all agreed to try to turn the angle around and focus on the positives of the camp.

Watching a bunch of snowbirds running around the beach kicking a massive soccer beach ball was a tough job. She laughed more than she had in days, which caused her side to pain her some. But it was totally worth it.

After that game, she walked over and got bottled water at the pool bar and met with a small group of people for a nature hike.

This was another favorite of hers: telling people about the flora and fauna of the surrounding area. To learn everything she knew, she'd taken a local class from the state park down the road. There was no better way to make a living than walking through the woods and doing something she loved. It was a far cry from the job she'd had working at her father's company. The travel alone had almost killed her. She'd been on a plane so often that she had sometimes forgotten where she was. Not to mention that flying that frequently had messed up her internal clock. She'd barely gotten a full night's sleep when she'd found out that Elle's grandfather had passed away. Dropping everything to come to be with her friend turned out to have saved her life as well. She supposed she'd always known she'd end up here with her best friends. They had been the only ones in her life who had ever mattered.

Growing up, she'd believed that she was the only one whose life was ruled and ruined by her parents. Yet since meeting Owen's dad, she could see a little of that in Owen as well. Just knowing they were in the same boat drew them closer.

She'd seen it the moment she'd met him. It was like finding like.

"Hannah!" Levi Grant called out to her as she made her way up to the main hall for lunch after her hike. Turning, she waited for the man to jog up to her. Levi was one of the best employees they had. Just like Owen and his brothers, Levi filled in wherever he was needed. He usually got everyone around him laughing at some of his jokes. The first talent show they had, he'd gotten up and done a stand-up comedy routine and had killed it. So much so that they had made him a regular in their shows. His strawberry-blond hair was shorter than normal now, since he'd cut off his curls and kept it short during the hotter months. He was one of the few employees who lived in Pelican Point. Elle had known him her entire life. He'd been raised by his grandmother, just like Elle had been raised by her grandfather. Hannah didn't know his whole story, but she understood that it was just as tragic, if not more so, than Elle's.

"What's up?"

"I was wondering—that is, I was hoping you would allow me to bring my gran tomorrow night?" he asked nervously. "Elle said it was okay if . . ."

"Yes." She touched his arm. "Of course. How is your grandmother?"

"She's okay—I appreciate being able to bring her. She's pretty lonely since her best friend, Robin, passed away earlier this year."

"Oh, I'm so sorry. Of course, your grandmother is always welcome."

"Great." He smiled. "I got my costume today. It's amazing! It was smart to request that guests not wear masks through the security line this time."

"Yes." She held back a shiver.

He must have noticed her concern, since he changed the subject. "How do you know all the right places to get these great costumes?"

She chuckled. "I have my . . ."

"Secrets." He laughed. "Yeah." He shook his head. "I have to go." He started walking backward toward the opposite side of the camp. "I'm helping . . ." He didn't get any farther, since Scarlett was rushing toward Hannah, and Levi bumped solidly into her. "Oh gosh, sorry," he said, turning around quickly.

Scarlett looked irritated enough that Hannah winced.

"Really? This is the third time today," she said, and it was then that Hannah realized that Scarlett had been holding a plastic glass of iced tea that had spilled down her top.

Instead of getting upset, Levi chuckled. "Maybe I like seeing you wet."

Hannah's eyes grew big, but instead of getting upset, Scarlett stepped closer to Levi. "In your dreams, funny boy." She stepped around him, and Hannah snapped her mouth shut before Scarlett could see her. Scarlett took Hannah's arm and started walking into the dining hall.

"What the heck was that all about?" Hannah asked, glancing back over her shoulder at Levi, who was watching their departure and grinning like a loon.

"He has a thing for me." Scarlett waved him off, and, when they stepped into the dining hall, Hannah turned to her.

"Duh," she teased. "You have one right back for him."

Scarlett laughed. "I do not."

"Is that man still standing?" She waved toward the closed door.

Scarlett frowned. "I don't go around slugging each guy that bumps into me."

"Three times in a day?" she asked.

"He's a klutz." She shrugged.

Hannah laughed. "Scarlett and Levi, sitting in a tree . . ." she started, only to have Scarlett hiss at her.

"Shut up." She glanced around. "That's the last thing I need around here—rumors about my love life."

Hannah's eyebrows shot up. "So, you do have a love life?"

Scarlett rolled her eyes. "No, and certainly not with the class clown."

"Why not? If my class clown had looked like Levi . . ." She wiggled her eyebrows at her friend.

"I came here to tell you . . ." She pulled Hannah into the hallway near the bathrooms. "I overheard Owen and Dylan talking. They're planning something for Monday."

"What?" She focused now.

"I don't know. They were whispering, and all I heard was, 'We'll deal with it on Monday.'"

"Okay?" She frowned and glanced around the room, spotting the three brothers grabbing their own lunches. "There's only one way to find out," Hannah said.

"Ask?" Scarlett said, her eyes on the brothers across the room as well.

"Heck, no." Hannah turned to her friend with a smile. "Sneak around and find out."

She walked off to the sound of Scarlett's chuckles.

CHAPTER
TWENTY-FOUR

Everything was set for Monday. Owen and his brothers had a solid plan for him to return to Destin without his father knowing. Their only hurdle now was Hannah and her friends. And at this point, it was looking more like a mountain instead of a hurdle.

Ever since yesterday during lunch, she'd been asking him questions about his plans with his father. He'd told her that they were still in a holding pattern, but something told him that she wasn't buying it any longer.

He'd figured that if he'd told her that he was planning on returning to work on Monday morning, she'd try to talk him out of it. Even his brothers were keeping that information from Zoey and Elle.

He hated keeping things from her but knew that it would be easier than arguing with her about going. He had to go. Nothing was getting done. Their plan was failing. He needed to be able to put all of this behind him so that he could move forward in life—to be with Hannah like he wanted, not to be with her because he was told to stay put by his father and the feds. He was done taking orders.

All day long, he'd helped Hannah and her crew turn the dining hall into a spectacular spooky hall of horrors, as she was calling it.

Once again, she'd outdone herself. She had a talent for pulling things like this together using only paper and tape.

She'd rented a huge blow-up spider they'd suspended over everyone's head. Its long legs had been a bitch to hang up, but now that he was done climbing ladders, he had to admit that it looked great.

As with the masquerade party, Isaac and his crew were making specialty items for dinner and the party. This time, however, the party would be limited to just guests.

He had never been one to get into Halloween, not really. Sure, he and his brothers had dressed up and run around collecting candy from neighbors, but as an adult, he'd never thought of the event as anything other than a night to see kids parading around his condo building doing the same.

He realized that he was actually looking forward to tonight's party. He still didn't know what costume Hannah had gotten for him, but she did tell him that he and his brothers would be wearing black shirts and pants underneath it, so he figured it couldn't be too bad. Could it?

"When do I get to know what I'll be dressed as tonight?" he asked as they walked out of the dining hall.

"You and your brothers' costumes are all down at the pool house." He groaned.

"Hey, you liked the last surprise, didn't you?" She stopped and turned toward him.

"Yes." He smiled, remembering how sexy she'd looked at the masquerade party. Then frowned when he remembered seeing the blood-covered dress pooled on the floor after it had been cut from her.

"Then, I suggest you head on down there and get ready." She rose up on her toes and kissed him. "We women have a lot more things to do, and we need you men out of our way while we change."

"Yes, ma'am." He smiled at her, and as he walked toward the pool house, images of Hannah in a sexy little outfit played in his mind.

Showering in a large shower room with his brothers was like being back in high school football. Still, after seeing the cool playing-card-king outfits the three of them would be wearing, he had to admit that Hannah had picked the perfect costumes.

There were notes attached to each one. He had the king of hearts, Dylan was the king of clubs, and Liam was the king of diamonds.

He wondered if there was a king of spades in the deck and what Scarlett and Aubrey would be dressed as, but since there were only three costumes, they all got ready. The black shirts and jeans formed the base; then they pulled on the rest of their outfits. When they all stood facing the mirror, he realized that they all looked so alike that it would be hard for anyone to tell them apart. The only differences in their outfits were the crowns.

"Wow, I never thought we looked alike until now," Dylan said with a chuckle.

"It's kind of freaky," Liam added.

"Do you think the girls did this on purpose?" Dylan asked. "You know." His brother wiggled his dark eyebrows. "To see if they could tell who was who?"

Owen chuckled. "They could spot a dork a mile away."

"Oh, so they can at least tell you apart from us," Liam pointed out quickly, earning him a punch in the arm from Owen.

"Good one, brother." Dylan slapped Owen on the shoulder. "We're supposed to help set up the food trays. It's buffet-style tonight."

"Yeah, have either Zoey or Elle been asking a lot of questions lately?" he asked as they walked toward the dining hall.

"They always ask a lot of questions," Liam pointed out.

"I mean, specific ones. Hannah has been all over me about Monday. It's almost like she knows something," he said; then Dylan stopped walking and looked at him.

"Yeah, Zoey was asking me this morning about my plans for Monday. I thought it was strange because I don't have the day off. So I told her it's just another day in paradise with my dream job and girl."

"Corny." Liam rolled his eyes. "Elle did ask me if we could have a special lunch on the beach on Monday. I didn't think anything about it, until now."

"They know." Owen sighed. "They have to. I mean, Hannah asked for my schedule, even though she can easily see it on the group calendar. Of course, we all knew you guys were going to cover for me, but still."

"Let's see how tonight plays out," Liam said, slapping him on his back. "If you still think they know after tonight, then maybe we should tell them?"

Dylan visibly shivered. "I promised Zoey I wouldn't keep secrets anymore. This has been killing me, and when I tell her . . . I may really die."

They walked into the main hall, finished setting up all the silver trays, and lit the oil lamps underneath them. As the food was being wheeled out, the women walked in.

"Wow." Liam backhanded Owen in the gut, getting his attention. When he turned and saw the five women standing in the doorway, he felt as if a sledgehammer had been taken to his gut.

"They look amazing," Dylan said, his grin practically reaching his ears.

Owen easily found Hannah; after all, there was a large red heart on the sexy white corset she was wearing. Zoey's top had the matching club, and Elle's diamond matched Liam's. Aubrey was the spade, while Scarlett wore a joker symbol.

"A full deck. Dibs on the diamond," he said, rushing across the room and taking Elle into his arms.

Owen shook his head as Hannah made her way toward him. "Wow," he said, admiring the view. Her short skirt flared out as black-and-white-striped nylons covered her long legs.

"Thanks." She smiled. "I didn't realize it would be so hard to tell you three apart in these." She reached up to kiss him, but he stopped her.

"How do you know you've got the right brother?" he joked before leaning in and kissing her.

"Is everything ready?" She stepped out of his arms. "No, that table doesn't go there." She rushed across the room to stop two employees from dragging a table in front of the stage.

"And she's off." He sighed and watched her and her friends finish preparing everything.

As guests started flooding into the room, he was pulled over to help make sure everyone knew how to go through the buffet line. It shouldn't be hard; after all, people ate at buffets all the time, right? So why was everyone constantly asking him how to do it?

The plates and silverware were first, followed by drinks and the main course, sides, and desserts. A little over an hour later, he realized it was seriously like herding a bunch of cats.

Less than two hours into the party, Owen was tired of hearing Michael Jackson's "Thriller," even though it was a really great song; he was just over it.

As he stepped out of the back door to get some fresh air, he ran into Dylan.

"It's stuffy in there tonight," he said, leaning against the railing of the stairs.

"Totally. How can it be raining and still eighty degrees out?" Dylan asked, combing a hand through his hair.

Owen chuckled. "Global warming." He shrugged and looked out over the foggy, spooky grounds. "Perfect night for a Halloween party, though. It's as if she has the ability to arrange the weather." He sighed.

"You've got it bad," Dylan surprised him by saying.

"Bad?"

"You're in love," Dylan blurted out.

"Yeah." He nodded, thinking about how much he cared for Hannah. How much it would hurt him if she wasn't in his life. "I love her."

"No." Dylan shook his head. "Not just love her, you're *in* love."

"Yeah." He frowned. "Same thing."

Dylan laughed. "No, it's not." He slapped him on the back. "Loving someone and being in love are two totally different things."

"Suuuuuuure," he teased as Dylan walked back into the dining hall.

Leaning back on the post, he thought about their relationship. Sure, he loved Hannah. He'd even told her several times now. He wanted a future with her; that much was true as well. It had scared the hell out of him when Ryan had attacked her. He would have done anything to protect her. Anything. What in the world was his brother talking about?

After he stepped back into the hall, it took a moment for his eyes to adjust to the darkness as he scanned the crowd for his queen of hearts.

Spotting Zoey, he made his way across the room.

"Hey." He pulled her aside. "Have you seen my queen?"

"She was just"—Zoey's eyes flitted over the crowd—"here some-where. She might have stepped into the kitchen." She started to move.

"No, I'll go look, thanks," he said. He moved to the back of the room and then avoided running into a few people taking empty plates into the kitchen.

"Have you seen Hannah?" he asked Scarlett, who was grabbing a bottle of champagne for some guests.

"No, not in the last half hour," she said.

"Where did you see her last?" he asked.

"With you by the stage—I figured you guys had snuck off into a closet." She winked at him and disappeared out the doorway.

He felt his heart skip. He hadn't talked to her since they had first arrived. She'd been too busy, and he'd been stuck helping herd the guests. Maybe Scarlett had seen one of his brothers talking to her and thought it was him?

After stepping back into the dining hall, he glanced around once more. Then, seeing both of his brothers talking to Elle, he made his way over to them.

"Any of you see Hannah in the last half hour?" he asked. "Scarlett says she saw her talking to one of us by the stage."

"It wasn't me. I haven't spoken to her all night," Dylan said.

"Me either," Liam added, and Owen had a sudden sinking feeling in his gut.

"We need to find her now." Urgency filled his voice and surged through his soul.

Hannah stood back and watched yet another successful party unfold. She loved making things come together, seeing the outcome of her hard work, watching people enjoy themselves. She was so happy that the guests had gotten into the fun of dressing up. Of course, there were a few who only wore their regular clothes, but at least the majority of them were dressed up.

Her friends had been so excited when she'd pitched the playing card idea. Finding the best outfits had been a little harder, since they needed all the same styles. She was lucky when she found three matching outfits for Dylan, Liam, and Owen. It took her a lot longer to find her and her friends' dresses. In the end, she had to order them from an online company instead of renting them, like she'd wanted to. But since she knew they would probably get more use out of them next year, she figured the cost was worth it.

With her worry about the case against Ryan in the back of her mind, she tried to focus on her future with Owen and the possibilities ahead of her.

The buffet was turning out to be a good idea, and she planned on adding that feature to a few nights a month. That is, if they could get guests to understand where the line started.

She watched Owen try to guide everyone to where they needed to be and could tell he was having a difficult time of it. She made a mental note to create signs that would help out next time. Maybe even order a sign online that said, "The line starts here."

Just as everyone had finished up with dinner, she spotted Owen near the stage and smiling and decided to see if they could have a moment alone together. He looked so sexy in his outfit. She was happy to see that he'd kept the outfit on all night. She knew he wasn't really one for playing dress-up, but at least he was easy enough to sit back and enjoy himself.

"Hey," she said, coming up behind him. Before he had a chance to talk, she pulled him into the back hallway and kissed him.

Instantly, she knew it wasn't Owen and jerked away to apologize, but then she saw it wasn't Dylan or Liam either. The man's arms tightened around her waist painfully, and just as she opened her mouth to scream, his fist plowed into the side of her head, sending her into darkness.

CHAPTER
TWENTY-FIVE

With all the lights on in the dining hall, and everyone still in their costumes, search parties were selected to start going over the grounds, looking for any clue of Hannah.

Since she wasn't officially missing, Reed and his friends took charge instead of the police. Brett had informed him that he couldn't spare too many people to help, since several fights had broken out at a large Halloween party and they were stretched too thin to spare many people. In the end, five uniformed officers helped out.

Later, Owen and his brothers had discarded their costumes, though Hannah's friends were still wearing theirs, too worried to even think about what they were wearing or heading up to change.

"I've tried calling her like a million times," Elle cried. "I even used the 'find my phone' app. It's like her phone is off. Or dead." She started to weep again and was immediately hugged by the rest of them.

"We'll find her. We're going to go cabin by cabin," Reed assured her. "Everyone has their designated areas. You ladies should stay here.

Maybe head up to your place and change? We'll all check back here in half an hour."

"Okay." Zoey started nudging them toward the doorway.

"I'll call you when we find her," Dylan said to her.

Owen followed his brothers out of the building and headed to their designated search area.

"Think we should call Dad?" Liam asked.

"Why?" Dylan turned to look at him.

"I don't know." Liam shrugged. "I mean, this could have something to do with . . . you know."

Owen's blood drained from his face, and he stopped walking. He'd thought of that, but his mind had blanked at the idea of Hannah in trouble again.

After pulling out his phone, he punched his dad's number and cursed when he hit the wrong digit three times.

"Don't you have it programmed?" Liam asked.

"Yes, but I thought this would be faster," he growled when he finally got it right.

His father's phone rang several times before going to voice mail.

"He's not answering." He hit the end button.

"Which could mean nothing." Dylan sighed. "Let's search here first and keep trying. Dad could be taking a piss for all we know."

"What about his buddy, the fed?" He pulled out his phone, and this time he did a search. Finding the contact for Ron Burgess, he hit the number.

The man answered on the first ring. "How did you get this number?" he asked.

"Ron, this is—"

"I know who this is. How did you get this number?" he asked again.

"From my father."

He heard a groan. "What do you want?"

"I don't know if this has anything to do with . . . what's going on with our dad, but my girlfriend is missing, and now our dad isn't answering—"

"Where are you?"

"The camp—" he started, but the man hung up the phone. "That went well."

He felt like throwing his phone but tucked it back into his pocket instead.

"You told him. Let's go make our sweep here before we jump to any more conclusions," Dylan said.

"Would you be so calm if it was Zoey?" he asked, his voice rising with each word.

"I'm not calm. I may look it, but trust me." Dylan laid a hand on his shoulder, and Owen could see he was telling the truth. "I'm scared shitless, but right now, we don't know if she's just delivering something to a cabin or . . . fallen down a well." He threw up his hands in frustration.

"There aren't any wells on the property," Liam said, earning him a glare from Dylan.

They each took point, separating groups of guests and sending them out to sweep, knock on doors, and search every cabin or building they had been assigned to. When the brothers returned to the dining hall, it was to find out that no one else had found her either.

"Where was she last?" Owen asked Scarlett again. The ladies had changed into jeans, T-shirts, and tennis shoes.

"There." She pointed to the now brightly lit area by the stage.

"Someone checked the hallway?" he asked, moving over to the spot.

A few people acknowledged that with a wave.

After stepping into the hallway, he flipped on the light and looked around. The small space was packed with extra chairs and tables, but just as he was about to turn around, he spotted something red and bent down to touch the drops of blood on the ground.

"Blood!" he called out as he rubbed it between his fingers. Looking around, he noticed a small red hat that had fallen between two rows of chairs. He reached in and retrieved the queen of hearts hat that had sat on Hannah's head.

His vision grayed as he looked down at his bloody fingers, and he knew without a doubt that something bad had happened to her.

When Hannah finally woke, she immediately started to gag on the piece of cloth that had been shoved deep down her throat. Blood dripped down the side of her face from a cut just above her eye. Already, she could feel the swelling from where the man's fist had connected.

Looking around, she tried to allow her eyes to adjust to the darkness. But with all the blood blocking her left eye, it was too hard to focus on anything.

She went to move but realized that her hands were tied behind her back. As she tried to free them, she found that whatever was holding her arms was also tied to her feet.

"There she is." She heard Joel's voice from somewhere in the room.

She tried to talk, to scream, but all that came out was a muffled sound.

"Oh, I wouldn't try talking too much. It dries the throat out." He chuckled.

She stilled. She hadn't known Joel that well, back when they had gone to school together, but she'd never known him to sound like this. Fear shot through her.

"You know . . ." His voice grew closer. "If it wasn't for your overbearing parents, I would have fucked you long ago." She felt a hand run up the side of her face, and she jerked away from it. "I take it you didn't know that your old man paid me off to stop seeing you? Got a cool ten grand out of breaking it off with you, but of course, I had fun seeing the hurt in your eyes first."

He gripped her face, pinching her cheeks tightly in his fingers. She cried out with pain, but he held her still. "I would have never imagined I'd be so lucky to get my hands on you again." He ran his hand down her chin and over her neck, squeezing enough that she cried out again, then moved farther down to cover her left breast. He pinched it hard once before stepping away from her.

"But there's no time right now to play," he said; then suddenly a phone's light filled the room, and she got her first look at him. He was still wearing an outfit matching the one she'd picked out for Owen. His eyes flew over the message on his phone.

"It appears that my dear brother's girlfriend has gone missing." He turned the phone off, and the room was once again flooded in darkness. "I'm going to have to drop everything—once again!—to help out for nothing. You'll be safe here; after all, you do want to keep *him* company." She heard him kick something; then a grunt came from someone else in the room.

Tears streamed down her face while she watched as a soft light from a doorway filled the room when Joel walked out. Then she was once again shadowed in darkness.

Instantly, she started wiggling, trying to break her hands free from the ropes that bound her. She turned from side to side, rolling around the ground, until she bumped into something solid.

She tried to speak again but gagged on the cloth, which caused her to throw up a little in her mouth. She swallowed the bile and shivered, then tried to steady her breathing through her nose. After flipping over, she used her hands to try to figure out who the other person in the room was. Unable to determine that, she felt the ropes binding his hands. If only she had something sharp, she could cut him loose; then, once he woke, he could get her loose as well, and they could escape.

She remembered the bobby pins in her hair and wondered if any of them were still around.

But then she felt the man's hands start to move over her ropes, and she held still while he worked on freeing her.

The dining hall was now flooded with even more people. Most of the guests, having been roused so that the search parties could look in their cabins, had flooded into the space, wanting to help look for Hannah.

More police had shown up, and they took the blood samples and Hannah's crown as evidence.

Of course, Owen and his brothers were questioned, along with Scarlett and the rest of them.

Even some of the kitchen staff sat around answering questions. He didn't see how this would help find Hannah, but since he didn't have any other ideas, he waited around.

Someone had gone to the house in Pelican Point to confirm she hadn't returned there. They came back empty handed, which made him even more anxious.

Joel showed up after Dylan had sent him a text message.

They still hadn't gotten ahold of their father, and Owen was beginning to wonder if his dad had anything to do with Hannah's disappearance.

Doubts of the past few months surfaced. Could his dad have planned the whole thing? His disappearance, the threats Owen had received when he'd taken over the company? Hannah's disappearance?

His father had told Owen about receiving his own threatening notes; he'd never really seen any of those firsthand. Then, there was the matter of the car exploding. He'd unlocked the car just as they had stepped into the parking garage. With an excuse to get Owen out of the way, he'd been free to take over again while giving Owen and his brothers a reason to stay put.

But why? If his dad was behind everything, why had he left in the first place? He had already been in charge.

Then, when Joel stepped into the dining hall, his mind cleared. It was as if his eyes had been opened for the first time.

"It's Joel," he said quietly, pulling Dylan aside. "It has to be. Scarlett said Hannah was talking to me. If it wasn't you or Liam . . ." He glanced over to the only other man who could have easily fit in with the brothers. Liam chatted away with Joel, seemingly unaware of the tension.

Dylan's face paled. "Shit."

"He's trying to ruin dad's business because he won't acknowledge him as his son." Owen's thoughts ran through everything. "He had a key to my apartment. Knew about the security codes. He could even rent the van under the corporate business card." He closed his eyes and took a deep breath. "He used to date Hannah in high school."

"What?" Dylan jerked his head toward him.

"Long story, but it's obvious now."

"What do we do?" Dylan hissed as Joel glanced their way.

Owen stepped in front of Dylan and waved to the man as if nothing was amiss. Then he turned back to his brother.

"We go along for a while until we can figure out what he did with Hannah," he answered.

"What about Dad?" Dylan asked.

"If he doesn't show up soon, then I'd say Hannah isn't the only one we should be worried about."

"Shit," he heard Dylan say just as Joel started walking toward them.

"I came as soon as I could. Liam filled me in on what happened." Joel looked concerned. If the man had had anything to do with Hannah's disappearance, there was no hint of it in his eyes.

"Thanks." Owen reached out and shook his hand. He wanted to pummel the guy and demand he tell him where Hannah and his father were, but instead, he turned away. "We're still waiting on the police at this point." He averted his gaze from Joel and turned to Dylan.

"Why don't you go fill Liam in on what we just found out. He's over there comforting Elle." He motioned to his brother across the way. Dylan left as directed.

"What did you just find out?" Joel asked.

Thankfully, Owen had prepared for the question.

"The blood we found in the back hallway was Hannah's blood type," he lied.

Joel shifted and glanced around. "What can I do to help?"

Owen thought about it while he looked around. "There really isn't anything any of us can do. If someone has her, we either need to wait for a ransom demand or . . ." He thought about the possibility of Hannah not coming back to him, whole, and shivered.

"Hey." Joel touched his arm. "I'm sure she's okay."

Owen's eyes met Joel's, and unless the man was the best actor in the world, he was telling the truth.

"I hope so, because if anything happens to her . . ." He let his words sink in as his eyes heated. Joel looked away quickly.

"Who is that?" Joel nodded toward someone across the room.

Owen took a moment longer to assess Joel before turning around and seeing who he had indicated.

"Reed Cooper. He used to be special . . ." He rubbed a hand over his jaw. "Never mind. He's been helping out around here with some security issues we've had." No point in tipping their hand.

"Nothing serious, I hope?" Joel asked.

"No," he lied again.

For the next few minutes, Owen stayed by Joel's side while his brothers kept their distance.

When the lead detective who Brett had told them was in charge asked everyone to return to their cabins, the small group of people who were left gathered in the employee dining room.

"You might as well head home," he told Joel, adding a bit of frustration into his voice.

"Yeah." Joel wiped his hand over his neck, as if he'd worked hard that day. Which he hadn't. "It looks like they don't have much to go on."

"Not yet," he said, and he watched Joel's expression change slightly. "But there's no reason for all of us to stay up all night. Thanks for coming out all this way." He shook his hand again.

"It's no problem. It's not like I had far to go." He smiled, then waved. "Night."

The moment Joel stepped out of the room, Owen's brothers rushed to his side.

"We're going to follow him," he said, and he nodded toward the women. "Did you tell them anything?"

"No, we thought . . . no." Dylan shook his head. "Let's go."

"I can't ask you . . ." he started to say.

"Fuck that; let's go." Liam walked toward the doorway.

After they stepped out, they watched Joel's truck drive out of the parking lot.

"We'll take my car." Dylan rushed toward his Tesla. "It's the fastest and the quietest."

They didn't argue but instead jumped in and sat back as Dylan punched it and flew down the driveway, catching up with the truck just outside town.

"Can you drive with the lights off?" Liam asked. "Like they do in the movies?"

"No, it's a safety feature now," Dylan answered. "But I doubt he knows we're back here. We're three cars behind him."

"Keep it that way if you can," Owen said, feeling his palms start to sweat.

"Should we have a gun?" Liam asked. "Or . . . some kind of weapon?"

"No, but I'm going to text Reed and let him know what's up. Then text him again when we get where we're going." Owen pulled out his phone and sent a detailed but quick message to Reed's phone.

Reed texted back immediately.

Let me know. I'm heading your way. Drop a pin on your phone's map when you get there.

Owen texted him which highway they were on and the direction they were heading. So far, they were only heading into the Destin area.

Then, after the bridge, Joel turned left instead of right, and Owen had a sinking feeling he was heading back to the office.

"Is he going to the office?" Dylan asked. "His place is to the right." He took the turn, barely making the light. They were four cars behind him now, and the streetlights were lighting up everything. Dylan reminded his brothers that Teslas weren't a standard occurrence on the roads around here yet and that he wanted to keep a bigger distance between them.

When Joel's truck pulled into the office building's empty parking lot, they parked across the street at the gas station and watched him get out of the truck and disappear inside.

"She has to be there," Owen said. "It took less than fifteen minutes to get here. He could have kidnapped her, dropped her off, and still had plenty of time before he showed back at the camp."

"Yeah," Dylan said, leaning closer to the windshield as if getting a better view of the tall building.

"The question is: What do we do now? That building is huge. Six floors, more than two hundred offices . . ." Liam started, earning him a glare from Dylan. "Sorry, it's just . . . I'm trying to be practical here."

"You're not good at it. Owen's the practical one." Dylan turned to Owen. "Well? What's our next move?"

Owen's eyes had been glued to the building, and when a light on the main floor turned on, his anger spiked, replacing most of the worry he had for Hannah. "We go in and confront him."

CHAPTER
TWENTY-SIX

Hannah stood with her palms to the wall, hiding the fact that her hands were now free behind her back, waiting for the door to open. She'd removed the gag from Leo's mouth and had been in the process of untying him when they noticed the lights go on again under the door. He'd pushed her toward the wall and told her to run the moment the door opened. She didn't know where he was now, but she figured he was going to prevent Joel from chasing her.

The fact that she didn't know where they were, which way to run, or even if she could run far scared her enough that her entire body shook while they waited for Joel to return.

She'd searched the room after getting free, but there was literally nothing in it. It was a five-by-five square room with not even a chair in it. They could have been anywhere.

"How did you get here?" Leo had asked her immediately when she'd removed his gag.

"Leo?" she mumbled.

"Yes. Hannah, right?"

"Yes. I don't know. I was at the party at River Camp, and then . . ." She shook her head. "Joel hit me over the head, and I woke up here."

Then she'd busied herself trying to untie Leo's ropes.

Now, she closed her eyes as she heard the door handle jiggle.

The moment the door swung open, Leo threw himself at Joel. The momentum of their bodies almost caused her to stumble as she jumped out the doorway and took off.

A smaller office with glass doors loomed. After pushing her way through the doors, she glanced around and realized she'd been here before. This was Owen's office building. His office was on the third floor. She didn't remember which floor she was on now but raced toward where she remembered the main bank of elevators was. As she glanced over her shoulder, she was imagining Joel running after her just as she bumped into strong arms that gripped her tight.

Fighting and kicking out, she was preparing herself to do anything to get free when she heard Owen's voice.

"I'm here, baby." He held on to her, and she heard the relief in his tone. "My god. I've got you."

"Owen?" she cried out, and she felt her knees go weak. He gripped her tighter.

"Shh," he said, kissing her hair and then her lips. "I've got you. You're safe now."

"Your dad," she said once the initial shock was over. "He's got your dad."

He turned to Liam, who she just realized was standing next to him, along with Dylan. "Take Hannah outside and wait for the cops." He handed her over to his brother and ran toward the room she had just flown out of.

When Liam started walking her away from them, she pushed away from him and followed Owen and Dylan into the office, where Joel and their father were still fighting.

It didn't take the brothers long to pull Joel off their father. The man's fists had been plowing into Leo's face relentlessly. Leo still had his hands tied behind his back and was sporting black eyes and a massive bloody lip.

"Dad?" Liam rushed over as his brothers held on to Joel.

"I told you to take her outside," Owen hissed.

"I'm not going to leave you in here," she said with authority. "I'm not some weakling that needs to be sheltered. I just escaped by myself."

"With a little help." Leo sighed as he leaned against the wall, letting Liam use his pocketknife to cut through the ropes still binding him.

"Fuckers!" Joel screamed. "You're all fuckers."

"That's enough." Owen pushed Joel into the office chair and jerked it forward until they were eye to eye. "We're going to start at the beginning while we wait for the cops to get here." Blood dripped from a large gash on Joel's lip, and it looked like Leo had headbutted him, since his nose appeared broken.

"Fuck you," Joel spat.

Owen raised his fist, his anger at the boiling point. But before he bashed the man's face in, he had to know why. Letting his fist fall to his side, he asked, "Is this because Dad won't acknowledge you as his son?"

Hannah watched as Joel smiled, opening the cut on his lip even more. "I'm not his son." He spat blood.

"He's not." Leo shocked them all by standing up, with the help of Liam. "He's my nephew."

"*What?*" Owen, Dylan, and Liam said at the same time.

"You're an only child," Owen pointed out.

"I am now." Leo sat down on the sofa across the room. "My sister, Stella, was fourteen years younger than me." Hurt and pain flooded Leo's eyes. "I was your age when my best friend raped her. She was only sixteen." He cried and put his face into his hands. "She gave birth to Joel, then, two months later, killed herself." Tears rolled down his face. "Robert Mitchell." He motioned to Joel. "His father, my best friend,

271

went to jail for five years. Only five years, after which he gained full custody of the only thing that I had left that reminded me of Stella."

"Did you ever have custody of Joel?" Owen asked.

"For the first three years of his life, your mother and I raised him as our own. We brought him home a year before we had you." He leaned back and took a deep breath. "But the Mitchell family had friends in high places back then, and shortly after Robert was released, Joel was ripped from our arms and raised by a monster."

"He wasn't a monster!" Joel shouted.

"Wasn't?" Hannah finally spoke. "From what I knew, you'd been adopted by a family in New York . . . Copeland . . ." She shook her head.

"Rhonda Copeland was Robert's sister."

Leo answered for Joel, who was just sitting in the chair looking at them. "Because of legal reasons, Rhonda officially adopted Joel, while Robert acted as guardian. Carl died shortly after Joel turned ten."

"How do you know all that?" Owen asked.

"Because, a few years back, I hired a friend to track Joel down. When I found him shortly after he'd graduated, I brought him here, hired him on, and tried to make everything up to him." Leo sighed.

Owen turned to Joel. "You're my cousin!" he shouted. "Why would you do something like this?" He motioned around them, at all the blood smearing the white tiled floors.

"It's what I do." He smiled. "Break up families." He chuckled, and Hannah felt a shiver rush down her back. Wrapping her arms around her, she stepped up to Owen.

"You tried to rape me too." Her eyes narrowed, and she felt Owen tense beside her.

"You son of a . . ." Owen raised his fist, but Hannah grabbed it and stopped him. "No, not now. Back in high school. It was the reason we broke up. He tried . . ." She sighed. "I should have known . . . I should have told someone, but you shamed me by having all your friends call me Cherry for the rest of the school year."

He chuckled. "I'd forgotten about that." His eyes flew to Owen. "So, did you pop that one—"

He didn't get any further, since Owen's fist sent Joel's head snapping back as more blood spurted from his now very obviously broken nose.

No one in the room made a move to stop Owen from hitting him the first time, but Hannah grabbed his arm and stopped his second blow. After all, Joel was still sitting in the chair with Owen hovering over him.

"He's not worth it," she told Owen.

"That's the whole point!" Joel shouted and laughed. "All this." He motioned around them. "Everything you have will be gone. Soon." His eyes narrowed.

"Why?" Liam asked. "We've taken you in, treated you like family."

"We *are* family!" Joel yelled. "And look at what you have; look at where I'm at. Do you want to know what happened to my dear stepfather who used to beat me? Carl Copeland was a monster. Robert, my old man, couldn't even be bothered to raise me himself, so he dumped me with my stepdad. All my stepfather ever did was come over and tell me how worthless I was. So, I slipped a little rat poison into Carl's coffee each morning after he'd beat me, until one day . . ." He made a choking sound and then laughed. "It felt so good to get away from Carl that, less than a year later, I added Robert to my list to be dealt with someday, since he'd abandoned me to that psycho." His eyes turned to Leo. "But when you came knocking on my door, I knew instantly who you were. All Robert could talk about was being betrayed by his best friend. My mother, the whore, had led my dad on. She was the one who had spread her legs, tempting him, begging him for sex." He laughed when Leo tried to stand up and rush him, but Liam held him back.

"Liar!" Leo screamed. "I caught him raping her. He had her tied down." He collapsed into Liam's arms. "She was only sixteen." He cried. "Robert was twenty-four. He should have rotted in that cell, instead of his freedom being bought by his wealthy parents. He never should have gotten custody of you. You should have grown up in a loving family, instead of being raised by that . . . bastard. I swore then and there that I would never let something like that happen to my own children or to anyone I loved ever again." Leo took a deep breath. "I only wanted to shelter you by keeping the truth hidden."

"You lied to me!" Joel screamed.

"No, I never lied. I never said you were my son."

"Lies by omission," Joel spat out.

"That's my fault. I should have told you the truth. I wasn't strong enough to tell you or my own sons. I thought by keeping it from you, the negative circumstances wouldn't prevent you from having a fresh start."

"Too late." Joel laughed.

"What about the espionage and the embezzlement? That was you too, wasn't it?" Leo asked.

Joel sneered at them, and Owen could see that no matter what his family had done, Joel had been too far gone to be helped. "It was so easy, after I gained everyone's trust. After all, since you hadn't confessed to being my uncle, everyone assumed I was your illegitimate son. They gave me access to everything around here. I had everything I could ever want." His eyes grew dark. "Except you and your sons stood in my way."

"What was your plan? To wipe us all out?" Owen asked.

"Yes, until Leo took off. It was so simple: a family vacation, something happening to the private jet, or better yet, a slow leak from the gas heater in the winter cabin you rented." He sighed. "So many possibilities, but when you took off with the rest of the money in your account"—he glared at Leo—"I knew you were onto me. Or at least onto someone. There were so many possibilities around here. After all, every member on the board was so willing to sweep you aside when Owen walked in." He turned and glared at Owen. "It was so much easier to fool you than your father, especially after he came back." His eyes turned back to Leo. "You kept asking so many questions that, the first day, I knew it was only a matter of time."

"You blew up my car," Leo said—more of a statement than a question.

"Yes." He smiled. "Mechanics class was good for one thing. Of course, I should have killed you both then. Then you sent the boys to the camp." He turned to Hannah. "And I got distracted."

Owen noticed the look of lust replace the anger in Joel's eyes and stepped between them, shielding his view of her with his own body.

"The cops are here," Liam said.

"They've been here." Leo stood up and wiped the blood from his face, then nodded to the hallway, where a man in black stepped forward. He walked over to Joel and pulled him to his feet. "Joel Copeland, you're under arrest . . ." he started to say.

Joel laughed. "My grandmother is still very powerful."

"Maybe at the state level, but I'm federal." The man smiled. "And your confession was just captured on more than one device."

Just then an entire team of men dressed in black rushed into the room. Two men hauled Joel away, while medics started working on Leo and a female paramedic took a look at and bandaged the cut on Hannah's head.

"What just happened?" Dylan asked after they'd been shuffled into the conference room down the hallway.

"Remember me telling you about wearing a wire?" Leo asked Owen.

"Yeah," Owen said, sitting beside Hannah. He was holding her hand, and she noticed a few bruises on his knuckles from where he'd punched Joel.

"Well, it wasn't just me that was wired." He glanced around. "Every room in the place has cameras or listening devices. I knew that when Joel kidnapped me, it was just a matter of time before Ron found me, but when Joel brought Hannah in . . ." Leo's eyes turned to her. "I'm so sorry you and your friends got pulled into this mess."

"I'm glad you're safe," she said.

He chuckled. "If it hadn't been for you . . . I was beginning to doubt Ron would get here on time."

"Hey," Ron said from the doorway. "We didn't bring enough people to have twenty-four-hour surveillance on this place." He sighed. "We missed it when Joel jumped you, and trust me, someone has paid for that mistake." His tone grew grim.

"Thanks." Leo shook the man's hand.

"We're just cleaning up . . . everything. We'll be out of your hair and your building by Monday morning."

"Thanks again," Leo said.

"What now?" Owen asked.

Leo leaned back, the bandages covering his cuts standing out under the bright conference room lights. "Now, I go on vacation while you boys take over . . ." The three brothers groaned, causing Leo to chuckle. "Okay. Now, I get back to work and do what I do while you boys figure out what you want to do."

Owen turned to Hannah. "I know what I want." He lifted her hand in his and placed a soft kiss on the back of her fingers.

"We're all set too," Dylan said.

"Sounds like my Elle had a very smart business plan. I may just have to see what I can do to make sure that camp stays open," Liam said.

"She'd love that." Then Hannah narrowed her eyes. "But don't expect us to pay you any franchise fees."

"What?" Leo shook his head in question as Owen laughed at her.

"I'll explain later, Dad. Right now, we're going to head home." He stood up and pulled Hannah up with him. Where he wanted to be more than anywhere else was with her. Anywhere, as long as she was in his arms. He didn't know what the future held, but as long as they were together, he figured he could live happily.

"That sounds amazing." She sighed. "You were talking River Camp, right?"

He held on to her, enjoying that they were both safe and whole. "It's where my heart is," he said, then kissed her.

EPILOGUE

Hannah watched the ducks land in the river and smiled as she pulled the light sweater closer around her shoulders.

"You're cold?" Owen said, picking up the blanket from the basket and wrapping it gently around her.

She shook her head. "I was just thinking about how perfect this Thanksgiving was." She sighed, remembering the day filled with wonder and family. Even though her parents hadn't made it down there, it was nice having everyone else, including Leo, all cram into the third-floor apartment and enjoy dinner together.

It was strange: as much grief as her parents had given her earlier about not going up to New York and wasting her time at the camp, and after everything they had gone through, her parents had fallen oddly silent about her not returning home. They had even briefly talked about trying to make it down there for Thanksgiving, but at the last minute, her father had had other commitments come up. Which, Hannah believed, was for the best. After all, some things would have to take a while for her to get used to. Of course, her parents' latest change in heart probably had a lot to do with the fact that Leo and her father were having serious talks about doing a project together.

She and Owen had moved into the house in Pelican Point full time. It worked out perfectly, since he was focused on starting his new housing project, Hammock Cove—a new neighborhood by Paradise Investments, just down the street from River Camp.

Sure, she'd gotten Isaac to make all the food for the Thanksgiving feast, since she and the rest of her friends had all needed to work most of the day, but still, it was enjoyable that they had all been together for a few hours.

"It was nice. I think it should be our new tradition," he suggested, then pulled her closer to his side as they sat on the little beach's shoreline.

"I agree," she said, looking over at him.

"I've heard you have a few of those around here," he said after a long silence.

"We do." She laughed, thinking about all the times she'd dunked Zoey in the water and all the times Zoey had gotten her back.

"There's one tradition of yours in particular that my brothers have sort of gotten in on . . ." he started, then pulled out a small box from his pocket. "I know that it's normally supposed to be delivered by your Wildflowers, but this time, they asked me to do it." He held out the small box and opened it.

Hannah smiled down at the little crystal unicorn that stared back up at her.

She reached down, pulled the ring out, and placed it on her pinkie finger. "It used to fit us all." She sighed and held her hand out to admire the ring.

"It's ugly." He laughed.

She turned and looked up at him. "Yes, it is, but then again, love isn't always pretty." She felt her heart swell when he lifted her hand to his lips and kissed her knuckles.

"With you, somehow I think it's going to be nothing but beautiful." He pulled her closer, and she melted in his embrace as the sun sank lower over the cool waters of their home.

ABOUT THE AUTHOR

Jill Sanders is the *New York Times* and *USA Today* bestselling author of the Pride series, Secret series, West series, Grayton series, Lucky series, and Silver Cove romance novels. She continues to lure new readers in with her sweet and sexy stories. Her work is available in every English-speaking country and in audiobook form, and her books have been translated into several languages.

Born as an identical twin in a large family, Sanders was raised in the Pacific Northwest and later relocated to Colorado for college and a successful IT career before discovering her talent as a writer. She now makes her home along the Emerald Coast in Florida, where she enjoys the beach, hiking, swimming, wine tasting, and—of course—writing. You can connect with Sanders on Facebook at http://fb.com/JillSandersBooks, on Twitter @JillMSanders, and on her website at http://JillSanders.com.